To Die for Her

TARA BRITT

Copyright © 2024 Tara Britt
All rights reserved
First Edition

Fulton Books
Meadville, PA

Published by Fulton Books 2024

ISBN 979-8-89221-612-8 (paperback)
ISBN 979-8-89221-614-2 (digital)

Printed in the United States of America

CHAPTER 1

The smell hit him first. It was a mixture of metal and rotten meat. Unfortunately, it was a smell he was familiar with. Holding back the instinctive gag reflex that accompanies the smell, his dark eyes adjusted to the semi-darkness of the old, abandoned warehouse. The boards across the windows several stories above the floor allowed in enough light through the slats that he could make out the bodies that were laying on the cold concrete floor of the warehouse. The August heat and humidity combined to make the perfect conditions for quick decomposition. His ears picked up the sound of flies buzzing around the bodies. The bodies weren't together or in a pattern. They were scattered around; a couple were lying next to the small wooden table and chairs to the right and two were off to the side, closer to the door. A couple of bodies lay deeper in the wide cavity of the warehouse, blood splatter and spray on the wall behind them.

Agent Mike Slade holstered his agency-issued Glock into his drop-down holster and reached into one of the pockets of the khaki cargo pants he was wearing and pulled out a jar of Vicks. He put a hefty amount on the inside of each nostril to kill the smell of the decomposing bodies while he took in the scene. He put the jar of Vicks back into his pocket, waiting for the others to do the same before they entered the warehouse together.

"Well, this is a mess," a short man with a buzz cut commented. He was built like a bull, his neck almost nonexistent, olive-skinned and sweaty. His dark eyes were solemn as he squatted down and got a closer look at one of the bodies near the door.

Slade glanced at buzz cut, a man who had accompanied him on multiple investigations, and grimaced. "Yeah, but completely disorganized. The two guys by the table were executed first and intentionally. If we can identify them, we can figure out if they were couriers or higher," he replied. He pointed to the two bodies deeper in the warehouse. "Those two were shot as collateral damage, witnesses. Maybe a different shooter."

Buzz cut nodded and stood up. "Yeah, these guys," he agreed, pointing at the two bodies by the wooden table, "have a single shot through their foreheads, but those guys," pointing to the bodies near the back of the warehouse, "have multiple body shots."

Agent Slade squatted down next to one of the bodies by the table. The entrance hole was in the forehead, but after rolling the body over, Slade saw a much larger exit hole in the back of the head, indicating a large caliber bullet was used, maybe a .38 or .357. He noticed the gray matter and pieces of skull behind the chair. "This guy was sitting in the chair when he was shot," Slade pointed out. Because of the decomposition, Slade hesitated to put a timeline to when it all went down.

A lean blond man with the same general uniform agreed. "You can tell these guys," pointing to the bodies by the table, "were shot first because they don't seem to be in a position where they were running, probably taken by surprise." He glanced around and focused on the bodies near the back of the dilapidated warehouse. "Those guys don't give the impression of running either. A second shooter makes sense."

Slade walked over to one of the bodies at the back of the warehouse and used his booted foot to roll one body over. "Look how he's zippered. Fully automatic weapon killed these two." He noticed the multiple shell casings that confirmed that statement.

A fourth agent was squatted down next to the two bodies nearest the door. "Looks like these two were making a run for the door when they got shot. Same zipper pattern but in the back," he commented. "They all have the same tattoo as the bodies last week too." He pointed out the green-and-black spider on a web on the left hand of one of the bodies.

Slade sighed and rubbed the part of his nose just below his eyebrows. The Kevlar vest he wore was heavy, and trickles of sweat started to slowly creep down his face from the St. Louis summer heat.

TO DIE FOR HER

"He's getting more efficient." He kicked one of the wooden chairs next to the table. "And who the hell keeps tipping him off!"

Four men in navy blue suits burst through the open door. The four agents inside turned their heads to look at them, half amused, half annoyed.

"No surveillance video. Cameras weren't working. They were just for show," announced one of the blue suits. His hair was cut short, his face cleanly shaven, and his shoes appeared to have recently been shined.

"No kidding. I bet if you check, you'll see the owner of this place hasn't been here in months, hasn't rented it out, and didn't give anyone permission to be here. He's trying to sell the place and hasn't had many bites," Slade informed them wryly.

"Yeah, how did you know that?"

"We already checked. Owner checks out. He gave us consent to search too. Rodriguez," Slade turned to look at the man with the buzz cut, "show him the consent form."

Rodriguez dug the document out of one of the pockets of his cargo pants, but the first man in the blue suit waved it off.

"Don't need to see it," he said, turning to face Slade. "Now what?"

"I think instead of chasing all these 'leads,' we need to find out who keeps tipping Ayala off. We find the leak, shut him down, then we can concentrate on catching Ayala before he moves his dope and money and maybe before he kills all of the witnesses that can help us close this case out and hand it over to the US attorney's office," Slade informed everyone. "Okay, you guys know what to do. I need photos, ballistics, the works."

He walked out of the warehouse to his government-issued black SUV with purpose, leaving the blue suits and his own men to gather and catalog the evidence at this latest crime scene. Ripping at the Velcro that held the Kevlar vest in place, Slade shed the vest and put it in his vehicle. Instantly, he cooled down. Slade ran his hand through his shaggy hair, feeling the sweat near his scalp. Who would have insider information to pass along to Ayala? Who could be feeding Ayala sufficient information to prevent his team from catching the drug trafficker red-handed? The questions bugged Slade. This was the third time in a month that he had pieced together sufficient facts to be able to put together a search warrant affidavit with enough probable cause to get said warrant only to come across the same scene. Dead bodies of men employed by Ayala, no drugs, no cash, and no evidence of where Ayala was or who was involved in the slaughter of his soldiers.

CHAPTER 2

Staci checked her appearance in the mirror in her foyer one last time before picking up her tote and keys. Satisfied, she stepped out of her condominium and turned to lock the dead bolt before descending the steps to the walkway. Her supervisor had messaged her the night before, telling her that he had a case that he wanted her to handle, one that was still in the investigation stage, and needed more attention than he could give it. Her supervisor, Max, had never asked her to specifically handle a case and, in fact, had rarely spoken more than a few words at a time to her. She had been an assistant US attorney for a little over two years now and had handled dozens of cases, most of them small drug or property crimes, but she worked long hours and put in extra attention that had so far paid off. If the defendants hadn't pleaded guilty and wanted a jury trial, she tried the cases, and she won. Because Max had reached out with this special situation, she wanted to look as professional as possible to instill confidence in both Max and herself.

She drove her American-made sedan to the offices down the street from the federal courthouse. The US attorney and his assistants, as well as numerous federal investigative agencies, were housed there, along with other federal court personnel. The parking garage was underground, and she pulled in slowly as the daylight was abruptly cut off when she drove through the employees' entrance. She glided into her usual parking spot, grabbed her briefcase, and locked the door. She ambled to the building entrance easily as she wore her power-walking shoes to and from work, changing into stylish heels once she was in her office. She smiled and waved at a couple of coworkers who were also headed to the entrance. She knew whatever case Max was getting ready to give her was going to be her ticket to moving up not just in the office but possibly even in the federal system. Her heart pounded at the possibilities.

Once in her office, she changed her shoes, grabbed a legal pad and a pen, and checked her watch. She had ten minutes before her meeting, so she had time to grab a mug of government coffee. Pouring the ebony liquid into her cup, she noticed a few of the paralegals were looking at her with what…sympathy? Curiosity? Suddenly, that good feeling started to be a little sour, and her stomach began to churn a bit. She stiffened her back, straightened her navy pencil skirt, and strode to Max's office.

He waved her in and finished up the conversation he was having on the telephone. "Yeah, Mike, I'll take care of it. I have to go. There's someone in my office," he told the person on the other end of the phone. Hanging up, he motioned to one of the chairs that were situated in front of his large mahogany desk. "Sit."

Staci sat in the chair but didn't relax. She was acutely aware that she was sitting forward in anticipation. Max took a sip of whatever liquid was in his mug, eyeing her over the rim.

"I will make this as brief as I can. We have a drug-trafficking problem in Missouri," he said matter-of-factly. "Hell, in the US. Unfortunately, one of the cartels has not only made its way to St. Louis, but it is pretty much running the entire drug empire here. There are multiple federal agencies trying to bring down the local distributor. There is a current, ongoing investigation, trying to locate, arrest, and indict the principal distributor here in Missouri, a guy named Miguel Antonio Ayala."

Staci nodded her head; she was aware of the ongoing war on drugs, and she knew that despite, or perhaps because of, all the legislative actions on the state and federal level, the Mexican and Central American drug traffickers were able to infiltrate the US narcotics market, drive local or small-time dealers out of business, and bring large amounts of cocaine, methamphetamine, fentanyl, and other dangerous drugs into the United States using the major highway systems, including I-44 through St. Louis.

"I don't have time to oversee the investigation and hopefully subsequent prosecution of this case. You've proven yourself efficient and capable of handling something this complex. I want you to finish up and hand off whatever else you are doing and focus solely on this case. Understood?" Max's eyebrows moved to accentuate his words.

"Yes, of course. We don't usually get this involved in the investigation though. What's that about?" Staci could feel the excitement growing inside her. If she handled this case successfully, her upwardly mobile aspirations would be jump-started.

"Yeah, well, it has been ongoing for a while, and the DEA and FBI finally asked for our help, mostly in the way of getting warrants signed, advising on procedure, and making sure no one screws up by violating anyone's rights so everything gets tossed out of court." Max pointed to four paper boxes stacked on top of each other in one corner. "That's everything we have right now. You will be meeting with the lead DEA agent this afternoon who can bring you up-to-date on everything. I suggest you start reading."

Staci's eyes widened at the task at hand, reality hitting her as to the enormity of the new assignment. She nodded and walked to the corner, lifting one box to judge its weight.

"You don't have to carry those. I'll get an intern to get a dolly in here to take those to your office." Max smiled at her. "I expect to have weekly meetings so you can update me on the progress."

"Of course." Staci sighed with some relief. "Will I have a paralegal or intern assigned to help me?"

"No. We don't have the extra resources for that. Sorry, budgets and all." Max didn't really sound sorry. He sounded like he was glad not to have to deal with this case anymore.

Staci marched to his door and told him, "Well, let's get these boxes to my office. I have work to do before this afternoon." Her back stiff, she left Max's office, trying to give off the sense that this was no big deal when in reality, she was terrified by the sheer bulk and complexity of this assignment.

CHAPTER 3

Staci had papers spread out all over her office, on her desk, the credenza, and even photographs on the floor. The intern had brought the boxes shortly after she left Max's office, and she had wasted no time in going through the first box. There were warrants, affidavits, police reports from local agencies, photographs, and endless narratives from federal, state, county, and city police documenting the multiple crime scenes. Making heads or tails out of all it was proving difficult. She ran her hand over her face and sighed. Maybe she had bitten off more than she could chew, she thought to herself. She abstractedly chewed on a fingernail as she looked at the debris covering her office. She leaned down to get a closer look at one of the photos on the floor. A knock at the door drew her attention away from the papers and photos, and she glanced up to see a tall square-jawed man dressed in cargo khakis, a T-shirt that stretched across broad shoulders and a well-muscled chest, and work boots. He had his firearm strapped to his hip and tied around his thigh in a contraption called a drop-down holster. Staci was fairly certain he had been looking at her butt when she was bent over but decided not to call him on that.

"Yes?" she asked impatiently.

"I'm Mike Slade. DEA. We have a two o'clock meeting?" He introduced himself as he walked into her office without her inviting him in.

Flustered, Staci recalled Max telling her there would be someone meeting with her. "Yes, of course. Have a seat." She gestured toward one of the chairs that had been moved against a wall to make room for all the documents.

Slade strolled into the room, noticing the photographs laying on the floor, photographs of the latest murders Ayala had committed, or at least ordered, at the warehouse. He had been so distracted by the view he had when he first came to her door, her bent over and that exceptional ass in the air, that he hadn't paid attention to what she had actually been looking at.

"You're starting backwards," he told her.

"What?"

"Backwards. Those photographs are chronologically the most recent."

Staci looked at the photos then at Slade. "I just opened the first box brought to me," she explained. "I think this meeting was a good idea. I hear you're the man in charge."

Slade smirked slightly. "Yeah, well, that's been the problem. No one seems to be in charge, and everyone is in charge. Because of the cross-agency issues, the multiple law enforcement types, every agency and law enforcement group has its own 'man in charge,' and it's screwing things up," he told her. "The left hand doesn't know what the right hand is doing or what they know."

"I thought the federal government was more organized than that," she replied.

Slade snorted and snatched the photographs off of the floor. "A little naive, aren't you?"

Staci immediately felt her blood pressure rise. *How arrogant this man was!* Rather than show him how much he riled her up with that comment, she slightly tossed her head and calmly replied, "Not really. I've been trying drug cases for two years, and I have never run into this much disorganization."

Slade scooted a chair up closer to Staci's desk and methodically straightened the pictures, tapping them on the bottom to align them. "Well, then let's organize it. How do you want to start?"

"Why don't you give me the story, start from the beginning, and that will give me an idea of how this case needs to go." She looked at Slade expectantly.

"Dope coming up I-35 out of Mexico. Hits the crossroads with I-44 and goes east and west. We know the path. We have chatter that there is one main bad guy who is directing things once it hits the Missouri state line. Apparently, this particular cartel has a 'director' in each state that the drugs enter. Our job is to find the guy in Missouri. We need to tie him legally to not just the drugs but also a number of murders that have been committed, pretty recently actually." Slade sat back in his chair and calmly explained the overall picture.

Staci nodded and made notes on her legal pad. "Okay. Got it. I understand you know who that person is?"

"Yep. Miguel Antonio Ayala. Born and raised in Mexico. Intelligence tells us he still has family there but that he has been in the United States since 2021. Crossed the border along with the thousands of immigrants that enter every day. Because of the sheer number, it's hard to vet everyone who enters, especially if they don't cross at the usual official spots." He stared at the degrees hanging on the wall behind her blonde head. "This isn't a political issue, not with us. Unfortunately, this is just one of the problems that has arisen, especially since so many states have either decriminalized or reduced criminal penalties for drugs. It created a market. And the cartels, and Mr. Ayala specifically, are now part of that market."

Slade continued, "It's a problem for multiple reasons. Cartels are lacing fentanyl in cocaine, meth, and marijuana, which is killing off people. One hundred and fifty people a day die to overdosing on fentanyl-laced drugs, most of whom don't even know it's in there. The cartel doesn't pay taxes on the dope they manufacture and sell unlike the distributors who register with the states who have decriminalized drugs."

"Okay, so you know who, how, and why," Staci asserted. "What is left?"

"Well, we can't find him. If we can't find him, we can't stop him, we can't question him, and while we can indict him, actually bringing him to justice is my ultimate goal." Slade's right eyebrow slid up. "And he's executing people whenever we get close. People he thinks are betraying him. These," he waved the photographs at her, "are examples of his work."

"My job is not just to help you get this investigation organized, but eventually, I am going to be the one to bring it to indictment and a jury. I need to piece this together, how did you get from point A to point B, etc.," Staci told him matter-of-factly. "The best way to do that is you and I are going to go through each of these boxes. We need to find the first box, the early investigations and incidents, and work our way to the present. Are you willing to do that?"

"If it means I catch this son of a bitch and you make sure he never gets out of prison, then yes." Slade's face was serious, his dark eyes making direct contact with Staci's green ones.

"Then let's start on the real first box today. You talk me through it. I need a whiteboard, some folders, and labels. I also need more coffee. You?" She got up from her desk with her mug in her hand and turned to face Slade as she approached the door.

He shook his head from side to side and stood up to look in the box closest to him. Standing, he realized Staci was much shorter, even in heels, than his six feet four inches. He smiled to himself, thinking her attitude was much bigger than her body. That could be good or bad.

When she returned with her cup of coffee, he pointed at the photographs. "See that pattern of bullet holes in these guys?" He pointed to the photos displaying the bodies found at the back of the warehouse. Staci nodded. "That pattern, bullet holes close together going straight up or down depending on your perspective, is called zippering. Someone had a fully automatic weapon and simply fired multiple shots in an upward or downward fashion. It's quick and easy. That means it was spontaneous. It's a quick and easy way to neutralize who you want to take out. The men who were killed prob-ably didn't even see it coming, it happened so fast. Same with these guys." Slade pointed to the bodies of the men that looked like they were headed to the exit and were shot in the back. "These men were taking off, headed out. Most likely saw the guys in the back shot and decided they were next and were running for the door. Someone near them simply shot them in the same way but in the back."

Staci took in the information. She was mildly aware of many of the terms he was using, but having him explain it in the theory under which they were working helped. Slade continued to explain each photograph and document with Staci taking notes.

Four hours later, Staci stretched and rubbed her lower back. She had kicked off her shoes long ago, hiked her skirt up as much as she could, given its style and fit, and sat on the floor next to Slade. One box was now completely cataloged, put in folders, marked in order of importance to investigation and prosecution, and photographs were placed in protective plastic sheets. A timeline had begun on the large whiteboard Staci had unearthed in a storage room, with prosecution witnesses' names beside each piece of testimony necessary to prove the enumerated evidence.

Slade glanced at his watch and stood up. He put out his hand to Staci, who gladly accepted it. "I think we should call it a day. We've been at this for four hours. My lunch wore off hours ago."

Staci smiled wryly. "I didn't eat lunch. I was too absorbed in this before you came and forgot."

Slade noted to himself that while she was thin, Staci didn't look anorexic. "You do that a lot?"

"No." Staci sat down in her desk chair and put on her sneakers. "I usually bring my lunch or have something delivered, but I was preoccupied today. I'll eat something when I get home." She gestured toward the box they had just completed. "Can I get your help getting that to my car? I'm taking it home."

"Why? We already went through it and sorted everything out." Slade lifted the box anyway.

"I keep work product at my home on occasion. That way if I can't sleep or get bored, I can open it up and comb through it again, or maybe we missed something." She shrugged and put her heels and wallet into her leather tote. She waited for Slade to exit her office before following him, pausing to shut off the light and close the door.

"How long have you been DEA?" she asked Slade while they rode down the elevator to the parking garage.

"Three years DEA. Before that, I was a cop in Dallas for ten years," he replied. "How long have you been an assistant US attorney?"

"Two years. Before that, I was a state prosecutor in Joplin for four years. I handled mostly sex crimes and drugs," she responded. "Law school at the University of Arkansas."

Slade didn't see a wedding ring on her finger, and he didn't see a tan line indicating that she wore one when she wasn't at work. It wasn't uncommon for people in their line of work not to wear a ring while at work; the less information a criminal knew about you, the better. He wondered if she had children or any family close, but he was not going to ask. This was a partnership that was better left to business hours, and in this day and age, she might take it wrong if he did ask. It didn't keep him from wondering what she would feel like naked underneath him.

The elevator door slid open, and Staci led the way to her car. She popped open the trunk and said, "Just put it in there. I can get it inside my condo once I get home and out of this skirt."

Slade nodded and set it down in the perfectly kept trunk. It appeared to have been vacuumed, and other than a small box with jumper cables and a first aid kit, nothing else was inside.

"Thanks," Staci told him as she opened her car door. "When do you want to go through the next box?"

"I can do it tomorrow. Right now, there's no chatter, and my teammates are re-interviewing some people. I don't need to be there for that."

Staci smiled and said, "Great! I will see you around 2:00 p.m.?"

Slade held her door open while Staci put her seat belt on. "Sounds like a plan."

He watched as she carefully reversed, then drove forward toward the entrance. "I need food, alcohol and gym time," he told himself out loud before walking to his own vehicle parked a few spots away.

Staci's drive home was short; it was one of the reasons she chose this particular condo. Close to work, a small yard in front, and it had a garage that led directly into the house. She tossed her keys onto the bowl that sat below the foyer mirror on a marble-topped table she had found at an antique shop. She was fairly frugal, but she had a weakness for solid antique pieces and would splurge once in a while if she found something that she just had to have. Heading up the stairs where the three bedrooms were, she brought her heels she had fished out of her tote to put away. Her bedroom was at the end of the hall-way, decorated in soft tans and sage green; it wasn't terribly feminine with the suede drapes and leather throw pillows, but it was peaceful. Staci felt like the room fit her personality well, not overly feminine but had just enough touches, such as the ruffled bed skirt and sage green Victorian chaise, that the room wasn't masculine either.

She opened the door to her large walk-in closet, complete with shelving, built-in dresser, and other amenities. She put up her heels, unzipped her skirt from behind, and carefully hung it up. She peeled off her blouse and tossed it into the hamper then grabbed a pair of white denim shorts and a tank top from the "summer side" of her closet. Flip-flops on her feet, she snatched a hair tie out of her bathroom and unbraided her wavy blonde hair, putting it up into a messy bun, and descended the stairs. She cut back through the door to the garage and retrieved the box Agent Mike Slade had put into the trunk earlier. It was heavy and bulky, but she managed to haul it into the condo and set it next to the sofa. She wanted to go back through it again, make notes on her own without Agent Slade there to distract her.

She had never been attracted to pretty men, and Agent Slade certainly wasn't pretty in the conventional sense. But he was probably the most ruggedly handsome man she had ever met. He had thick dark brown hair that was a bit overgrown around the ears and in the back along his collar, with curls on the ends, and large, deep, and soulful brown eyes. He had that square jaw and the slightest dimple in his chin. She even noticed once when he smiled slightly that he had a dimple on the left side of his lips, which were not too thin, not too thick. His nose had obviously been broken on at least one occasion as it had a slight hump, but that didn't distract from the nobleness of it. Once upon a time, that strong nose was probably his best feature. He was tall and muscular but not the bulky muscles you see with a bodybuilder. He was leaner, more compact. Staci bet that under his clothes, one would be able to see definition of the various muscle groups.

"What are you doing!" Staci whispered out loud. She shook the thoughts out of her head. Yes, the man was attractive in a very masculine sort of way, but she was a professional. She was going to be working with him for however long it took, and sitting around, fantasizing about him, was not going to get this case solved and prosecuted.

On the other side of town, Mike Slade was in the gym near his apartment. It was supposed to be "leg day," but he was edgy. He needed to do upper body and legs today to make himself tired. His mind was busy, first on the Ayala case, but then, surprisingly, he started thinking about that little assistant US attorney. He appreciated pretty women, even had had himself a few, but there was something different about this one. Something he couldn't put his finger on. Yes, she was educated, articulate, appeared to be completely professional, but there was something else under those clothes that fit her like a glove and showed off her curves. There was something under that peachy skin and in those jade-green eyes that were almost almond-shaped. He couldn't put his finger on it, but she intrigued him. Too much. And that was why he needed extra time with the weights tonight.

Neither of them slept well. Tossing and turning, they thought about the case, the timelines, the players, and they kept seeing the scenes in the pictures of the bodies taken at the various crime scenes across the state. They also thought about each other.

Staci's mind kept replaying how Mike's smile didn't reach his eyes, how he was tense like a cat about to pounce, and how he was always guarded and looked at her without trust or confidence. She could hear his baritone voice, low, almost a growl. She worried how they would be able to work with each other long term if he didn't open up. She knew, felt in her bones, that he was keeping something from her.

Mike Slade, on the other hand, couldn't stop his mind from replaying over and over how her eyes were smoldering pools of dark green that were hypnotic, how her pink tongue licked her bottom lip when she was absorbed in something she was reading, and how a faint scent of something soft and sweet wafted over to him with each movement she made. He wondered how she tasted and felt. He cursed himself, aggravated at how obsessed he had become after just one meeting with her. No woman had ever gotten under his skin this fast and this much. He had a job to do, and she was a distraction that he didn't need.

CHAPTER 4

On this particular afternoon, they were both staring at the whiteboard that Staci continued to add to as they scoured the evidence boxes. They had reached the end of the evidence boxes, and now they needed to figure out what the next step was. Staci was looking for it just to make sense. Slade was trying to fit in pieces that were missing to help figure out who was tipping off Ayala.

"This might sound amazingly stupid, but if I understood the organization better, it would help," Staci admitted sheepishly.

"Well, there are more than ten known cartels, all out of Mexico, Central, or South America," Slade told her. "The one you have probably heard more about in the news is the Sinaloa Cartel."

Staci shook her head.

Sighing, Slade continued, "Ever hear of El Chapo?"

"Oh, yes!" Staci's eyes lit up at something she recognized.

"Okay, he was the head of Sinaloa until his capture. They are the most violent, even killing their couriers for losing product, getting caught skimming money. They do it in ways to warn others in their organization about the dangers of doing so. They even go after their families," Slade said. "So all of the cartels have clear lines of authority and the responsibilities of that authority. Some are vertical, where one individual is in charge, with underbosses whose main job is to pass along the decisions of the boss but also insulate the boss from legal responsibility. Below them are captains or lieutenants who are in charge of people lower than them," Slade explained.

"But others don't have the vertical ranks. They are more horizontal. That just means the authority for making decisions doesn't flow downward. They work more like international corporations.

The cartel you and I are working on is more horizontal. Remember we talked about Ayala being the distributor in Missouri?"

Staci nodded her head.

"Right, well, each state has such a distributor. They are like regional managers. They each have the authority to make decisions in their own territory not incumbent on any other distributor."

"So they don't answer to each other. Do they answer to anybody?" Staci asked.

"Sure, just like all international corporations, there is a board of directors although that 'board' is usually just one or maybe a couple of individuals. As long as the projected profits are met and the individual distributor isn't bringing too much heat onto the cartel, more than what they are used to anyway, the 'board' lets the distributor stay in his or her position and continue making most of the day-to-day decisions." Slade stood up and stretched. His legs were cramping from all the sitting they did today, and he could feel his stomach start to rumble.

"There are rules of operation, however. Mostly unwritten, and some have been verbally communicated. Anyone who breaks those rules are violently punished, usually by one of the lieutenants. They don't write the rules down, evidence, you know. They generally pass on communication and orders through personal contact. Because there is such personal coordination with this type of communication, they are flexible. They adapt. That is what makes it so hard for law enforcement to shut them down. We might arrest a higher up here and there, but there is always someone in training, and because of the close relationships, everyone seems to know when they will have to step up or when law enforcement will be showing up."

Staci watched him pace around slightly, and then he shut the door. He turned and looked at her, his dark eyes solemn. "Everyone has a skill or you aren't part of the organization. They promote from within and particularly if someone has a specialization that sets him or her apart from everybody else. This assures that the most qualified people are placed where they can be of the most use and the best use for the organization. They don't share information across responsibility lines to ensure that no one person knows too much, so if caught by law enforcement, they only can share limited information, and there is little impact on the entire operation. There is someone involved in this investigation whose sole job is to provide to Ayala the movement of this investigation so he can stay one step ahead of us."

Staci's eyes widened. "You don't think it is anyone in your agency, do you?"

Slade shrugged. "I don't know. He or she could be in your office or the FBI or anyone who has access to government files. I've stopped documenting most of my theories and investigation on government computers. I have a backup system I'm using. I suggest you do the same. Cartel members are very careful to plan everything out down to the last detail. They make contingency plans. They don't let on to their plans, and they are very organized." He ran his long fingers through his thick dark hair. "These people are psychopaths. They have a total disregard for others. They have no respect for law and order, and they have zero empathy for other people. But they can hide in plain sight. They come across as your normal individual. They can be charming, like domestic abusers. But like domestic abusers, when crossed, they mete out violence swiftly and without impunity. You need to be very careful."

"I'm just the prosecutor. I would think you were more at risk," Staci replied.

"Not necessarily. Yes, I am in danger if I get too close, but since we are working more like a team on this one, the bull's-eye is also on you. And no offense, you are female." He put his hands up as if to ward her off when he saw her eyes flash. "The culture they come from is very machismo, very sexist. They see you as a weak member of this investigation. That makes it more dangerous for you than for me."

Staci dug her smartphone out of her tote and took pictures of her whiteboard. She then pushed a button, sending the photo to her email. Slade watched as she dug a blue thumb drive out of her tote, inserted it into her laptop, and copied the email she sent herself onto the thumb drive. She noticed him watching her.

"I've been copying everything in these boxes when I take them home to make sure I have them protected." She deleted the email and then clicked a few more tabs on her computer. "I also know how to delete them on my laptop so they can't be recovered by a cyber expert."

Slade nodded admiringly. "Smart girl. Who all knows about the theories we've come up with while we were going through this stuff?"

"Just Max and probably his legal secretary. I have to report to him once a week, and we've only met once," she replied.

"Good. Keep it that way." Slade started picking up the scattered papers and photographs to put into the last box. He stared at the photograph on top. Something about it bothered him, something nagged him, like he was missing something.

Staci noticed he was staring at one particular photo. "What is it?" she asked.

"I don't know. I feel like there is something we are missing, something in this picture."

"Keep it. I have it saved." She smiled. "It'll come to you when you least expect it."

Slade sighed and folded the eight-by-ten photo small enough to fit into one of the pockets of his khaki cargo pants. "Yeah."

Staci had worn flats today, with her slim black pants, so she had room to put the rest of the photos into the tote rather than her usual heels. Slade noticed that the pants showed off her tight, well-rounded bottom, and he caught himself just before he started wondering what it would feel like in his hands.

"Hey, want to grab a bite to eat?" he asked. Seeing her eyes widen and her hands freeze, he assured her, "We both have to eat, and it wouldn't hurt to talk about this someplace other than here, a different environment."

"Oh, uh, sure." Staci was flustered and embarrassed that he might think she thought it was a date. "Where do you want to go? I have to put this box in my car, and I can meet you there."

Slade picked up the box. "I'll carry it for you. It's heavy."

They rode in silence in the elevator down to the employees' parking lot. The box wasn't that heavy, and he hadn't bothered to carry the last two, just the first one, which she had asked him to carry. There was definitely something on his mind; his eyebrows squinted together, and he was just staring at the buttons on the elevator panel. Staci breathed a sigh of relief when the doors opened in the garage.

Slade carried the box to her trunk, which she had popped remotely when the elevator doors opened. "There's a diner about four blocks from here. You will have to park on the street, but you can't miss it. Leo's Diner," Slade told Staci.

She nodded and replied, "See you there in a few minutes."

She slid into the driver's seat and started the car. Slade shut her door and stepped back to let her back out of her reserved spot. He was still thinking about the photograph, and he started to formulate a whole new theory.

Staci found a parking spot just across the street from the diner. Slade was right; she couldn't miss it. Lots of neon light and reminiscent of the old diners from the '50s. Red-and-white checkered pattern on the signs in the windows, and she could see red vinyl booth seats from where she parked. Locking her car, she looked both ways before jaywalking across the street to the curb in front of the diner. The door actually faced the corner, almost in a triangular fashion, which was a kind of quirky Staci found charming. She opened the door, and she was not disappointed. The diner smelled like fried food and pie. There were tables and booths and even a counter with red vinyl and chrome barstools. Several pies were stacked inside a glass pie keep on the counter, and the cooks even wore those white soda fountain hats someone might see in a Norman Rockwell poster.

"How many?" A young woman, probably not more than eighteen, suddenly appeared in front of Staci.

"Oh, two." She looked around to see if Slade was already here, but she didn't see him.

"Follow me." The young woman grabbed two menus and two sets of flatware and walked toward the back of the diner. She stopped in front of a booth that looked out onto the street where Staci had parked. "This okay?"

"Yes," Staci told the woman as she slid into the booth facing the door.

Another young lady, this time a little older and wearing a lot more eye makeup, marched over and asked what Staci wanted to drink.

"Ice water, no lemon, please," Staci answered.

She heard the bell above the door and looked up. Slade was coming through the door, looking around for her. Staci waved slightly at him, and he strode down the aisle toward the booth. Staci noticed that every single female working in the diner had, for a brief second, stopped and watched Slade. She rolled her eyes.

"What's with the eye roll?" Slade asked her as he got to the booth. He didn't sit.

"Nothing." Staci was not about to tell him about how the women reacted to his entry. Noticing him just standing there, she asked, "What?"

"I need you to sit on the other side."

"What?" Staci moved while she asked the question. She settled her tote on her left side and looked at Slade who had slid into the booth where she had just been sitting.

"I need to be able to see the door. I don't want my back to it," he explained. "It's a cop thing."

"Okay." Staci picked up a menu and looked at it. "What's good here?"

"Everything. What kind of food do you eat?"

Staci made a face. "What kind of question is that?"

"Well, if you are a vegan or vegetarian, they have different salads or this veggie wrap thing. I'm neither, so I haven't actually eaten any of that," Slade explained.

"Yeah, I'm not vegetarian or vegan. Have you ever had any of the burgers?" Staci responded.

"Yeah, the bacon cheeseburger with blue cheese is great. I usually have that when I eat here, which isn't that often by the way." Slade didn't know why he offered the last part. It really wasn't any of her business how often he ate here.

The waitress with the heavy eye makeup reappeared, holding some sort of drink in her hand. She set it down in front of Slade.

"Got your sweet tea, Mike. Want your usual or going in a different direction today?"

Staci smirked at Slade. He had the sense to blush slightly as he answered, "The usual."

Nodding, the waitress asked Staci what she wanted to order, and Staci took Slade's advice and ordered the bacon cheeseburger and fries. "And water, no lemon," she reminded their server. Waiting until the waitress had walked back to the counter, Staci smiled full on at Slade. "For someone who doesn't eat here that often, you sure have a 'usual.'"

"Okay, I probably eat here more than I should," he conceded. "Now, let's get to why I suggested we get out of the office to talk about the case. Something about the photos has been bothering me, but I couldn't put my finger on it. I know what it is." He reached into his pocket and pulled out the photograph Staci had told him to keep earlier. He unfolded it and turned it so she could see it. "See this?" He pointed to the hand of the man that had been deemed as executed rather than collateral damage. Staci looked at the photograph.

"It's his right hand. He has a gold pinky ring on with some sort of insignia."

"Right. So did the other four men who were intentionally shot in the head. None of the men killed who were lower in rank have that ring."

"Okay, and what is the significance?"

"Well, first, he is only executing the men directly under him. That sends a message," Slade replied. He leaned back, gently pulling the photograph off the table and down to his lap as the waitress put their plates on the table in front of them. Staci's water was plunked down in front of her. The waitress asked if they needed anything else.

Slade answered for both of them, "Nope, this looks great." With a nod and smile, the server turned to another table.

"I don't know what the significance is other than the rank that is being targeted. Intelligence suggests that Ayala believed they were skimming money." Slade took a bite of his cheeseburger and looked at Staci with expectation.

TO DIE FOR HER

"How does that help us?" Staci salted the french fries that accompanied the burger and popped one in her mouth.

"Well, let's think about this from his viewpoint. Why do I think these men were skimming money or maybe drugs?"

"Someone told Ayala they were. Someone Ayala trusts even more than these underbosses."

"Who would benefit from telling Ayala that his underbosses were skimming?"

Staci finally bit into the cheeseburger. It was juicy and melted in her mouth. She unconsciously moaned slightly from the deliciousness in her mouth. Slade heard it, and his mouth suddenly went dry. That moan. All thought about the investigation was gone. All he could focus on was Staci's mouth, chewing, her tongue darting out to lick the juice from the meat from her lips. He needed to hear that moan again.

"Hey, Slade, who would benefit?" Staci's impatient question snapped him back to the investigation.

"Sorry, I was trying to think about the options," he lied. "Someone who either really did skim and has to deflect the blame to someone else or someone who is trying to take over Ayala's position?" Slade shrugged and took another bite.

"Maybe both?" Staci ventured.

Slade nodded. "Another question we need to answer is how are they getting tipped off to where we are."

"If we had those answers, this investigation could be over shortly. I feel like the answers to those questions lead us to what we need to get an indictment." Staci finished off her fries. "I have to say, this place does have good food."

Slade looked at her plate. Except for a bite or two of the cheeseburger, Staci had polished off a lot of food. Raising an eyebrow, he asked, "Did you really just eat all of that food?"

"Yes, I did." Staci stiffened slightly. "What about it?"

"Whoa, tiger, no judgment. Just surprised, is all. You're what, a size 2? And you ate all of that? Where did it all go?" he chuckled.

"I run. And, no, I'm a size 4, if you must know." Staci suddenly felt self-conscious. "I don't usually eat this much food. I guess I was just hungry tonight."

"Did you eat lunch today?"

Staci shook her head.

Slade followed up with, "When was the last time you ate lunch?"

"Okay, so I don't usually eat lunch. I lied that first day. But I eat breakfast, and why is my nutritional behavior any of your business?"

"It's not." Slade motioned for the check. "I guess I stepped over a line."

"Yeah, well, I'm an adult. I know I need to eat regularly. I just get distracted."

Slade was looking through the plate-glass window and noticed that a dark-colored sedan had been parked two cars behind Staci's car. Nobody got in or out of the car since it had parked shortly after he had arrived at the diner. His eyes narrowed. He took his change from the waitress and stood up. "Let's get out of here. Go home, think about what we talked about."

Staci offered Slade a ten-dollar bill to pay for her meal, but he shook his head. "Put that back. Next one is on you." He started walking to the exit, and she followed.

Once out on the street, she turned to look at him and asked, "Are the personal belongings of all the victims still available? Not turned over to the family or anything?"

"Yeah, they are available, probably at the coroner's office. Why?" Slade kept one eye on the dark sedan.

"Can you bring them all to my office tomorrow? I want a close-up look at them." She remembered some other things in the photographs, and she wanted to get home to look at the photos. "Not just the underbosses, but the couriers or lower-ranked guys that were also killed. I need all of it."

"Yeah, sure, I can check it all out and bring it to you." Slade held onto her elbow as he escorted her across the street and into her car. "Drive straight home."

"I'm sorry?" Staci furrowed her eyebrows at Slade.

His demeanor had changed suddenly in the diner around the time he was paying for the food, and she wasn't sure what was happening.

"Drive straight home. Go inside and shut any blinds or curtains. I want to check something out," he told her.

Staci nodded, started her car, and pulled away from the curb in the direction of her home. Slade walked down the street and around the corner to where his SUV was parked, which happened to be in the same direction Staci was driving. He got into his vehicle and watched as the dark-colored sedan also took that same direction. Slade picked up his phone, dialed it, and waited for the call to be answered as he turned his vehicle in the same direction that Staci and the dark-colored car had driven.

Fifteen minutes later, Staci pulled into her garage, lowered the door, and unlocked the dead bolt between the garage and her foyer. The bottom of the stairs were between the door and the foyer, with a large plate-glass window facing the street. Staci lowered the blinds and closed the drapes. Not sure why Slade went all cloak-and-dagger on her suddenly, she shivered. She double-checked the dead bolt on the front door and went upstairs to change. She wanted to review those photos, all of them, again, before she went to bed.

Slade drove slowly down the street adjacent to Staci's. It was dark now. He parked his SUV and got out, quietly shutting the door. He walked slowly, silently toward the corner, using the bushes and a fence to hide himself. Her condo was the second one from the corner across the street from where he was hiding. He watched her close the blinds and drapes. He also saw a light turn on upstairs a few minutes later. Then he looked around and saw the sedan. It was parked across the street but two condos down on the same side of the street Slade was hiding. He couldn't make out the license tag in the dark, and he didn't want to tip off whoever was in the car that he was onto them. Not yet. But this confirmed what his hunch back at the diner had told him. Staci was being watched.

He sneaked back to his vehicle and backed down the street before using a driveway to go back in the direction of his own home. He stared at his phone for a second then dialed Staci.

Staci had the photographs spread out on her dining room table. She saw a common denominator and couldn't wait to tell Slade. At that very moment, her phone rang.

"Hello?" She didn't recognize the number that popped up. It was quiet. "Hello!" she said a little louder and a little more forcefully.

Then Slade's voice, "Hey, just making sure you got home okay."

"Yes, I did. And guess what—" she excitedly started to tell him her discovery when he cut her off.

"Save it for later. I will explain tomorrow." And the phone went dead.

He is the oddest man, Staci thought to herself as she stacked the photos together and put them in her tote. She carried the boxes back out to the garage and put them in her trunk. She paused as she went to shut off the garage light. Did she hear something? She listened. Nothing. She shut off the garage light and closed the door, making sure the dead bolt was secure. She set her alarm and turned off the lights downstairs. Climbing the stairs, she yawned. Morning would come early, and she was exhausted.

The man in the dark sedan watched the lights go off one by one. When the light upstairs also went out, he dialed a number on his phone. "She's all tucked in. We are good to go." And with that, the sedan pulled away from the curb and disappeared into the night.

CHAPTER 5

The next morning, Staci hurried off the elevator toward her office. She knew Slade would be bringing the personal effects of all the murdered men, and she was anxious to see if her discovery was among them. As she approached her door, she noticed it was slightly ajar. *That's odd*, she thought. She knew she had locked her office when she and Slade had left to grab dinner. She slowly pushed the door open, and her mouth and eyes flew open in shock. Papers were strewn everywhere, her computer was on, and drawers were pulled out. She immediately crossed the lobby and went to Max's office.

"Max," she barged in.

He was in his office. Two of Slade's men were there, Rodriguez and a guy named Carmichael that she had seen in passing. They stopped talking and turned to look at her.

"We have a problem. Come to my office."

She left, followed by the three men, and when they got to her office, she pushed the door open wide and gestured with her left arm. They looked in, looked at each other, and then at her.

"What the hell?" Max asked her at an elevated volume.

"Exactly. I locked my door when I left last night, and I came in this morning to this." Staci gestured wildly with her hands. "Somebody broke in and ransacked my office!"

"Is anything missing?" Rodriguez asked.

Staci stormed into her office and started looking through her drawer and cabinets. "Not that I can see." She typed something on her laptop and frowned. "Whoever it was tried to hack into my laptop too. It doesn't look like they were successful though."

"What a mess," Carmichael commented. He started picking up some of the documents that were on the floor. Rodriguez jumped in to help, too.

"Wait a minute! Leave everything where it is. I need the FBI or the marshals up here to take pictures, fingerprints, and a report." Max stopped them. He turned to someone in the secretarial pool. "Get someone up here!" The three men waited with Staci.

"Thank God the Ayala files weren't in here," Max commented. "That could have been disastrous."

"Nope, those were safely in my car. Good thing," Staci muttered.

Several men in blue suits came off the elevator in a rush and hurried in Staci's direction.

"Where's the crime scene?" one of the men asked.

Staci pointed in her office. Max and Rodriguez and Carmichael all excused themselves so the FBI boys could process the scene and take statements. One man took photos, another dusted for fingerprints, and a third one asked Staci questions: What time did she leave last night? What time did she arrive this morning? Was she sure she locked the door when she left? Is anything missing?

The elevator dinged, and Staci turned to see Slade exit the elevator.

"Rodriguez and Carmichael just told me what happened." He looked around her office and saw the other agents processing the scene. He was carrying a bag that had a local bagel restaurant's name on the side. "When they're done, call me. I'll be back." He turned, taking the sack with him.

"I could eat now," Staci quietly told him.

He shook his head, "No, I'll bring it back. Too much going on right now." He strode back to the elevator and pushed the button.

The doors closed, leaving Staci alone with the FBI agents and two legal secretaries who were gazing curiously at her from their desks in the lobby. Staci reached into her tote and pulled her red heels out, replacing her sneakers with them. She smoothed her loose bun and sat down in one of the chairs in the lobby.

After what seemed an eternity, the agents told her they were done. She entered her violated office and started picking up the papers on the floor and the desk and put them back in the folders from which they came. She had a few cases that were set for sentencing, so she signed onto her computer to work on the sentencing briefs that were due in a few days. It was unnerving that someone could break into a federal government office unseen after hours. It was even more unnerving thinking about what could have happened if she had chosen to work late as she often did. Shivering a little, she tried to focus on the brief. She double-checked the camera to make sure it was off even though she knew she had installed enough firewalls and other security, thanks to her sister who was a computer genius. A knock on her door interrupted her thoughts.

"I'm back." Slade was holding that bagel bag and standing in her doorway.

She waved him in, and he entered, closing the door behind him.

"Hey, sorry about earlier. I want to tell you what I saw last night," she started before he put one index finger in front of his lips, warning her to stop talking.

He reached into the bag and pulled a small, odd-shaped device out. She watched as he ran the device over walls, all the surfaces, and then started running it over electrical outlets, her desk phone, in each drawer and in cabinets, on picture frames, throughout her office. Finally, he stopped and put the device back in the bag.

"Um, you just swept for bugs," she needlessly pointed out.

"Yep, you're good. For now," he replied. He reached into the bag again and pulled out multiple plastic bags full of jewelry, wallets, and other personal effects. "I believe you were wanting these?"

Staci's eyes lit up. She grabbed one of the bags and peered into it. "Yes! Thank you!" she exclaimed. "Last night, I looked over all the photos. Everyone who died was wearing one of these!" She reached into a bag and carefully, using a napkin she had pulled out of drawer, removed a silver ornate cross. It was about four inches long, three inches wide, had a lot of shiny stones interwoven with silver, and it was on a heavy silver chain.

"There should be one of these in every bag."

"So?"

"Imagine, once you are part of the crew, you are gifted with one of these, along with being tattooed a spider in a web." Staci pointed to the hands in the photographs that she had pulled out of her tote.

"Okay, hear me out. Tracking device. At first, I thought there might be one in the rings, but that would only count if whoever is gathering the data is tracking the underbosses. Way more people have these crosses, and if they get them once they have earned a spot in the inner circle, you can keep track of more people, including couriers, accountants, even secretaries. Anyone who might have access to records or information," Staci explained. "I called someone last night to double-check the possibility." She didn't mention she called her computer genius sister who was a complete tech nerd. "It's been done with watches and even written about in spy novels. The CIA used to use fake coins and put computer chips in them. So we need to take one of these apart and see if there is anything in them that could be a tracking device."

"Not here. Why did you think of a tracking device?" Slade's interest was definitely piqued.

"Staying a step ahead of you. Those were your words," Staci said.

"Yeah, ahead of us. Not them." Slade gestured toward the deceased men in the photos.

"Right, but you said Ayala might believe someone is skimming, money, drugs, or both. How better to keep an eye on his people when he isn't around than to track their movements? If you develop an informant, his movements can also be tracked. If someone goes anywhere they can't explain, Ayala will know it, and his suspicions are raised. Did you, by any chance, have an informant or two?"

"We've had a couple. They haven't been found dead, but they are off the grid for sure. We figured they are in hiding at this point."

"They aren't in hiding completely if they are wearing one of these." Staci dangled the cross at Slade.

"Assuming there is an actual tracking device in all of them."

"Correct. We need to start taking them apart to see." Staci studied the front of the cross carefully.

TO DIE FOR HER

Slade took a cross out of a different bag and started turning it toward the light. "We need a jeweler's loupe to see anything. Everything is so tiny."

"I can order one online, have it shipped to my house overnight. Not a problem."

"Let's say we find something that could be a tracker. We need to find who is gathering the data. That is the direct link to Ayala, I think. How can we find that out?" Slade put the crosses back in the bags.

"I might know someone who can help with that if we actually find something in the crosses." Staci smiled mysteriously. "You aren't the only person who knows 'people.'"

Slade put everything back in the bagel bag.

"You don't happen to have any actual bagels in that bag, do you? Or cream cheese?" Staci looked longingly at the bag.

"Actually, yes." Slade pulled two bagels, one that was a cheese bagel and one that had everything on it, out of the bag along with single-serving cream cheese containers and a plastic knife. "Just in case anyone got curious about what was in the bag."

Staci picked the cheese bagel and started covering the two halves with cream cheese while Slade opened her office door.

"Everyone can watch us eat bagels out of the bag." He smiled at her and began slathering his bagel with cream cheese.

Staci laughed softly and bit into hers. She had skipped breakfast this morning because she was so anxious to get to work and tell Slade about her ideas. The cream cheese was tart but smooth and put her in a much better mood.

"Where do you suggest we examine the items?" she asked.

"Somewhere private," he said when he stopped chewing.

"Wow, not many places for that. Pretty much leaves your home or mine," she observed. "Unless you have a wife at home." She raised her eyebrows at him and took another bite.

"No wife. But, yeah, your place or mine is pretty much where it's going to have to happen," Slade told her. "I can come over to your place about 8:00 p.m. I have some reports I need to finish, and I want to follow up on some leads that came across my desk recently."

31

"Sure. Eat before you come over. I haven't gone to the grocery store this week."

Slade smiled, that dimple on the left cheek prominently displayed. "This is work. Not a pickup."

"I didn't think that. But you have to agree, sometimes you can eat and work at the same time. That's all I meant." Staci immediately felt his disdain at thinking she was coming on to him. Even though she wasn't, the rejection still stung.

They finished off the bagels, and Slade stood up. He snatched up the handles of the bag and looked around for a trash can to throw away his napkins and the plastic knife they used to smear the cream cheese. Staci pointed to a gray cylinder next to her desk.

"So tonight? Eight, okay?" Slade asked as he threw away the garbage.

"After seven. I have an appointment after work," Staci told him as she cleaned off the desk where her crumbs had fallen.

Nodding, Slade took his bag and left.

At exactly 6:30 p.m., Staci rolled into her driveway and then her garage. She grabbed her tote and the gym bag from the back seat, pushed the button to lower the garage door, and unlocked the door. She had yoga every Wednesday evening after work, and tonight was no exception. The quiet class gave her peace and let her stretch her muscles, releasing the tension from her job, and since she had been assigned this particular project, she especially needed the class. Only eight other people were in her class, and she enjoyed the small group. All women, and most of them worked outside the home; they had nothing in common with each other except for the fact they all came to yoga on Wednesday evenings.

Staci put her tote down in the foyer and ran up the stairs to unpack her gym bag. She was sorting through what could hang back up and what needed to go into the laundry when her doorbell rang. *Shoot*, she thought to herself. *I thought I had enough time to grab something to eat and change.* Sighing, she walked back down the stairs, peered out the peephole, and saw Slade standing there with his bagel bag. She opened the door and told him to come in.

TO DIE FOR HER

When Staci opened the door, Slade was taken by surprise. He had never seen her in clothes other than her work clothes, always professional and not a hair out of place. Tonight, she had on a neon pink tank top that showed off her surprisingly toned arms, a pair of gray leggings, and her hair, although still in a bun, was coming loose, with blonde tendrils framing her face that looked devoid of makeup.

Seeing his obvious surprise, she gestured with her hand to enter and told him, "I have a yoga class every Wednesday evening after work. I got home like five minutes ago."

Recovering from his surprise, Slade said, "Yeah, I know I'm early. Traffic wasn't as bad, and the diner was quick tonight. Didn't take as long as I thought."

"Good, you ate." Staci took the bag from him and walked into her living room and put it on the coffee table.

Slade had hung back, looking at the photos hanging on the wall above the foyer table.

"This your family?" he asked the obvious.

Staci walked back to where he was standing and pointed at a photograph of an older woman and man, the man wearing the uniform of a military officer. "That's my mom and dad. Dad literally just retired from the Air Force last year."

"A pilot?" Slade studied the medals on the man's uniform.

"Yes. He flew in Desert Storm and then a couple of times over Iraq after 9/11. The last ten years he oversaw flight training at various bases. That," she pointed at a photograph of six women, "is me and my sisters."

Slade's eyes widened and he smirked. "You have five sisters? Your poor dad," he commented.

"Yep. That one," she pointed to a woman with dark curly hair and dark eyes, "is the oldest. Meredith. She's a doctor. She was born in Texas at Lackland Air Base. This one," Staci pointed to a blonde whose hair was straight and whose eyes were also brown, "is the second oldest. Allison. She's an accountant. She was born in England."

"Who's that?" Slade pointed to another woman who had straight dark hair and the same jade-green eyes that Staci had.

"Third oldest, Isabella. She's a computer engineer. She actually works for NASA, writing most of the code, now. And these two," she pointed to the two remaining women who had the same curly blond hair that she had and the same eyes. "These two are my younger sisters, twins. Casey and Cassidy. They were born in Aviano, Italy."

"What do they do?" Slade stood back and looked at the photo. All the women, although their hair and eyes might differ, had many of the same features. Their eyes twinkled, their smiles were wide.

"Casey is a stay-at-home mom. She married a professional athlete that she met when they were both in college, and they decided when they had their first child that the best start they could give their children was for mom to be home and hands-on since dad has to travel so much with his team." Staci walked to the kitchen and took a bottle of Chardonnay out of the refrigerator and poured a healthy amount into a wine glass. "Cassidy is a teacher. Everyone but Casey and Isabella lives here in Missouri, which is where my dad's last assignment was before he retired. Casey lives on the East Coast. Izzy lives in Houston."

"I wouldn't have pegged you as someone who came from a family that large," Slade commented.

"Want a glass of wine?" Staci offered. Slade shook his head. She smiled, reached into the refrigerator, and pulled out a bottle of beer. "What about a beer?"

Slade grinned and said, "Now you're talking."

"I think my parents were trying for a boy, at least after my older two sisters. The twins were kind of a surprise to be honest. All of us older four are two years apart. Casey and Cassidy are six years younger than me. So I don't think they were exactly planned. But my mom and dad always told them they were a blessing, so who knows." Staci shrugged.

Slade looked at a piece of mail that was on the bar between the kitchen and the living room. "Your real name is Anastasia?"

"Yes, Anastasia was my great-grandmother's name."

"You moved around a lot as a kid, huh?"

"I was born in Germany. Dad was stationed there. Four years later, we moved to Italy. Six years later, we moved to Hawaii to the

TO DIE FOR HER

air base there. Four years later, we moved to Little Rock, Arkansas. I managed to graduate from high school and go to college before my dad's last move to Whiteman Air Force Base, south of Kansas City."

Staci took her glass of wine and walked into the living room. She sat on her brown leather sectional and started pulling the plastic bags containing the personal effects of the murdered men out of it. "I enjoyed the moving. It gave me a chance to literally start over every four to six years, experiment with who I was. My older sisters hated it, the twins always just rolled with everything, so I don't think it bothered them. But me," Staci smiled and leaned back a little, "I got to change who I was every time we moved."

"Why would you want to do that?" Slade joined her on the couch, sitting perpendicular to her location on the L-shaped sectional.

"Girls, especially pre-teen and teenagers, struggle with who they are and who they want to be. They want to be popular or maybe they would rather be known for being smart, maybe it would be cool to be goth or preppy." Staci took a sip of her wine. "I had been exposed to so many different cultures that I wasn't sure who I was. So whenever we moved, I would change into who I thought would be the coolest. It took me a while to find who I really was."

"And who is that?" Slade was curious. He sipped his beer and watched her reaction. He hadn't really expected her to be so open about herself and her family tonight; she was always the prim and proper, always professional, cool, calm, and collected Staci.

"Just me. I am a little bit of everything I wanted to be. I'm smart, and I know that sometimes intimidates others. I'm kind. I try to think of others, but I also like excitement. I don't like boring, but at the same time, I like the routine I've made for myself," she answered. "What about you?"

"What about me?" Slade set his beer bottle on a coaster on the coffee table and picked up one of the crosses.

"Who is Michael Slade? What's your story?

"Born and raised in Texas. Suburb of Dallas. My mom was a homemaker. I have two siblings, a younger brother and a younger sister. My dad was law enforcement in that same suburb. Nothing exciting." He shrugged.

"Are your parents still living?" Staci also picked up a cross and started looking at it through a magnifying glass.

"My dad is. He retired, is living in that same suburb, keeps busy with making sure the grass is not less or more than half an inch high." Slade grinned at the thought. "My mother died five years ago of breast cancer."

"I'm so sorry, Slade. Were you around when she was sick?" Staci turned her attention to Slade.

"Yes and no. I was in Dallas still, so I would come by regularly and check on her, but she was stubborn. Didn't want people to feel sorry for her or treat her any differently. She cooked us Sunday lunches right up until she was hospitalized that last time." Slade gazed soberly at the wall across from him, remembering. "All of us kids and my dad were with her when she passed away. I think that made her happy, that we were all together with her."

Staci put her hand on his arm. "I'm sure it did."

Slade snapped back. "That was when my dad finally retired. Said he wanted to enjoy his life and spend it the way he wanted to while he still could. My siblings went on with their lives. I was lost though. That's why I finally went to the DEA and away from Texas. I had to find my purpose again, and I had to do it alone."

"And did you? Find your purpose?" Staci asked softly.

Slade looked her in the eyes. "Yes."

Staci turned her attention back to the cross she was holding. The magnifying glass was awkward to hold when studying the cross, but the jeweler's loupe wouldn't be delivered until tomorrow. She narrowed her eyes as she studied the heavy silver. It was quite ornate. There were markings on the back, delineating the designer. At the juncture of where the two pieces that formed a cross met, there was a round, raised piece that almost looked like a flower, but the petals were pulled in, like a flower that had not yet bloomed. She fidgeted with that piece, pulling and twisting. She looked closer at the base of the flower. There was a definite line of demarcation that went all the way around. Slade watched as she got up and walked back to the kitchen. The leggings she was wearing were tight and gripped her bottom like a second skin. His maleness appreciated that. She had an amazing backside, and he found himself watching it admiringly as she walked.

She grabbed something out of a drawer and started digging at the cross at the line at the bottom of the flower. With a small snap, the flower came off the cross and bounced on the countertop. She picked it up and looked at it. Rushing over to the coffee table, she picked up the magnifying glass and looked inside the bottom of the flower.

"Aha!" she grinned. "I knew it!" She leaned over, holding the silver flower, and pointed. "Look!"

Slade leaned in, and Staci put the magnifying glass over the flower. Sure enough, the tiniest dot, bluish and rough, lay in the center. They both began going through the rest of the crosses, and in each, the same dot was found. After what seemed hours, they both leaned back, contemplating what their discoveries meant.

"So how do we get them to activate or track so we can triangulate where the data is going?" Slade asked.

Staci stared at the ceiling. "Well, they aren't activated now because whoever gave them these crosses knows they're dead. As far as figuring out where the data was going, that is going to take a computer expert. That is way beyond my knowledge."

"I don't want anyone at the agency messing with these. Not until I figure out who to trust," Slade told her.

"Yeah, I think I know someone. Someone we can trust."

"Who?"

"My computer nerd sister." Staci reached for her cell phone. Slade put out his hand and stopped her.

"I almost forgot. Wait," he told her. He dug in the bagel bag and produce two cell phones. "These are burner phones. Not in either of our names. My number is programmed into yours and yours into mine. If you want to talk about this case, use these. I don't know who might be listening on our other phones." He handed her a simple flip phone. She took it and looked at it skeptically. "Call your sister on this."

Staci punched in her sister's number, and it rang three times before she heard her sister's voice on the other end. "Hello?"

"Hey, Izzy, it's me, Staci," Staci responded.

Slade watched as Staci walked to the foyer and then took a left, and he heard a door open and shut. She was gone about fifteen minutes when he heard the door open and shut again. Staci rounded the corner past the stairs to the living room. "I'm going to overnight one. Make sure you are there to sign for it. How long will it take you to figure it out?" Staci listened as her sister responded. "Great! Hey, thanks for doing this. How is David?" David was her sister's cat. Again, Staci listened to the answer as Slade watched her walk back in his direction.

"That's really great, sis," Staci told her sister. "I gotta go for now, but when you get it, call me on this phone, not the other one. And tell David I said hi." She closed the phone and smiled. "So you are going to take one of these. Package it up, overnight it to my sister. She's going to examine it and see if she can tell us anything about how to trace it back to whoever was tracking the men. You have to do it because of the whole chain of custody issue."

Slade nodded. They put the rest of the crosses in individual plastic baggies that Staci had in a drawer in her kitchen, and Slade labeled each one with the name of the deceased cartel member who wore it.

"I can't take these with me, and I can't leave them here. What am I supposed to do with them?" he asked.

Staci replied, "Well, obviously, my office isn't an option considering what happened last night."

"What about a PO box?" Slade asked.

"That's good for temporary storage, but I was thinking, what about a safe deposit box?"

"Great, but I don't have one."

Staci smiled. "I do, but I can't get there until tomorrow morning."

She placed everything back into the bagel bag. She ran upstairs and retrieved the gym bag that she had unpacked earlier. "Here, let's put this bag in here. You can take it with you, but meet me at Waterford Bank on Union Street at 9:00 a.m. as soon as they open."

TO DIE FOR HER

She picked up the first flower that she had popped off. "Let's get this packaged up and addressed."

They made quick work of wrapping the flower multiple times in tissue paper then slid it into a tiny velvet bag Staci brought down from her bedroom. She had kept her grandmother's cameo necklace in it, but she was sure Grandma would approve of her using the velvet bag for this precious cargo instead. She surprised Slade by producing a cardboard envelope with a popular courier's logo on it and slid the velvet bag into it. Noting the look on his face, she smiled and told him, "I use them a lot to send things to my sister and nephew on the East Coast. It made sense to have a few around instead of going there every time to get one only to go back to send it."

Slade nodded.

Staci addressed the envelope and handed it to Slade. "They open at eight thirty. Get this sent off before you meet me at the bank."

"Yes, ma'am," he replied, and somewhat subdued.

This woman was a mix of efficiency, vulnerability, and surprise. She was also a bit bossy. It all intrigued him.

CHAPTER 6

At exactly 9:00 a.m., Staci exited her car and strode toward the doors of the bank. She looked around before opening the doors, surveying the parking lot for Slade. She didn't see him, so she went inside to wait. She had just reached the sofas off to the right where customers could sit while they waited for whatever banking business they had to begin when Slade entered the bank carrying the gym bag. She nodded her head at him once and walked to him.

"We have to go to the desk over there to get escorted back," she told him as she started in that direction.

She approached the woman behind the desk and got her driver's license out of her purse. The woman pushed the clipboard in her direction to sign while looking Slade up and down appreciatively. For some reason, that irritated Staci. A balding man in a suit that was a little too baggy approached her and asked for her name.

"Anastasia Everly," she replied and showed him her driver's license as well.

Nodding, the man turned toward a hallway and walked to the third door. He opened the door and paused, looking at Slade.

"He's with me," Staci informed him.

The man nodded and let Staci and Slade enter before he walked to the wall of metal doors. He waited until she put the key in and turned it. Once it clicked, he left, shutting the door behind him. Staci opened the door and pulled out a long box. She set it on a countertop behind her and opened the box's lid. Slade reached into the gym box and pulled out the baggies with the crosses. They put them into the box, replaced the box in the wall, and Staci shut the door, turned the key, and then reached for the gym bag. She stuffed it, barely, into her tote.

40

TO DIE FOR HER

"You go ahead and leave. I'll wait ten minutes, and then I'll leave, just in case we were followed," Slade told Staci.

He knew she was being watched, but he didn't want to spook her. She nodded and left. He strolled out into the lobby and sat on one of the sofas. He picked up a real estate magazine that had been left on a side table and pretended to read it while he kept an eye on the doors. After ten minutes, he put the magazine down and walked out of the doors, looking around the parking lot, making sure Staci was gone. He didn't see anything suspicious. He walked over to where he parked his SUV and got in. He had some people to interview and a meeting in a couple of hours. He backed out of the parking space, turned onto the street, and headed to the office.

Staci reached the employees' parking lot half an hour later. She pulled into her usual spot, pulled the gym bag out of her tote, and threw it into the back seat. She took a moment to bring her blood pressure down. All this cloak-and-dagger stuff was exhilarating but terrifying at the same time. She had a search warrant to draft for the silver flowers on those crosses, and she wanted to research the origin of where they might have been ordered. It didn't take long to get an elevator and make it to her office since she was late to work today. Most everybody was already inside and working already. She waved to the legal secretary assigned to her and three other assistant US attorneys and unlocked her office. Looking around, she noted that everything appeared to be in order unlike the day before. Satisfied, she changed into her heels and took a folder out of her tote. The folder had her to-do list for the day, and she wanted to make sure she stayed productive. She was a list maker. She bordered on OCD but was too flexible to be completely there. Her lists, however, kept her organized, at work and in her personal life. Today's list included researching the silver crosses, drafting the warrant after Slade had brought her his affidavit, and filling in the timeline of investigative activities in the event she needed it for court later.

She turned on her computer, and while she waited for it to warm up, she thought about yesterday evening. Slade had become more human, opening up about his family, his mom's death, and its effect on him. She liked thinking about him as a person with emo-

41

tions and baggage rather than the driven machine intent only on solving this case and then moving on to the next. He rarely smiled, but when he did, his whole face changed. He became approachable, not as threatening, and as sexy as he was when he was so intense, his sexy gauge when he smiled went well past a ten. That dimple was particularly mesmerizing.

A knock on her partially opened door interrupted her thoughts. She looked over to the door and saw Max standing there.

"You busy?" he asked.

"Just getting my day started. Come on in." Staci turned away from her computer, which was angled away from anyone sitting across from her.

Max entered and took a seat in one of the two chairs in front of her desk. He casually crossed one leg over the other and looked around.

"I just thought I would check in on you. You've had a pretty busy couple of weeks," he commented.

"Yes, I now understand why you had to pass it off to someone else. This case does tend to dominate most of my time," she told him as she picked up her coffee mug and took a sip.

"So anything new to report?"

Staci wanted to tell him about the tracking device development, and her theories, but until she had something concrete, she didn't want to share. Once they had found either Ayala or the person in his organization that was tipping him off about the DEA's progress in their investigation, then she would fill him in. Otherwise, it was just speculation and not particularly helpful. She shook her head in the negative.

"No, Slade keeps following up on past leads and is reinterviewing some people, but we don't really have anything. The good news, however, is no more bodies have turned up." She smiled at Max.

"How are you and Slade getting along? He can be a handful," Max asked.

Staci shrugged. "He can be that," she agreed. "But the good thing about him is if you explain things from the legal standpoint,

TO DIE FOR HER

how a judge would rule or what the rules of evidence say, he usually complies."

Max nodded. "That's good. That's really good. I wasn't sure if he would run roughshod over you when I assigned this to you."

"You may have misjudged me, Max. Don't mistake professionalism for weakness." Staci's smile became stilted and no longer reached her eyes. This is how Max thought of her? Timid and weak? "I spend all my time on this case. Weekends, evenings, and, of course, here at the office. I will bring Ayala down and prosecute him in a case so legally tight that no appeal will give him relief. You can count on that. Having to spend a little time with Mike Slade isn't going to veer me off course."

"Of course! I didn't mean to imply that he would scare you off the case. I just meant I was afraid he wouldn't work with you and follow your legal advice in this, that's all." Max put his hands up, palms toward Staci as if warding off an evil spirit. "Are you still lugging those boxes back and forth or have you found a home for them?" He put his hands back down.

"Still lugging them back and forth, but I'm about through with that. I have gotten everything out of them that I can at this point. Why don't I prepare you a memo detailing the categories to be used, like what can be a piece of physical evidence, what witnesses are really relevant versus people who have nothing to add or exonerate? Something like that?" Staci offered.

Max's demeanor visibly changed from almost bored to leaning forward in his chair with an eager smile. "That would be great! We can forego our meetings if you just prepare me a memo every couple of weeks. I know people around here don't really like meetings."

Staci responded with a wry, "You said it, I didn't."

Max stood up and told her he would see her later and left. Staci paused before she turned back to her laptop. What an odd conversation that was. Max never came to her office; it was always the other way around. And him bringing up how Slade was treating her, what was that? She had dealt with some of the worst jerks in other cases, and no one really cared. It was an unwritten rule that unless it was obvious harassment, you just did your job and moved on to another

43

case. Usually, the attorneys only had to deal with the investigative side when preparing for trial and, of course, during trial. Shaking her head, Staci typed in her search words to start her research. She needed to focus on this case.

Seven hours later, Staci shut down her laptop. She had learned quite a lot about those silver crosses and looked forward to filling Slade in. The warrant was done, had been emailed to Slade for him to get a judge's signature, and she was looking forward to a quiet evening at home. Tonight she had no intention of working on this case. Football preseason was starting, and she wanted a glass of wine and some Chinese takeout and to relax in front of her television, cheering on her favorite team. She changed out of her heels and put them in her tote, grabbed her keys, shut off her light, and closed the door. It was just after 5:00 p.m., so she had to wait for the elevator for a few minutes, and the ride down to the garage took a few minutes as people came in and out of the elevator on its trip below. Once it reached the garage level, Staci exited with two other people she recognized as working in the building but on other floors and in other agencies.

She made the left turn toward the main parking area and started toward her car when she heard steps behind her. She stopped, and the steps stopped. She turned to look around. Seeing nobody, she continued to her car. As she approached the driver's side, she clearly heard steps behind her. She slowed down but continued steadily. She moved her keys into her fist, each key protruding between her fingers. As she reached the car door, she saw the man's reflection in the window of the vehicle. His hand reached out and gripped the top of her shoulder. Taking a deep breath, Staci jammed her right elbow into his midsection as hard as she could. She spun around and punched the man with her right fist, keys impaling him in the cheek. She shoved her left hand up and connected with his nose. She had dropped her tote, and she took a small step backward and then kicked the man in the groin as hard as she could. She heard an "Oomph" before he dropped to the ground. She saw that one of her heels had fallen out of her tote when she dropped it, so she grabbed the heel, pulled it back, and leaned over the man, ready to put the stiletto in his face.

TO DIE FOR HER

Slade had decided to call it a day after he had gotten the judge's signature on the warrant Staci had emailed him earlier. He needed some time away from this case, just to get some perspective, and tonight was the perfect night. He would grab some dinner and beers with his team at a sports bar and watch the preseason football game tonight. *Some quality team bonding*, he justified to himself. He got off the elevator and turned to the garage and then stopped in his tracks. A man with dark hair, medium height and build, wearing dark pants and a dark jacket was following Staci. They reached her car before he could yell out and warn her. As Slade lunged forward to run to Staci, he saw her spin. The man's head jerked back twice, and then the man doubled over, finally collapsing to the ground. He watched Staci pick up one of her heels, kneel over the man, and raise the heel above her head, ready to smash it into the man's face.

"Whoa! Hold up there, Sugar Ray!" Slade had pulled his firearm and had it pointed at the man groaning on the ground. He rushed over to where the man lay moaning.

Staci heard Slade's voice just as she was about to bring the heel down on the man. She looked up, her hand still holding the shoe above her head. She saw Slade approach, weapon aimed at the man on the ground, so she slowly lowered the shoe. She stood up, straightened her skirt, and picked up her tote. The man on the ground was saying something in Spanish, and Slade answered him while he rolled Staci's assailant over and cuffed him.

Once the man was cuffed, Slade put away his pistol and asked Staci, "Are you alright?"

Staci shrugged, hiding how shaken she was, and replied, "Yeah, I'm good." She watched Slade lift the man up off the floor to a standing position.

"Do you need a statement from me?" she asked.

Slade shook his head. "No, I watched the whole thing. This," he splayed out his hands somewhat in bewilderment, "happened so fast before I could react. Where did you learn to fight like that?"

"I have five sisters." Staci smiled wryly. "I don't think I can drive right now. Adrenaline, you know?" Staci told him.

He smiled and agreed. "Yeah, I know. Let's go back inside. I want to question this guy before we book him. You can watch."

With that, he turned back the way he came, one hand on the man's elbow, guiding him to the elevator. Staci breathed in through her nose and out through her mouth, yoga style. She closed her eyes for a second, focused solely on her breathing. Once her breathing returned to normal, she caught up to Slade and the detained man. She studied the man, noting that he looked Latino, with dark hair and eyes, ill-fitting jacket; he was sweaty, and a glint of silver could be seen to the side of his open collar. She looked up and caught Slade's eyes and then cut her eyes back to look at the man's collar. She looked back at Slade, and he nodded.

The man said something else in Spanish, and Slade told him in English, "Shut up. You'll get your chance to talk in a few minutes."

The elevator door opened, and Slade jerked the man forward. "This way."

A couple of people were still in the offices where Slade's people worked. They turned their heads to watch Slade escort the handcuffed man down a hall, and then they turned back to what they had been doing, not the slightest bit fazed. Staci tentatively followed Slade although she kept a distance between her and the two men, not sure where she should be going.

"In here," Slade told the man.

He shut the door behind them, leaving Staci in the hallway. She stood there, unsure what she should do. A minute later, he opened the door, and she could see her attacker behind him sitting at a table, handcuffed to it. Slade opened a door next to the one he had just come out of. A large window facing into the room where the handcuffed man was seated was on one wall.

"He can't see you," Slade told Staci.

She nodded and wrapped her arms around herself. It was cold in the room. Slade shut her in the room and returned to the handcuffed man.

For the next half hour, not much happened. Slade established the man spoke both English and Spanish. He presented a document and read it to the man. It was the man's Miranda rights information. Slade had the man initial after each paragraph, signaling that he understood each right. He agreed to waive his right to remain silent or have an attorney present. The man's name was Joaquin de la Cruz Gestado. He was not a documented citizen or resident alien, and he was from Guatemala. He was thirty-five years old. He still had family in Guatemala, and he worked for cash, under the table, doing odd jobs and carpentry work. All this was mundane stuff. But when Slade asked him about Miguel Ayala, the man's face changed. Fear? Anger? It was hard to judge. He denied he knew anyone by that name, and then suddenly, the man reverted back to speaking in Spanish.

"*¿Dónde está Miguel Ayala?*" Slade asked again. "Where is Miguel Ayala?"

"*No sé,*" Gestado repeated. His face was emotionless.

Slade leaned in.

"*¿Por qué intentaste lastimar a esa señora? ¿Quién te envió a agarrar a la mujer?*" Slade asked him why he tried to hurt Staci and who sent him.

The man shook his head and refused to answer. This went back and forth for the next two hours. Who sent him, who does he answer to, who gave him the order. Still, Gestado refused to say. Finally, Slade reached across the table and exposed the silver cross around Gestado's neck.

"*¿Quién te dio esa cruz?*" Slade asked the man who gave him the cross.

The man said nothing. Slade reached over and yanked it off Gestado and held it up in front of him. "Who gave this to you? I know you work for Las Arañas." Slade opened the man's shirt slightly and lightly tapped the tattoo of the spider in the web on his pectoral muscle. "Tell me about this," he demanded, shoving the cross closer to the man's face.

When the man still did not answer, Slade sat down in the chair across from the man, calmed himself, and informed him, "They already know where you are. These contain little GPS trackers, so they know where you are at all times. If you think that not answering my questions is going to keep you safe, think again. They already know where you are, and you've been here way too long to have just done what they sent you to do and left. They know. And whether you talk to me or not, they're going to think you are talking. So you may as well tell me what I need to know."

The man's face whitened, and his eyes grew large. "*Por favor.*" His heavy accent was even heavier now. "It's not me I am worried about. I have an old mother and two sisters in Guatemala. They are the ones at risk. I am not afraid to die, but I can't let my family suffer. I became one of them to make money so my family can live in a house with electricity and running water and so they never go hungry." He held his hands palms up in a sort of plea.

"Then just give me a name. If you don't know where Ayala is, have you been present when orders were given?" Slade pressed gently as if sympathetic with the man's dilemma.

Gestado nodded.

"Was it Ayala?"

The man shook his head and lowered his eyes.

Slade sighed. "Can you give me the name of the person who you heard give orders or not?"

The man nodded ever so slightly. The man gestured at Slade, imitating writing. Slade knew immediately that he wanted paper and pen, so he reached over to a desk in the corner and handed the items to Gestado. Gestado wrote one word and handed the pad to Slade. Staci watched as Slade read the word, and his face visibly paled as he stared at the word. Slade tore off the paper and shoved it into his pocket. Gestado put his index finger in front of his lips. He gestured toward the cross. Slade took the cross and set it out in the hallway and returned.

Gestado told him, "Sometimes, they know what you say. I will not tell you anything else. I want a lawyer." He leaned back in his chair and looked at Slade expectantly.

Slade knew the man was through talking, and he had uttered those magic words: I want a lawyer. Questioning was over. He left the room and entered the room where Staci had been watching.

"What did he write?" she asked him.

TO DIE FOR HER

Slade wasn't prepared to tell Staci what Gestado had finally given him because it didn't make sense. He needed time to check it out.

"It was a street name. Not an actual name. I need to do some digging to find out who he was referring to. It could just be a desperate man saying stupid things."

Staci was livid. She had grown up in a house of secrets. She hated secrets. And now she and Slade were supposed to be on the same team and working together. Now was not the time to have secrets. She told him so in so many words and stomped out of the room. She snatched up the cross he had laid in the floor next to the door. "And you need to check this out too!"

She marched down the hall and got onto the elevator. Slade sighed, but he couldn't go chasing after her. He needed to get Gestado booked in the local county jail, put a federal hold on him, and then get him transferred somewhere for safekeeping.

Turning back to the room, he told Gestado, "Let's get you booked."

The next morning, Max called Staci into his office. When she knocked softly and stuck her head in the door, he motioned her inside. "I heard what happened yesterday evening. Are you alright?"

Staci smiled and told him, "My knuckles are a little sore, but I'm fine."

"This is getting too dangerous. Normally, prosecutors aren't targeted. You have any idea why they are going after you?" Max asked, casually sipping his coffee.

"No idea. I know Slade and his men are making some progress, but I have no idea how I figure into it." Staci sat in the chair across from Max's desk. She crossed her ankles and took in Max's demeanor. He didn't seem overly concerned; he was more curious about the situation. "Maybe I should reassign this case. I wouldn't want anything to happen to you," he suggested.

Staci's eyes narrowed slightly. "No, I have this. I've already spent so much time on it. I don't want to just hand it off at this point."

"What about the guy who tried to attack you? He say anything?"

Alarm bells went off in Staci's head. She didn't know why. But she knew she didn't want to give anything away at this point. She shook her head and replied, "Not that I know of. I don't speak Spanish, and the guy only spoke Spanish. Slade didn't mention anything to me about him giving up any information."

Max nodded slowly. "Well, they don't usually. Their families are usually threatened if they talk. They would rather go to prison than talk. The families are taken care of if they go to jail instead of turning."

"The double-edged sword of cartel life, I suppose." Staci looked over to the door, ready for the conversation to end. "I need to get back to work. I have some motions to work on for the few remaining cases I still have."

Max waved her off. "Of course, go. I just wanted to make sure you were okay and not scared off."

Staci laughed slightly. "It will take more than that to scare me off."

She walked to the door and let herself out. She tried to walk out like she didn't have a care in the world, but the longer she was in Max's office, the more uncomfortable she became. She didn't know why. It wasn't that Max did or said anything inappropriate or suspicious. The longer she worked on this case, the more paranoid she was starting to become. *My goodness*, she scolded herself. *I'm becoming just like Slade.* She shook her head and strode to her office.

CHAPTER 7

"Manny, phone." The prison guard gestured to a heavily tattooed man working out in the yard.

The prisoner set the weight bar down and wiped his brow with his forearm. Scars of torture and war dotted his forearm among the many tattoos. He walked slowly, taking his time, toward the guard, walking with the swagger that only prisoners have, showing the rest he was the baddest man in the yard that day. He followed the guard inside and down a hallway where a pay phone was located. He picked up the receiver.

"Yeah?" He spoke into the phone.

The guard stood patiently next to him. He looked around and saw that the lone guard was the only person in the hallway.

"It's me. I need a favor," the deep voice on the other end of the line informed him. "A prisoner was transferred there last night. Do you have access to the prison library?"

"Yeah." Manny kept his answers short and noncommittal.

"I'm emailing you pictures of him and his family. He's there in the medical unit. His family is in Guatemala. I need to know what he knows."

"I want out of here," Manny told the voice matter-of-factly.

"I promise. You make this happen, you're out."

"Do you care how it happens?" Manny smiled at the guard, trying to catch him off guard and determine if he was listening.

The guard rolled his eyes and turned sideways away from Manny.

"I need him alive. Otherwise, no. Do you know how to contact me?" the voice asked.

"Yeah." Manny sighed. He had been at the federal prison in Springfield for three years. He was ready to blow this pop stand.

"Let me know."

The click on the phone let Manny know the conversation was over. Manny hung up the telephone and gestured to the guard, ready to go back to the yard. He casually strolled to the door, bobbing his head and bouncing on the balls of his feet in anticipation.

*****

Staci printed off the photographs of the six men, folded the paper they were assembled onto into her tote. Some things weren't adding up, and she was calling in a couple of favors later. She heard a knock at her office door and looked up to see Mike Slade standing there, dressed in a navy blue suit, white shirt, and red power tie. He had shaved off his usual stubble, and his hair, which was usually tousled, was neatly combed. She had never seen him in anything except khaki work pants and T-shirts. Even though he was devilishly handsome in that usual work attire, he exceeded the word "handsome" today. He was magnificent. So much so he took her breath away.

"Wow! What's the occasion?" she asked him when she could breathe again.

"I had to testify at a grand jury earlier this morning." He sauntered inside and shut the door. "You were going to tell me about something the other night, and I cut you off. What was it?"

Staci had to think for a second, then her face lit up and she smiled. "Oh yeah, so those crosses. Made from Mexican silver. Taxco, Mexico, specifically. Apparently, there are a lot of silver mines in that area. And there are three jewelry shops that sell jewelry made from that particular silver in the St. Louis area." She pushed a piece of paper across her desk toward Slade. "I don't know if they make the designs on-site or if the crosses are made somewhere else and shipped up here to sell, but I bet you and your team can find out."

Slade reached over and picked up the paper and read the short list of jewelers. "We'll check this out." He tucked the paper into his pocket and changed topics. "To get to a grand jury, what exactly will suffice?"

Staci thought for a second. "Well, someone to testify to the volume of drugs, the money made, who manages the operation, and, if we are pursuing all the murders, who made the orders. Remember, the burden for an indictment isn't beyond a reasonable doubt."

Slade nodded and stood up. "Well, I guess I will follow up with these jewelry shops." He turned to leave.

Staci stopped him when she said, "Thank you for being there last night. I might have really hurt that guy. Survival instincts are funny things."

Slade turned slightly to look at Staci. Sitting behind her desk, with her blonde hair pulled back into a single braid, dressed in her black pencil skirt, pastel blouse, and fitted black blazer, she looked prim and proper and so very innocent. He wouldn't have guessed that she would have been able to take on Gestado like she did. And when she lifted up that stiletto heel, ready to bring it down on the man's face, a little bit of her fortitude shone through. She surprised him on a regular basis, either with her wit, her intelligence, or her demeanor. She kept his interest, and that could be good or bad. Either way, not many people could keep his interest very long.

All he said to Staci was, "Yeah, no problem." Then he left her office.

*****

Several days passed before Slade and Staci saw each other again. She kept to her usual routine, closing out the last of the cases she had been working on before being assigned to the Ayala project. She went home, ate dinner, and tried not to think about Slade and what he was doing.

One night, she made a phone call to a good friend who was working in Europe. She had been wrestling with whether she wanted to dig into Slade's team or not since Ayala had been tipped off so much, and now that she was on the case, the murders had stopped. It seemed like someone told Ayala to lay low for a while. If that was the situation, someone who had knowledge about the progress of the investigation had to be involved. Her friend in Europe had some ties to various intelligence groups, and Staci wanted to rule out the people on Slade's team.

"Hey, girl!" Staci greeted her friend when she picked up. "What's going on?"

"Aнннн!" her friend yelled into the phone the same way she always greeted Staci. "How are you? There is so much going on! Did I tell you I think I met *the* one?"

Staci laughed and said, "No! Tell me about him!"

For several minutes, the two women chatted back and forth, catching up on family and personal lives. Staci always enjoyed talking with her friend, and she always made Staci smile and feel better about whatever was going on. Finally, Staci got to the heart of the call.

"Listen, I need a favor. Are you going to be in St. Louis in the near future? I have something I want you to look at and find out some information."

Her friend excitedly replied, "You know what? How lucky are you? I will be in St. Louis at the end of the month."

"So this is one of those super secret things. I'm pretty sure there might be someone following me, so we need to use discretion," Staci advised her friend.

"Ohhh, okay." Her friend switched into playful work mode. "Let's meet at our fave hangout before I moved back to Europe. I can text you the date and time."

Staci gave her friend the number for the cell phone Slade had provided. "Use this number when you do. Ciao!"

"Ciao, darling!" The line went dead.

And then came bedtime. The condo was dark and quiet, and Staci was left completely alone with her thoughts. More and more, those thoughts were about Mike Slade. More and more, her dreams involved Mike Slade as well. No matter how she tried, she couldn't get him out of her head. She knew that she was going to have to get

TO DIE FOR HER

him out of her system, and there was only one way to do that. But that particular thought scared her the most.

*****

Slade drove his government-issued vehicle down I-44 as fast as he could. It wasn't daylight yet, but when the call came in that Gestado had been assaulted and wanted to talk to him, he couldn't get there fast enough. He wanted to talk to Gestado before the other man changed his mind. He wondered why Gestado had had the change of heart, but he wasn't going to push it. When he saw the signs for the exit in Springfield, he sat up straighter and focused on the road. The drive up to the prison was typical, gun towers, barbed wire, multiple stop stations. He showed his badge at each stop station until he got to the parking lot for visitors. He grabbed his tape recorder, made sure he had plenty of tapes, and checked the batteries. He didn't want any interruptions once Gestado got to talking.

He walked to the front gate, flashed his badge, signed in, and waited to be escorted inside. He had to check his firearm, went through a metal detector, and finally, the captain, the person in charge of the prison, met him and showed him to the medical side of the prison. The federal prison in Springfield was primarily for providing medical, dental, and other health care to federal prisoners. However, the medical units were divided up, and Gestado appeared to be in a single-person unit.

When Slade entered the room, he saw Gestado on the bed, with IV's hooked up. He looked pale, but he was awake and gestured Slade over. Slade turned to his escort and asked for privacy. Once the captain had left and the door shut behind him, Slade took the tape recorder out of his pocket and showed it to Gestado who nodded. Once everything was set up, Slade asked Gestado in Spanish, "I hear you want to share something with me."

"Yes. I thought I would be safe here, but someone came while I was sleeping and stabbed me in the side." He pulled the hospital gown over slightly, showing Slade the wide bandage on his rib cage. "They did this to me, and I did not even tell you anything."

55

"Yeah, well, appearances. They will always assume you did."

"Moving me here made it worse, I think," Gestado sighed. "But it doesn't matter. I met someone here. He came in the middle of the day, like he owns this place."

"Who?" Slade leaned forward slightly.

"His name does not matter. But he belongs to a rival business of Ayala. He said the people he works for wants to take over Ayala's business. They are not afraid of Ayala's bosses." He breathed in a ragged breath. "He had pictures of my family." Gestado continued in Spanish, "He said his bosses would move my family and provide for them if I helped them take over Ayala's territory. Family is everything."

"So why did you want to talk to me?"

"The best way to take over Ayala's business is to remove his business from him. If you kill him, there is always another person to take over the business. If you take the business, there is nothing. I will give you names and where they are. I cannot make them talk to you. I am just a soldier, not anyone of importance."

"He promised you a higher position in his organization?" Slade asked.

Gestado shook his head. "No. He promised me my mother and sisters would be protected and that I could join them when they were moved."

"That's a lot to promise. Does he work here?"

"No, he is a prisoner here. But he has connections to the outside."

"What makes you think you can trust him to fulfill those promises?"

"He knew things. Things he should not have known."

"Did he threaten you?"

"No. But I know how these things work. If I do not do what he wants, my time will be very hard, very dangerous. He might even tell others I am a snitch." Gestado swallowed and closed his eyes. His breathing calmed.

Slade was afraid he might be dying, so he shook him slightly. Gestado opened his eyes and looked around the room.

TO DIE FOR HER

"Here are the names of the people who know things." And he rattled off four names. He told Slade where they lived, where they worked, and who was around them. Slade did not interrupt Gestado; he let him talk as long as he wanted.

When Gestado stopped talking, Slade asked him, "The other night, when you were arrested, I asked you for a name and you gave me 'Zorro.' What is that?"

"It means fox in Spanish." Gestado looked confused.

"I know what it means. What or who is Zorro?"

"Zorro is the person who is pulling Ayala's strings, gives him ideas. Gives him advice. He laughs and says he calls himself Zorro because he is the fox in the henhouse." Gestado breathed out deeply and groaned slightly when he tried to move up in the bed.

"Have you seen this Zorro?" Slade continued to press Gestado.

Gestado nodded. "I have seen him two times. Once was when some men were killed at a warehouse because the police were closing in. He suggested that certain people close to Ayala had to be responsible and needed to be eliminated to protect the business. Once was when he told Ayala that the woman was too focused on him and she needed to be scared away." Gestado smiled wryly. "I did not know she would hit so hard."

Slade's jaw hardened. Whoever this Zorro was, it was on his order, not Ayala's, that Staci had been attacked. It was also on Zorro's order, not Ayala's, that those men were killed. Ayala might be the person who actually issued the orders, but this Zorro was planting the ideas into Ayala's head, controlling him.

"Why would Ayala listen to Zorro?" he asked Gestado.

Gestado shrugged. "That is beyond what I am allowed to know." He looked around the room and then came back to focus on Slade. "How long am I here?"

"At least until I check out this information you gave me. I'll check on your family as well. Don't talk to anyone else about what you told me. Don't even talk to that other prisoner. You don't know who you can trust here."

Slade stood up and put the tape recorder into his pocket. He turned to Gestado, but the man seemed to be asleep, snoring slightly.

Slade went to the door and knocked. After a short time, a guard opened the door and let Slade out and began escorting him to the exit. As they walked down the last hallway, Slade saw a heavily tattooed Latino leaning on the cement block wall. The man's eyes narrowed as he watched Slade, and Slade noted that his ink reflected his membership in a known Mexican prison gang. As Slade passed him, the man continued to watch Slade, finally pulling himself away from the wall and walking in the opposite direction, whistling as he went.

On Slade's drive home, his thoughts vacillated between the information Gestado gave him and Staci. The sooner he could give Staci enough information for an indictment, the sooner he wouldn't be working as closely with her. The thought did not give him the peace he had hoped. He decided he would call up an old friend, someone who always managed to make him forget whatever was going on in his head even if it was just for a night. He could deal with his physical urges and his emotional ones at the same time. He picked up his cell phone and scrolled for her number. He hesitated for a moment. Was this really what he wanted? He and Roz both knew the score, knew this wasn't a relationship, no strings. That's the way he wanted it. Why did he hesitate then? Disgusted with himself, he pushed the button to call Roz.

"Hello?" Roz's voice answered the phone.

"It's Mike. You have plans tomorrow night?"

Laughing gently, Roz replied, "Been a long time, Mike."

"Yeah, but you want to get together or not?"

"You know I do. My place?" Mike Slade knew she was smiling that cunning smile. She knew how to get him going, and she knew it.

"Great. Nine-ish okay? I have some work I need to finish up first."

"Sounds yummy. See you then!"

The line went dead. *There*, he thought to himself. *I will work this out the way I always do.* He reasoned that once he had exhausted his body with Roz, Staci wouldn't be as much of a temptation. It was just a physical response to a nice-looking woman, and once that was satisfied, he'd be able to focus on this case and not think about Staci, at least not in the ways he had started thinking about her.

TO DIE FOR HER

The next twenty-four hours flew by. He and Rodriguez surprised the four cartel members whose names Gestado had given him. Most had been caught with something illegal, making holding them in custody easier than anticipated. Only two talked at all. He had only needed one of them to talk, so Slade left Rodriguez with the last one, the one who got scared the easiest when they showed him photos of the dead men in the warehouse. He was a nerdy little guy, not Latino at all. He looked exactly like his job: the moneyman. Thick glasses, thinning hair, small, and wiry. Slade felt like this investigation was now moving at a much better pace. Gestado, this accountant, and the third suspect were all going to be placed in separate places around the area to be moved every so often to keep them under the radar and away from exposure and harm. Slade decided that while Rodriguez was interviewing the bean counter, he would go home, shower, and then drive over to Roz's house.

Slade's and Roz's rendezvous did not, however, go as planned. Slade sat on the side of the bed, naked and frustrated. Roz ran her long fingers up his muscled back, across his left shoulder, and down his arm, tracing the barbed-wire tattoo that wrapped around the muscled bicep with her red painted fingernails.

"It happens," she reassured Slade.

"Not to me it doesn't," he retorted, angry and confused. He was aggravated with himself and humiliated. Every time he had reached for Roz, he found himself being repulsed by the thought of having sex with her. So he tried closing his eyes. Instead of Roz's long dark hair and flashing brown eyes, he saw wild blonde hair and green eyes in his mind, and his body rebelled.

"She's a lucky girl," Roz told him quietly.

Slade whipped his head around and glared at her. "What are you talking about?" He knew what she was referring to, but for some reason, he dared Roz to say it.

"There are usually only a couple of reasons a man has difficulty getting hard. One is a physical reason," Roz smile at him. "You are the epitome of health." She sat up in the bed and pulled the sheet up over her voluptuous breasts. "Another reason is stress."

"That's probably it. I've been working on a case that has been slow and frustrating. I have to constantly be analyzing the next step," Slade relaxed a little. That was it. He was stuck in this case and was ready for it to be done.

Roz clicked her tongue against her teeth and softly chuckled. "Nope. How many times have we gotten together when you needed to get rid of the stress of your job? You've never had a problem satisfying both of us, multiple times, on those occasions." She sighed, blowing out a slow breath. "I knew this day would come. I dreaded it."

Slade turned his body to face her. "What?"

"The other reason a man can't perform is when another woman has his heart."

"That's ridiculous. Men cheat on their wives and girlfriends all the time."

"No, men cheat on wives and girlfriends who no longer have their hearts. You, my friend, are no longer the keeper of your heart. Whoever she is, she holds your heart in her hand." Roz leaned over the side of the bed and snatched up Slade's T-shirt. He caught it when she tossed it to him and slid it on.

"I think you're wrong. I'm not dating anyone." He stood up and pulled his jeans up.

"You don't have to be dating her. You just long for her." Roz wrapped her silky robe around her naked body. "If you're smart, and I think you are, you need to show her your hand. Let her in."

Slade didn't answer. He slid on his boots and started to tie the laces. Roz just watched him from the other side of the bed, smiling sadly, knowing that their relationship was at an end. Once Slade was finished dressing, she walked with him to the door. She put her hand on his arm as he reached for the doorknob.

"Slade, you have to start trusting people with your heart. I don't think you're the kind of person who would fall as hard as you have fallen if you didn't trust this woman. You've literally never fallen for any woman your entire life, so you've never had your heart broken. I don't know what keeps you holding back, but you need to figure it out and then let it go. You are missing so many opportunities for happiness." Roz stared up at Slade's face, earnest in her advice and wishing only for the best for him. She had loved him for a long time, but she also knew he didn't return the feelings, so she had taken the part of him he was willing to share. She knew it was time for both of them to move on.

"Yeah, well, I guess you don't know me as well as you thought," he responded, but he knew she was right. It was a scary proposition, letting go, losing control. It was scarier than kicking in a door with a felon on the other side; it was scarier than having a gun pointed at him. Those situations he knew about, could plan for, but matters of the heart were completely outside of his wheelhouse. "I have to go." He opened the door and walked out to his car.

Roz just watched him leave, laughing softly at his denial.

CHAPTER 8

The next two weeks flew by. Slade had the recorded interviews with the two cartel members and Gestado transcribed and hid the tape recordings in his gun's lockbox. He kept it close. He also had the two witnesses' silver crosses although he had ripped out the transmitters almost immediately. He needed to get the transcripts to Staci and have her add the crosses to her safe deposit box, but he had been actively avoiding her since that disastrous night with Roz. Sighing, he got off the elevator at her floor and walked to her office. The door was closed and locked. He glanced at his watch and saw that it was after five o'clock. Of course, she had left. After five and on a Friday. Considering his options, he decided he would join his team's Friday poker game instead of driving over to her house. He left to go home and change clothes, calling Rodriguez on his way out to confirm he would be playing poker and offering to pick up food or beer.

He found himself driving by Staci's condo on his way to the poker game. It was almost seven o'clock now, and his poker game was on the other side of town. He wasn't sure why he drove by, but now he was frowning. The place was dark. She clearly was not home. Not that it was any of his business. Shaking his head, he turned his car at the next stop sign and made a beeline to Rodriguez's house.

Rodriguez lived with his wife and three children in the quiet suburb of Webster Groves. His home was an unassuming one-story house with a basement, and the weekly poker game occurred in that basement. His wife, Josie, always fixed them snacks, and when Slade knocked on the door holding a six pack of beer, she opened the door with a wide smile on her face.

"Mike! So good to see you!" She ushered him in. She was short, not more than 5'2", and after giving birth to three children, she had

TO DIE FOR HER

put on a little weight. She wasn't fat by any means, but Slade had seen photos of her and Rodriguez's wedding, and she was definitely more filled out now. He could hear some sort of chaos coming from down the hall. He smiled. Rodriguez had two boys and a girl, and the boys were always into mischief. Whatever they were doing now was causing the little girl to cry.

"Boys! Stop it!" Josie yelled down the hall. She smiled and shrugged at Slade. "Those boys will be the death of me, I swear."

The little girl, a dark-headed five-year-old whose big dark eyes were wet with tears emerged from one of the bedrooms. "Jason broke my Barbie," she said and held up a doll that no longer had a head. She saw Slade and immediately stopped crying.

"Uncle Mike!" She galloped down the hallway and into Slade's arms when he squatted down. She hugged him and somberly said, "My Barbie doesn't have her head now."

"Hmmm," Slade surveyed the damage. He didn't know the first thing about fixing broken dolls. "Where's the head?"

"In my room." And the tiny child ran back to the room where she had come from.

Josie emerged from the same room with two boys, Jason and David. They looked appropriately chastised, but when they saw Slade, they smiled. Slade smiled back. He didn't know how Rodriguez stayed sane with all the chaos that came with a house full of kids, but in Slade's mind, it made Rodriguez the bravest man he knew.

The little girl reappeared, holding the doll in one hand and its head in the other. She held both out to Slade. Slade panicked and looked up at Josie. The child's mother laughed at Slade's expression and told the child, "Lacey, I can glue it back on, but you won't be able to turn the head anymore."

Lacey gave her mother the doll and the head and said, "That's okay, Mama. I don't need her to turn her head. I just need her to look fabulous."

Josie nodded and told Slade, "You know where to go. I need to glue this together."

He grinned and stood up. Carrying the beer, he descended the stairs to the basement. It was dark, illuminated only by the three lamps situated around the room. The poker table was off to one side, and all the members of his team were present.

"There you are! What took you so long?" Rodriguez stood up and took the beer from Slade. He passed out a bottle to each of the team and opened the one he kept.

"Just had to run home and change clothes," Slade responded as he took a seat at the table.

Carmichael began dealing each of them their hands. Slade surveyed his team. He had handpicked Rodriguez and Mark Saenz. Carmichael, Westbrook, and Vaughn had transferred in at the beginning of the Ayala investigation. Since that time, they had spent time bonding as well as working together since they had to trust each other to have each other's back. Saenz and Westbrook were also married with children, and Slade had met their families at various social events: weddings, the occasional dinner, and once at a dart-throwing contest in a local bar. Steve Vaughn was a serious man. He rarely smiled, but he was a hard worker, and he could make good decisions. He was a lady's man, to be sure, as many women were attracted to his blond, good looks. He was the youngest of the group and looked like a California surfer. Carmichael smiled all the time. Nothing seemed to ruffle his feathers, and he was quick on his feet. He didn't join the rest of the group socially as much as the others, and he had never introduced anyone he was dating to them, choosing to always attend the gatherings alone.

Smiling, Slade pushed in his first chips, telling the group, "I'm in. Let's see where this goes."

*****

Staci parked her car on the street, a block from La Chere. It was a nightclub on The Landing that she and her friend, Monica, had visited on many occasions before Monica had moved to back to Europe. She and Monica and another couple of friends had frequented this club right after Staci had passed the bar exam, but when Monica took the job in Brussels and Staci's job had moved her to Joplin for a while, she and the rest of their group never got back to

TO DIE FOR HER

going dancing at La Chere after Staci moved back to St. Louis. The excitement of seeing her friend after so long was making her heart beat a little faster, and the idea of letting loose, dancing, and enjoying the company of someone other than coworkers was exhilarating. She opened the doors and looked around in the dimly lit room and immediately saw Monica. Red hair, long and flowing, wearing a tight purple dress and thigh-high boots, Monica grinned when she saw Staci. She waved Staci over to the empty barstool next to her.

Staci flounced onto the bar stool and announced, "I'm parched!"

On cue, a handsome bartender appeared and asked, "What can I get for you, ladies?"

"Dirty martini," Monica ordered.

"Make mine a Pink Lady," Staci told him.

Then both women giggled and hugged.

"I have missed you!" Staci declared.

The bartender produced their drinks and placed them on napkins. The women took a second to sip their drinks then smiled at each other. "When will I meet this handsome devil you told me about on the phone?" Staci asked her friend.

"Liam?" Monica rolled her eyes and fanned herself. "He is the most handsome man I have ever met. He's on assignment at the moment, but as soon as he has some downtime, I definitely want to bring him 'across the pond' to meet you!"

"He sounds amazing," Staci told her. She took a healthy gulp of her drink.

"What about you? Are you dating anyone?" Monica sipped her martini, looking over the rim of the glass.

Staci immediately thought about Slade. His tall, muscular body, square chin, perfect nose. His intelligence, his dangerousness. She shook her head, "No," she replied truthfully. "No one."

"Hmm, interested in someone?" Monica raised her eyebrows and smiled slyly.

Staci tipped her head slightly. "He's not interested in me. And he's a work person. Off-limits, but to be honest, he is about the sexiest man I've ever met."

Monica laughed softly. "Liam was…is a work person. And I find it hard to believe this guy isn't interested in you. Every guy in this place is interested in you, and most of them are gay." She waved her hand around to encompass the room.

"So finish that drink and let's go to the restroom," Staci suggested. She downed the remainder of her cocktail and gestured toward the ladies' room with her head. Monica gulped down her martini and followed Staci.

Once in the restroom, Staci looked under each toilet stall. She sobered up immediately and took the piece of paper with the six DEA team members photos out of her tiny cross body purse. "I need you to find out about these men. One of them is not like the other." She handed the paper to Monica.

Monica stared at it briefly and then asked, "Why don't you just ask your—"

Staci cut her off. "No. I want to handle this on my own. He doesn't need to know anything about this. He always makes such a big deal out of things."

Monica shrugged and put the paper in her own purse. "Okay. When do you need the information?"

"As soon as you can get it to me. Their names and personal identifiers are on the backs of their photos."

"Are you in danger?" Monica stared at Staci, looking for any tic or other giveaway.

"I don't think so. But I think one of them is purposely messing up an investigation I am part of." Staci didn't consider the attack by Gestado being in danger. She saw it more like a warning.

"Got it. Now we planning on being in here all night, or do you want to dance the night away?" Monica purposely lightened the mood.

"Let's dance!" Both women laughed and left the restroom for the lights on the dance floor.

*****

TO DIE FOR HER

The heavily tattooed man, Manny, was out of prison. He was standing directly across the street from La Chere, watching. He pulled his cell phone out of his pocket and dialed a number.

"Yeah?" the voice on the other end answered.

"I'm watching her. She went into a nightclub called La Chere on The Landing."

"Got it. Just stay there."

"I have shit to do."

"I know."

"I'm leaving by ten o'clock."

"Got it."

Manny hung up his phone and put it back in his pocket. He had only been out of prison two weeks. Sprung as promised but with strings.

*****

Slade was starting to get bored. He had excused himself to go to the bathroom, and upon entering the basement again, he noticed the other men were putting up the chips and cards.

"You through taking my money?" he jokingly asked.

Rodriguez replied, "Yeah, apparently Vaughn has a late date, and Westbrook's wife is wanting him home. Something about peak ovulation or some nonsense."

Slade looked around the room. "Where's Carmichael?"

Saenz shrugged and said, "He said he had to go. Probably had a date too."

"Okay, well, I could use some sleep myself, so I will see you guys on Monday unless we get called out this weekend." Slade put away the chair he had picked up and saluted the men remaining in the basement. He climbed back up the stairs where the house was now quiet.

He hugged Josie. "Thanks for the snacks and letting us take over your basement again," he told her.

"Yeah, sure. Anytime. Now that the kids are in bed, I'm off to bed myself. Take care of yourself, Mike. Find you a woman," Josie told him.

Slade just laughed. He walked to his car. This was his personal vehicle, an American-made muscle car. He didn't own property, and his apartment was a one-bedroom in a loft downtown that he didn't spend a lot of time in or money on. But this car was his pride and joy. He had bought it right after he had started with the DEA, and he babied it. He smiled when he started the engine, listening to its perfect timing. He paused before backing out. He wanted to hand over these transcripts to Staci before Monday so she could upload them onto her flash drive. He also just wanted to see her. It had been two long weeks. He took out his burner phone and texted her: "Hey, it's Slade. I have something to tell you. You home?"

A few seconds later, she replied: "No. La Chere. Dancing."

Slade thought about that reply. *Dancing? La Chere? What in the world?* This he had to see. He backed out and drove in that direction.

*****

Staci smiled as she put the burner phone into her purse. *That would probably blow his mind*, she thought. She picked up her third Pink Lady and sipped it.

"Ooh, what's with the sly smile?" Monica grinned.

"Oh, nothing. Just screwing with someone's head." Staci laughed. "Oh! I love this song! Let's dance!"

She threw back the rest of her drink, and she and Monica walked to the dance floor. Staci loved to dance. She didn't think she was that good, but she loved all types of music. Usually, she had classical music playing over the sound system at home, she worked out to heavy metal, and now, this electric dance music had her wanting to sway and move to its beat. The beautiful thing about La Chere was it was considered a "crossover" bar. Most of the couples in it were gay, and the reason it was so popular with Staci and her friends was because they could come and dance and drink and socialize, and very few men were going to hit on them because they were women.

Staci and Monica could dance, and everyone just assumed they were "together," so no one bothered them.

When Slade walked through the doors of La Chere, he noticed a few things. First, the couples inside were mostly same sex. This didn't bother him. Another thing that he noticed was that some of the women appeared to be almost as tall as him, wore heavy makeup, and had Adam's apples. Their clothes were flashy and exaggerated, lots of bright colors, miniskirts, and fishnet hose. A lot of them were looking at him like they wanted to eat him for dinner with their lined lips. Drag queens, Slade noted. He found them to be very witty and philosophical individuals.

One of them was sauntering toward him, smiling seductively. She stopped in front of Slade and reached out to put an enormous hand on his bicep. "Hey, handsome. Are you lost or just looking for love in all the wrong places?" she asked.

Slade looked down at the hand adorned with long glossy fingernails and then back to its owner. "While I'm flattered, I'm here on business," he told the queen.

The third thing he noticed was a blonde woman dancing about fifty yards away. Her blonde hair was just past her shoulders and very curly. She was dressed in what appeared to be vinyl or faux leather black pants that were skintight. Her back was to him, and he could see the waistband of the pants barely came up past the crack of her butt. The music changed to a little faster beat, and that bottom started bouncing and shaking, and suddenly, like a bolt of lightning had just hit, he knew that he recognized that ass. The blonde woman was Staci. He stood there for a few moments admiring her ass. Then he strode with purpose over to her and just stood there, arms crossed. A red-haired woman who was dancing next to her stopped and just looked at him. Staci noticed the redhead's gaze and turned around. Her eyes widened in surprise, but she smiled temptingly at him through lips that were dark red. Normally, she wore nude or pale lipstick, but tonight, those lips were red. Slade had never noticed how full and plump her lips were until now.

"Hey! I didn't think you would actually come here!" Staci yelled at him over the music.

"Let's just say I was curious," Slade told her in an equally loud voice. He gestured toward her outfit. "This is a new look."

Besides the tight pants, she had on red stiletto heels and a black top that laced up the front. The laces were tight and together at the bottom, which came to just above her navel, but the higher you went on the top, the looser the laces were and the wider the gap. Two half-moons that were her breasts were clearly visible. She wore more makeup than she did at work, and the double coat of mascara made her green eyes pop. Slade noticed that she had a glint of metal at her navel. A belly button ring? He suppressed a groan. This woman held a lot of surprises.

Staci introduced Slade to Monica. "This is my best friend from all the way back when we lived in Italy. Her dad was in the military with mine."

Slade nodded, and Monica yelled, "Nice to meet you."

Then the music changed again, slower with a deep bass beat. Staci grabbed Slade's hand and pulled him toward her. "Dance with me," she demanded.

Reluctantly, Slade obliged. He pulled her close, ran his hands down her back, and let them rest on her hips, holding her next to him. He caught the beat and moved his hips against hers, letting the music guide his movements. He breathed in, knowing he was playing with fire. His body started to respond like it wouldn't at Roz's house, and he closed his eyes, willing it to behave. Staci felt the stirrings of Slade's body and smiled. Maybe it was the three Pink Ladies, maybe it was the fact it had been so long since she had been with anyone, or maybe it was realizing the power she now had over Slade, but suddenly, she wanted him to want her as much as she wanted him. She turned around so her back was against him and ran her hands up over her head. She moved her rear end against him, still in time with the music, grinding. He ran his hands from her hips up her sides and then grabbed her arms. He yanked her away from him, almost angrily.

"It's time for you to leave," he told her. She had him on fire. His body was rebelling, betraying how she was affecting him. He was frustrated and pissed off, all at the same time.

TO DIE FOR HER

Staci laughed at him. "You aren't my father or my boss." She started to pull her arms away from his grip.

"I'm not kidding. You've had too much to drink. You don't know what you're doing," Slade started to pull her off the dance floor.

Staci yelled at Monica, "Call me when you know something!"

She walked with Slade to the door but not before she heard Monica laugh and say, "Oh, I'm pretty sure he's interested."

They got outside before Staci yanked her arm away from Slade. Her mood changed from carefree to angry. "What the hell do you think you are doing?"

"Little girl, you are poking the bear. You need to go sleep it off before you get yourself into trouble," he told her. "Where's your car?"

"Oh, I'm too drunk to dance but not too drunk to drive? Do you realize how dumb that sounds?" Staci reached into her purse and retrieved her keys.

"I have no intention of letting you drive. I'm going to drive you and your car to your house and then have someone come get me and take me back to my car," he told her as he snatched the keys out of her hand.

As they walked, Slade spotted her car about a block away. He pushed the auto-start button on the key fob. A loud explosion permeated the cool late September night air. A massive fireball erupted from Staci's car, and the heat and sound wave of the explosion knocked both her and Slade off their feet. For an unknown amount of time, Staci couldn't hear anything. Everything and everybody was moving in slow motion. She finally picked herself up and noticed Slade doing the same. They both turned to look at the melted, molten mess that had been Staci's car with shock on their faces.

"Well, shit." Staci's calm statement summed it up.

"Indeed," Slade agreed.

For the next two hours, police and firemen smothered the area. They took statements and put out the fire. Staci pulled her own cell phone out of her purse and took pictures of the burned-out shell that used to be her car.

"What are you doing?" Slade's voice was behind her.

71

"Taking pictures. My insurance agent isn't going to believe this," Staci retorted.

She had already gotten the incident number for the police report so she could get it and provide it to her insurance company. She knew on Monday when she reported this to Max that he would be furious because the boxes of evidence had been in the trunk, but fortunately, everything was preserved on the flash drive she carried everywhere. She shivered, but she didn't feel cold.

Slade's hands came up on her shoulders. "You're in shock. We need to get you home."

He turned to the agent in charge. "You have everything you need? Can we go now?"

The agent nodded, and Slade guided her around the corner to his car. He put her inside and closed the door. Staci felt numb. If Slade hadn't have come to the club tonight, hadn't have been the one to push that button…

"Can we get food?" she asked him when he closed his door and started the car.

Surprised, he answered, "Yeah, what do you want?"

Staci started laughing. At first softly then louder until she was almost hysterical. Slade sighed, and reached across the center console, taking her into his arms.

"It's alright, Staci. We're both still alive and kicking."

Sniffling, Staci moaned. "But if it wasn't for you—"

Slade didn't want to think about what-ifs. The thought that Staci would have been killed if he hadn't been there burned in his soul. "But I was there. You are okay," he told her, his calm assurances belying the torment he was feeling about how close Staci came to being blown up. "Now what do you want to eat?"

"Mexican food. Tacos," she answered. She had to pull herself together. It was embarrassing, crying in front of Slade.

He laughed. "Tacos it is." He pulled out into the Friday night traffic, headed for the nearest all-night taco stand.

*****

They pulled into Staci's driveway a short time later. She exited the car carrying the bag of food, digging for her keys. She got the front door open and walked into the kitchen. Setting the bag on the counter, she sighed and opened the drawer on the end of the island. It was the designated junk drawer, and after rifling through it for a moment, she pulled a garage door opener out and held it in the air triumphantly.

"Ah-ha!" she exclaimed. "I found my extra opener!"

Slade glanced up and smiled. It was the littlest things that seemed to make her happy.

Staci set it back down on the counter and asked Slade, "Would you mind very much if I ran up and took a shower before we eat? I feel gross."

Slade shook his head. "No, go ahead." He was envisioning her in the shower, naked and wet. He needed her out of his presence for his own sanity.

"Great," she told him as she ran up the stairs.

Slade looked through her cabinets until he found a plate and a wine glass. He poured Staci a glass of her favorite wine and put her tacos on the plate. He wandered around the living room for a few minutes, looking at her knickknacks and photos. He looked at the mail thrown onto the island: Anastasia Nicole Everly. She had a laptop opened on the coffee table, but it was in sleep mode. He didn't dare try to wake it up. He didn't want her to know he was snooping. He went to the front door and bolted the dead bolt and then checked the door that led to the garage. He was studying the windows that were between the front door and the garage door. These could be an issue if someone was really targeting Staci.

"Bullet-resistant glass," Staci's voice floated down the stairs.

Slade turned toward the sound of her voice, and his breath was caught in his throat. She had scrubbed all the makeup off, her hair was in a messy bun, and she was barefoot. She had put on gray cotton gym shorts that came to the middle of her thighs, but the waistband sat under her navel. Her pink tank top sat just atop her navel, exposing that damn belly button ring. Well, not a ring. A shiny little bar. And Slade desperately wanted to run his tongue against it.

"What?" he asked instead, pulling himself away from those thoughts.

"When I bought the condo, my dad came, and we installed some extra security stuff. The dead bolts, the alarm system, and we replaced all the windows with bullet-resistant glass." She floated down the stairs. "All of his years in the military made him overly cautious about keeping the castle safe." She walked to the kitchen and saw the plate of food and glass of wine. "Thought you told me I was too drunk to dance?"

"Yeah, well, someone just blew up your car, so I figured one more glass to help you sleep couldn't hurt." He shrugged and helped himself to a beer in her refrigerator.

They walked to the living room where Staci sat cross-legged on the sectional. Slade joined her, keeping some distance between them. He watched her devour the first taco. She looked like a teenager now, not a temptress.

He smiled and waited for her to swallow before he asked, "When is your birthday?"

Surprised by the question, Staci paused and then answered, "December 24th. Yours?" She took a sip of wine.

"October 14th."

"So coming up in a couple of weeks. Interesting." She took another sip of wine. "While we're asking invasive questions, why aren't you married with a couple of kids?"

Slade shrugged. "Never met a woman I wanted to spend the rest of my life with. My parents' marriage was solid. If I ever marry, I want my marriage to be as good as theirs was."

"So you are using their marriage as an excuse for your fear of commitment. Interesting," Staci made the observation as she finished the glass of wine.

"What about you? No husband, no long-term commitment? What's your excuse?"

"Oh, I thought I had found my prince when I was in law school. We dated for a couple of years, even lived together for about six months, but," she shrugged, "it wasn't meant to be."

TO DIE FOR HER

Slade was curious. He took a gulp of beer and asked, "What happened?"

Staci smiled wistfully. "He blacked my eye."

Slade choked on his beer, and a rage he didn't recognize started to build inside. "Excuse me? He hit you?"

Staci nodded. "He was a nasty drunk. One night, he came home after drinking with his buddies, and I made the mistake of pointing out that he was home late. I guess that was enough for him to punch me in the face and throw me across the room."

"Did you call the police?" Slade noticed his grip on the beer bottle had tightened, so he concentrated on relaxing it.

"Nope. I left him. Told him if he ever contacted me again, I would report it to the bar examiners as well as the police. That would have ruined his career. I also went out and signed up for my first kickboxing class the next day. I still go every Saturday morning. I was determined that the next man who put his hands on me would pay physically," Staci told him. "So I guess my excuse is I haven't found a man I completely trust."

"Wow. So it was the kickboxing classes, not your sisters, that taught you how to kick an attacker's ass?"

"Yes and no. I was a scrapper, my dad calls it. I would throw down with the best of them, but he and my mom got me into sports as a way to channel some of that. My sisters and I did fight, but it wasn't organized. It was reactionary. Kickboxing taught me how to organize the fight. How to instinctively have a plan," Staci responded.

"What sports?" Slade continued with his questions. She was probably the most surprising female he had ever met.

Staci shrugged. "Soccer, track, volleyball. I was like the son my dad never had because I enjoyed watching sports too. I love football and hockey. Not as big a fan of more mundane sports like tennis. I went to a Division I college on a soccer scholarship."

Slade was sure the surprise showed on his face. "So you have some favorite teams?"

"Of course. But what about you? Did you play sports when you were in school?" Staci decided the interrogation needed to be returned.

"Football and baseball. All Texas boys try one or both at least."

"Let me guess, quarterback?" Staci only half-teased. He had the confidence she had seen in the quarterbacks she had known.

"Nah, I was a linebacker. Defense all day long," Slade's drawl was showing now, telling her that he was relaxing around her a bit.

"Why defense?" Staci set her plate down, another taco still on it, but she wasn't hungry anymore. She was fascinated with this conversation. He was letting his guard down, being someone other than Agent Slade.

"'Cause you get to hit people, of course!" He laughed and finished off his beer.

The room became quiet as he looked around, knowing he needed to leave but not wanting to. Staci felt the awkwardness too. As he stood to leave, she quietly said, "Can you stay the night?"

Slade stared hard at her. He was trying to figure out what she meant when she noticed his dark eyebrows almost knit together in a scowl. "I mean, someone just blew up my car, and I would have been in it. I'm a little nervous to be alone right now," she explained. She looked up at him, her green eyes wide, feeling a little foolish but admitting her fear all the same. "I have a guest room, or you can sleep here on the couch. I just don't want to be alone right now."

Slade slowly sat back down next to her and took her hand in his. He brought the palm up to his lips and gently kissed it. He looked at her across her hand, his eyes smoldering. "Darlin', if I stay, I won't be on the couch or in the guest room." He ran his tongue softly across the palm of her hand.

Staci sucked in her breath. Fire ignited from somewhere inside her. Her eyes darkened into a deep dark green, and she ran her tongue across her bottom lip. Slade thought he would explode right there in her living room.

"Tell me, Staci, am I leaving or am I staying?" He pushed for her answer, knowing what he wanted her to say.

Staci knew what she should say, but the heat in Slade's eyes overwhelmed her. She took a minute to make the decision, but when she made it, she was all in. "Stay," she whispered.

TO DIE FOR HER

Groaning, Slade moved closer to Staci, put one hand on the back of her head, and pulled it toward him. He leaned down and placed soft butterfly kisses on her quivering lips. He held back the power he felt growing inside himself. He didn't want to scare her off, not when he was this close to what he instinctively knew would be unlike anything he had ever experienced.

Staci, however, overcame whatever timidness she might have felt at first. As soon as Slade's lips touched hers, she was ravenous. She wanted, no, needed more. She put both hands alongside his face and demanded more with her lips. Slade responded by parting her lips with his and expertly sliding his tongue in her mouth. Staci matched his eagerness and then broke away from his lips. She began placing wet kisses along that magnificent jawline, down his neck, and along his chin.

Surprised, Slade found himself out of breath. That mouth was tormenting him, making his body react in a way that almost scared him. He had never gotten this hard this fast. He brought her mouth back to his and kissed her again, this time picking her up and setting her on his lap so that she was straddling him. He ran his hands up the back of her T-shirt only to find she didn't have on a bra. The realization almost caused him to erupt right there. Wanting to slow things down, he pulled his mouth away from Staci's mouth and leaned back. Her nipples were hard points behind the T-shirt, and he leaned forward again, this time taking one of the nipples into his mouth through the cotton shirt. He sucked and lightly bit the nipple, and Staci sucked in a deep breath.

She was on fire. Everywhere he was touching, kissing, felt like small explosions. She could feel herself getting wet between her legs, and she felt a desperation she had never before experienced. When she caught her breath, she smiled slightly and reached down to the bottom edge of her shirt. She pulled it over her head, exposing her breasts to Slade. Slade moaned, and his eyes became as black as onyx. She was more beautiful than he had even imagined. Her breasts were high and firm, larger than he had thought, with their dark pink areolas and erect nipples. He closed his eyes and took one of her nipples in his mouth, willing himself not to climax.

Staci could feel him between her straddled legs. He was hard and pulsing, larger than her limited experience had known. When he took her nipple in his mouth, she couldn't help the soft squeal that burst from her throat. The sound thrilled Slade and drove him to be more ravenous with the other nipple. Staci stopped him momentarily, pulling on his shirt and demanding that he take it off. Slade quickly obliged, tossing it off to the side. Staci ran her hands over his chest, brushing his own nipples with her thumbs and laughing softly when she heard his swift intake of air. She leaned down to flick one with her tongue and then kissed her way up his chest, up his throat, and back to his lips. Slade greedily kissed her back, letting her know he was as eager as she was for what would come next.

Staci lifted her hands up to her hair bun and took it out of the elastic tie, shaking her wild blonde mane. Slade muttered something unintelligible and buried his hands in her hair, pulling her face to his, and smothering her mouth with his. Staci knew she had come too far to turn back, so she gently pulled away and climbed off his lap. She had never suffered from self-image problems; she had always been in shape because of sports, so when she stood before him and put her thumbs into the waistband of her shorts, she paused. Teasing him slightly, watching his eyes flash and his tongue dart out to lick his lips in anticipation, she lowered the shorts to the floor and stepped out of them. She stood before him in only the baby pink bikini panties that she wore under her shorts.

Slade's breath left his body, and all he could say was, "My god." She was magnificent. She had defined abs and thigh muscles; she was perfectly proportioned, and that damn belly bar glinted in the light. Even though she was smiling at him, he could see the shyness behind her eyes.

"You're perfect," he told her and started to reach for her.

She backed up slightly and told him, "I showed you mine. Now show me yours."

Slade almost choked. He undid his belt and his jeans while he watched her watch him. He slid his shoes off and leaned up slightly to pull his jeans down along with his briefs. Instead of waiting until he had taken them all the way off, Staci straddled him again when

TO DIE FOR HER

they had reached just beneath his knees. He had intended to take them all the way off, but now that was impossible.

He could feel the heat radiating from between her legs, could feel the wetness. She was pushing herself against him, promising him paradise and torturing him at the same time. Slade wasn't sure how much longer he could hold out. He took her hand and put it on his erect penis, telling her, "Touch me."

Staci wrapped her fingers around him as best she could. She was a little frightened and a lot excited to find out that not only was he blessed with length but also girth. As soon as she had him in her hand, she moved it very slowly, tentatively. As soon as she heard him make a guttural sound that assured her he was enjoying her touch, she held him tighter and moved more deliberately.

He snatched her hand away, telling her, "That's enough of that. You're going to make me explode."

And before she could react, he took a nipple into his mouth again, running his teeth and tongue on it while he moved a hand between her legs.

Staci felt the anticipation build as she felt his hand cup her, and then she felt a single finger trace along the split of her vagina. She closed her eyes and shivered when she felt the fingertip touch her engorged clitoris through her panties. She knew she was on the precipice, and she was ready to fall. After a few short strokes, he paused. She opened her eyes and saw hesitation.

"I need these off," Slade told her, touching the waistband of her panties.

"Mmmm, yes, you do," Staci purred back at him.

Although reluctant to break the connection between them, she stood up and yanked her panties down. She straddled him a third time, and this time, there was nothing between them. She moved slightly against him, teasing him, feeling his erection jerk. He reached between them again and rubbed his finger against her clitoris again, feeling it skin to skin. His finger was rough, but it rubbed Staci exactly the right way, and when Slade slipped that lone finger inside her, she felt all the tension leave her body. She shuddered as she climaxed, letting go of everything that was holding her back.

Slade felt her tighten around his finger, and then he felt the vibration of her climax. Suddenly, his entire hand was wet as her orgasm spent itself. He could no longer wait. He needed to be inside her. He paused only long enough to demand, "Say my name."

When she softly said "Michael" in his ear, he groaned and put a hand on each cheek of her butt and lifted her slightly then down onto himself. He slid into her and almost lost himself. She was so tight, and the heat was so intense he wasn't sure how long he would last. He closed his eyes, willing himself to go slow. She arched against him, taking him even deeper, and then using those perfectly muscled thighs, she began to ride him. She moved slowly at first, and he held her butt in his hands to guide her. Suddenly, electric shocks overtook him, and a primal need to bring them both to climax spurred him into holding her tighter, lifting her up and down, faster and faster until he felt the vibrations start inside her again. She was keeping pace with him, and when her climax started, he felt her not only ride him faster but also harder, grinding onto him until suddenly, he felt her shudder, felt the moisture, and heard her release the most intense growl from her throat that he was almost sure he had hurt her physically. Before he could explore that possibility, his body betrayed him, and he released himself with a mighty hiss, thrusting upward as far inside of her as he could reach.

For a few moments, neither of them moved. Her forehead was on his shoulder, his hands still on her hips. Finally, Slade opened his eyes and tried to focus. He had never lost himself like this before, never lost control. Staci had awakened something in him that both excited him and terrified him. He felt her pull herself off him and saw her grab his shirt that he had thrown to the side. She slid it on and gave him a small smile.

"Now what?" she asked.

"Maybe we should move this upstairs," he suggested as he pulled his jeans back up over his hips.

She nodded and waited for him to get his pants buttoned before offering her hand. Staci knew she should be completely satiated. Slade had been masterful, knowing how and where to touch her. But she was greedy and wanted more. Her head told her this had to be the only night they would spend as lovers because she couldn't compromise the case that had brought them together. She had to get this out of her system, had to get *him* out of her system so she could concentrate and finish this case and move on with her life. Her legs still wobbly and her heart pounding, she led him up the stairs.

As he was walking up the stairs, Slade frowned. He had lost control to the point that he had not put a condom on. He never forgot a condom. Now he was chastising himself for being so irresponsible. Even as a teenager, he had always taken control to ensure that whoever he was with was safe and protected.

Staci glanced back at him and saw his frown. Was he regretting it already? She paused on the stairs and asked, "What?"

Slade glanced up at her and saw the worry and insecurity on her face. God, she was beautiful. She was kind and intelligent. She was also probably the only woman in the world who didn't realize how incredibly sexy she was. And the sex. Slade had no words for the way she responded to his touch, how alive she became whenever she was experiencing the pleasure. And her eyes. How deep dark green they got, almost as if they were glowing with an otherworldly light. Looking at her now, he gulped and breathed in her essence.

Grinning his devilish smile, dimple in full display, he told her, "Just thinking you were walking awfully slow."

Staci smiled back at him, her eyes flashing. "Then come on!" And she ran up the stairs.

Following her, Slade promised himself he would be smarter the rest of the night. He followed through with that promise as they brought each other to the brink, over and over, the air punctuated by moans and sighs and squeals. Finally, in the wee hours of the morning, they fell asleep, snuggled together, their bodies fully satisfied and their minds free of the stress and fear with which they had started the night. Right now, it was just the two of them and no one else.

CHAPTER 9

Thunk, ka-thunk, ka-thunk. Slade opened one eye. Then he heard the screaming guitar and throaty moans of a heavy metal band. *What the hell*, he thought to himself. He reached for Staci, only to be met with an empty bed. He sat up. It was still dark outside. He glanced at his watch. Five thirty in the morning. He continued listening to steady, rhythmic thuds and loud raucous music, trying to wake up, his mind intently trying to figure out what all that noise was. After a few minutes and no closer to recognizing the *ka-thunk* noise, he got out of bed, pulled on his briefs, and opened the bedroom door. The noise and the music got a little louder, so he followed it down the hallway to the second door. It was very slightly open, and he pushed it open enough to peer inside. Staci was running on a treadmill, steadily, making good time. Her hair was pulled up into a haphazard ponytail, and she was wearing a gray sports bra and those tiny shorts marathoners wear. She had her phone perched on the treadmill, and she was shiny with sweat. *Well*, Slade thought to himself, *that explains her ass*. He watched her for a few seconds and then decided he might as well take a shower since he was up.

He walked back to the bedroom, gathered up the used condoms he had carefully placed on the floor, and threw them in the garbage. He grabbed his jeans and walked to two doors facing the bed. *One of them has to be a bathroom*, he told himself. He reached for the one on the right. It opened up into an enormous closet. He studied it for a moment, noting how organized it was, color-coordinated, shoes lined up just so. It screamed OCD, and Slade smiled. Staci wasn't exactly OCD, but she definitely was organized, and she liked order. Closing the door, he opened the door on the left. This was the bathroom. Enormous shower, big enough for two, he noted to

TO DIE FOR HER

himself, double sinks, towels neatly hanging on the rods, decorations to a minimum. The color scheme of sage green and tan spilled into this room, the walls a soft khaki, the towels and mats the sage green, the floor seemed to be a light-colored slate. He closed the door most of the way, leaving it open just enough to let steam out, and started the water, allowing it to warm up. He grimaced when he noticed the soap was a variety of body washes: lavender, citrus, vanilla. None of them very manly. Sighing, he reached for the vanilla-scented body wash. This was probably the least likely to make him smell like a female.

"Whew!" Staci blew out a breath as she turned the treadmill off. Five miles. She ran every morning except Sundays. Running let her work things out in her head, and when her head was too full, running let her clear it. She could run off stress, worry, just about anything. She really liked starting her day with this clean-slate status. She turned off the music and walked back to the bedroom. She could get a shower before she woke up Slade. They were going to have to have a conversation about last night and how it could not happen again. Smiling slightly, she didn't regret it. He was as fantastic a lover as she had fantasized, but this would compromise the case, and they had come too far to have that happen. Busy with her thoughts, she pushed the door open slowly, her mouth opened a little too wide. She hadn't paid attention when she entered the bedroom or she would have noticed the bed was empty. Now as she peered through the door, Slade had his back to her, obviously fresh out of the shower, drying off. His legs were long and powerfully muscled. But it was his back that took her breath away. She had always been a fan of the latissimus dorsi muscle group. Great lats had always been sort of a weakness for her. Slade's lats were magnificent. They were strongly defined and made his shoulders look even wider. She gazed at the barbed-wire tattoo around his left bicep, and there was some short of shield on his right shoulder blade. His hair was still wet, and when he bent over slightly to run a towel over his head, Staci slowly closed the door back to how she had found it. She backed up quietly and sat down on the edge of the bed to wait for him to finish so she could get her shower. She definitely had to stop this now before it was too late.

Slade emerged from the bathroom with a large grin on his face. Damn, that dimple made her knees weak, Staci admitted to herself.

"I thought you might join me in the shower when you were eyeballin' me," Slade teased.

"How did you know I was there?" Staci knew it was pointless to deny it.

"Always be aware of your surroundings. After a pretty short time as a cop, you start to get a sixth sense about being watched." He shrugged and walked around the bed, looking for his shirt.

"Slade, we have to talk," Staci began. She took in a breath, her semi-practiced speech ready to go.

"Uh-oh, that doesn't sound good." Slade slid his shirt over his head and looked at her expectantly.

"Last night was amazing," she began. "But it can't happen again."

Slade crossed his arms over his chest and leaned back against the bedroom wall and smiled at her, his eyes flashing. "I was kind of hoping it would happen at least a couple of more times."

"Yes, well, I can't compromise this case. If the lead prosecutor and the lead agent are sleeping together, it makes your credibility an issue. And it draws my ethics into question," she told him. She stood up and faced him. "I really don't know what your intentions are, but until this case is tried to completion, not only can this, whatever this is, not happen again, but no one can know."

Slade mulled over what she was telling him. He knew she was right. He didn't want her to be right. Finally, he nodded. "Okay, I respect what you're saying. I agree with you." He walked slowly over to where she was standing, her eyes that deep old jade green, showing her uncertainty about his purpose. "But when this case is over, promise me we can re-examine this." He leaned down, and Staci's heart pounded. If he kissed her, her resolve would melt. But he only placed a light kiss on her forehead.

"Go get a shower. I'm hungry and need breakfast," he told her.

"Actually, I have a kickboxing class I have to get to, and then as soon as my insurance agent sends me the information, I have to go pick up a rental car," she replied.

TO DIE FOR HER

Slade closed his eyes. She could be the most obtuse woman. "Fine." He snapped open his eyes. "Get a shower. I will drive you to your class."

Staci almost ran to the bathroom to put space between them. He oozed a sexuality that she was not prepared for. She closed the door and let out a sigh. A hot shower would do wonders, she told herself.

Slade made his way downstairs and looked in her refrigerator for something that could tide his stomach over for a while. For someone who apparently took health and exercise seriously, the contents of the refrigerator belied that. She had a couple of bottles of wine, some cheese, some butter, several Styrofoam containers with leftovers from various restaurants around town, and a pizza box. He looked in the pizza box and found several slices of what appeared to be Italian sausage and olive pizza. He sighed. That would have to work.

Next, he opened cabinets to find a plate to put the pizza on in order to microwave it. He saw a blue thumb drive sitting slightly behind the stack of plain white plates. His eyes stayed on the flash drive for a few seconds, pondering its contents. He'd ask her when she came downstairs. He put the pizza on the plate and stuck it in the microwave for less than a minute. He looked around and didn't see a coffee maker. What did this woman drink in the morning? He looked in the refrigerator and saw a small container of milk. He pulled it out and opened it, and immediately, his head snapped backward from the smell of rotten milk. Gagging a little, he poured it down the sink and threw the bottle away. He found several unopened bottles of water on the lowest shelf of the refrigerator, so he grabbed one of those. He stood at the countertop, eating the leftover pizza and washing it down with the water, watching the stairs, waiting on Staci.

He didn't have to wait long. He heard her before he saw her, her feet heavy on the steps as she half-walked, half-ran down them. He glanced up and saw her as she got to the landing. Her wild curly hair still wet but thrown into a messy bun, sneakers on her feet, sweatpants, and a T-shirt that read Property of University of Arkansas football. He half-smiled, thinking that Staci made even sweatpants look sexy.

"Okay, ready?" she asked. She saw him scarf down the pizza he was eating and set the plate in the sink. "Really? You couldn't wait a few minutes?"

He smiled and shrugged. "I worked up an appetite last night." He watched her face turn red.

She averted his eyes, grabbing a purse that was next to the table in the foyer. She slammed her phone inside. Slade made a mental note that flirting with her and teasing her was a lot of fun, and now that he knew he could get under her skin, he intended to do a lot more of it.

He drove her to the gym where her class was held. As she got out of the car, he told her, "I'm going home to change clothes. When do I need to be back to get you?

"A couple of hours. I should be done by ten," she told him.

She shut the door, and he waited until she was inside before driving away. As he drove toward his apartment, he remembered he had never gotten around to telling her about the interviews they had conducted, how they probably had sufficient evidence to start the process of indictment, and, probably the best news, the most probable location of Ayala. Smiling at the memory of why he had forgotten to tell Staci the good news, he plotted how he would find more time to spend with her.

A little less than two hours later, Slade opened the door to the gym. It was really warm inside. It smelled like a gym. Noise bounced around inside of it like a gym. He could hear some grunts to his right, so he turned to see the grunts coming from Staci. Every time she landed a blow with her fist or a foot, she grunted. She had taken off the sweatpants she had had on earlier and was wearing shorts similar to the running shorts she had been wearing this morning when he watched her on the treadmill. Her T-shirt was also gone, and now she only wore the bright red sports bra she had been wearing underneath it. She was dripping in sweat, and her bun was even messier, with strands of hair escaping from every angle. She was hitting the bag hard, her knuckles wrapped in sports tape. Her shoes were off,

TO DIE FOR HER

and her bare feet landed on the bag in precise movements. Slade stood there, admiring her technique for a few moments before her trainer acknowledged him with a nod of his head. Staci stopped her assault on the oversized bag and turned in his direction. Her chest was raising and lowering with her heavy breathing.

She walked over to him and asked, "Has it been two hours already?"

He breathed in and was amazed that even as sweaty as she was, she smelled delicious. He nodded and told her, "If you get dressed, we can go get brunch."

Laughing, she retorted, "Getting dressed isn't going to make me smell better. You sure you want to be seen in public with a chick who is sweaty and gross?"

"You aren't gross," he lied. He watched as she slid on her sweatpants and T-shirt and then her sneakers.

Her trainer came over, stuck out his hand, and introduced himself. "Hey, I'm Jake."

Slade shook the offered hand and replied, "Mike."

Jake tossed his head in Staci's direction. "She's pretty driven. Come a long way since she started here."

"She tell you about the guy that tried to attack her in the parking garage?" Slade asked.

"No, I haven't heard that story." Jake shook his head, clearly interested.

"Yeah, guy came up behind her. Just as he reached for her, man, she got him with an elbow in his solar plexus, hooked him with a fist, and kicked him in the nuts. Took her seconds to get him on the ground." The pride in Slade's voice was apparent.

"Damn. I'll have to ask her about that. I'm certain she can give almost anyone more than they bargain for." Jake laughed.

Staci strolled up to the two men and looked from one to the other. "What are you two talking about?"

Slade grinned at her. "Just telling Jake how you kicked that guy's ass in the parking garage."

Staci rolled her eyes. "Great. You can tell that story at my funeral."

The two men laughed, and Slade asked her, "Ready to go?"

When Staci nodded, he led the way to the door and held it open for her. They walked to his car. When Staci was inside, she looked at Slade curiously.

"What?" he asked as he started the smooth motor of his car.

"What's with this car? I noticed it last night, but I was preoccupied by my own car blowing up," she asked.

"It's my personal car."

"Yeah, no kidding. It's kind of flashy for you, don't you think?"

"Flashy? No. High performance sports car? Yes. I have an appreciation for well-made American muscle cars. When I was in high school, I found a 1969 Camaro with a split front bumper, but it needed some work. I got a job and worked my entire sophomore year in high school to save up for the car. My dad matched what I saved. Then I spent my entire junior year fixing it up. Every dime I made went into that car. I drove it all through college. When I started on the force in Dallas, I sold it to buy a newer car. I have regretted that decision every day."

Slade pulled into the traffic and headed toward the newest restaurant district just west of downtown. "So when that car died, I decided my next purchase was going to be something that was more like me and more reliable."

"And this is what you chose?" Staci was attempting to tame her hair and not doing a very good job.

"Yeah. Listen to that engine? Purrs like a kitten," Slade bragged.

"My insurance agent got back with me. I need to go to the airport to pick up a rental. Maybe you can help me decide what to get while my claim gets settled," Staci suggested.

"Sure." Slade shrugged. He pulled into a parking lot and put the car in park. Shutting off the engine, he let himself out and was walking around to open Staci's door when she opened it herself. Sighing, he put a hand on the door and offered the other to her. She took it.

"You're killing me," Slade told her.

"What?" Staci looked up at Slade, confused.

He smiled wryly at her. "I'm trying to be a gentleman, but you keep screwing it up."

TO DIE FOR HER

Staci gasped slightly and then blushed. "I'm sorry. I'm used to being independent."

Slade snorted quietly. "Independence is one thing. Not recognizing a guy's attempt at chivalry is something else." He gently grabbed her elbow, guiding her to the door of the eatery.

The restaurant was busy, but the service was top-notch. Slade's fried eggs and steak were cooked perfectly. Staci's Eggs Benedict melted in her mouth. She looked around the restaurant as they ate, noting that the clientele appeared to be mostly middle-class individuals either coming from or going to their children's sports events. The women all wore similar clothing, leggings and sweatshirts or jeans and a sweater. The children wore various sports jerseys and shin guards. The noise level was above normal, and Staci wondered if she was going to get swallowed up in the chaos. Slade used the noise, however, to bring her back to focus.

"I was looking for you last night to catch you up on the latest developments in the case," he told her between swallowing a bite of food and taking a healthy gulp of coffee. He liked his coffee black and strong. He had made a pot of it when he had gone to his apartment to change, and now it was kicking in. He could feel it.

Staci returned her focus to him. "Oh? What?" She nibbled on a piece of the buttery biscuit that had come in a basket before their food arrived.

Slade told her about his interviews, about getting them transcribed as well as having them recorded. "Saucedo explained that the bulk of the money came in, that small increments, under ten thousand each, were deposited in a variety of small banks around the state. Anything more than that has to be reported and raises red flags with the feds. After the money sits in the accounts for three to five days, it is transferred to a variety of off-shore accounts. There is a guy named Zorro, who gets a cut, and the money is transferred to his account before any money goes to the other accounts. Once the money is transferred to the off-shore accounts, it sits there long enough to be credited then more transfers until it makes it to Mexico."

Staci pondered the information. "Zorro? Really? And who is Saucedo again?"

89

"Saucedo is their accountant. He has the legit books as well as the not-so-legit books," Slade explained again. "He takes his orders directly from Ayala. He says Ayala is getting more and more paranoid, and he blames this Zorro person for it. He claims Zorro plants ideas in his head. He also gives Ayala information no one else has. That's why he gets a cut. He lets Ayala know when the feds are moving in or where, and he gets paid for that protection."

"But Zorro? I mean that's kind of cheesy." Staci took another bite of her breakfast.

"It means fox in Spanish," Slade informed her. "Another informant told me it's his own private joke, that he is the fox in the henhouse."

"I wonder what that means. What henhouse?" Staci sipped her juice thoughtfully.

"You know, it could mean either the organization or some other henhouse."

She looked meaningfully at Slade. They both had strongly considered that there was a mole in the federal government, probably in Slade's own unit.

Slade frowned slightly. "I know. I've thought about that."

"What did the other guy tell you?" Staci asked.

"He's the product guy. He receives it and delivers it to be divided up, weighed, and then delivered to the various transportation units. Again, this Zorro has his fingers in that. Again, gets a cut."

"Can anyone identify this Zorro?" Staci asked.

"Yes, all three of them can," Slade confirmed.

"Do you have these persons where they are protected?" Staci knew the answer. Slade did his job very well. Every detail was planned, contingencies were considered.

"Of course." Slade finished his breakfast and leaned back.

"I don't want to know anything about that. I don't want to know where the tapes are. All I need are the transcripts. I can get this put together and take it before the grand jury in a week. But I don't want anyone to know in advance," Staci told Slade.

She was starting to form an idea, but until it came to fruition, she didn't want to share. She hated secrets after having grown up

TO DIE FOR HER

in a home where not only did her father have to keep secrets about what he did in the military, but she and her sisters also had been taught early on how to keep secrets from others to protect the family. She had vowed that once she was out of that environment, she wouldn't have secrets. Her mother had told her once, when she had complained about not being able to tell her friends where they were moving, that it was because her father loved her and her sisters that they kept certain information to themselves, that she had to trust her parents to do the right thing. It didn't take the sting out her prepubescent predicament, but Staci did what she was told. Now when she no longer lived with her parents, she found herself back to keeping secrets to protect others.

Slade signaled the waitress for the check, but Staci took it when the server put it on the table. "You bought me tacos last night. I'll pay for breakfast," she told Slade, smiling at his surprised look.

He relaxed and nodded. "Ready to pick out your temporary car?"

"Absolutely!"

Two hours later, Slade stood next to the driver's side window of Staci's rental car.

"You sure you can handle it?" he teased her.

"No. But it was in the price range allowed by my insurance," she assured him. Contrary to what Slade had hoped to find for her, Staci was sitting in a modest sedan that got good gas mileage and met all the necessary safety standards. Slade just laughed at her morose expression.

"Can I drive your car someday?" she asked him. "That might make this a little more palatable."

Slade laughed even harder. "Absolutely not."

"Okay, well, I need a shower, and I'm missing college football," Staci informed him. She wished she could think of a reason to delay leaving.

"Then I guess you better get going," Slade told her.

He was torn between wanting to spend more time with Staci and putting as much distance between them that he could. He genuinely enjoyed her company. He found her interesting. She could talk about a variety of subjects, and she listened when he talked, asking follow-up questions that assured him that she wasn't just hearing him but was actually listening. She was witty, the intellectual dry wit that he appreciated but rarely found. It was easy being around her. She gave off a calm that he hadn't experienced in a long time.

Staci started the reliable sedan and rolled up the window, giving Slade a slight wave and wistful look as she drove down the aisle of cars in the parking lot. Slade watched her drive off before he began the trek back to his own car.

*****

Monday morning came faster than Staci would have liked. She was going to have to tell Max about her car blowing up with the boxes of documents in it. As she unlocked her office and changed her shoes into navy heels, Max's personal secretary knocked on her door. Looking up, Staci saw Dana stick her head in.

"Max wants to see you in the conference room," she announced. "Now." She looked directly at Staci.

Staci nodded, stood, and straightened her navy pinstriped suit. She took in a breath that was supposed to be calming but did not, in fact, calm her down, and grabbed a blue flash drive from her desk. She walked to the conference room and opened the door. Surprised, she saw not just Max but Slade and his entire team sitting at the conference table.

"Come in, Staci," Max waved her in.

Staci came in and sat down. Slade caught her eye and made an almost imperceptible shake with his head. He was trying to tell her something, but what, she didn't know.

"These men were at my office, first thing this morning, and told me your car blew up Friday night," Max quietly stated.

"That's true," Staci confirmed.

"And those boxes of documents that were evidence to this cartel case, they were in the trunk of your car?"

"Also true," Staci looked around the room. This was an ambush. The other men just stared at her, no expressions on their faces.

TO DIE FOR HER

"Were you alone?" Max asked.

"No, Agent Slade was present when it happened," she told him.

"Give me context," Max quietly demanded.

"I was out with a friend, and Agent Slade had texted me. He had additional information he wanted to share about the case, so I told him where I was. He showed up. When we were walking to my car, he had my keys and pushed the auto-start button, and my car blew up," she recounted.

"What information did he want to share with you?" Max kept prying.

Staci glanced in Slade's direction, and again, his eyes were boring into hers and then narrowed.

"I don't know. It was too loud in the club to talk, and we didn't have an opportunity to discuss anything about the case because my car blew up while we were walking towards it, outside. That kind of distracted us from whatever information he came to relay," Staci answered.

"Have I not discussed with you the dangers of keeping those boxes in your car?" Max turned slightly in his chair to look directly at Staci.

She felt rage building inside her. He was trying to embarrass and humiliate her in front of the agents.

"Yes, you have." Staci didn't deny it. She was trying to decide how to handle this. She could be professional or she could throw caution to the wind.

"Now because of your negligence and insubordination, this case is done. There is nothing we can proceed on. How do you think I should handle this?" Max was smiling slightly, thinking that she was going to fold and walk away.

Staci made up her mind and decided caution was overrated.

"Well, Max, since you asked," Staci started. "The only reason I kept those boxes close was because between being attacked in the parking garage in this building and my office being burglarized here as well, it became obvious that security at this building was mediocre, at best. Additionally," she produced the blue flash drive and set it firmly on the table in front of her, "every single document that was in those boxes, every photograph, every statement, every report, everything, has been backed up on this flash drive. The fact that you brought me into this little Star Chamber to attempt to show these gentlemen how little you thought about my competence, how dumb you think I am to not take precautions in the event of something happening to the evidence, really demonstrates how misogynistic you really are."

Staci stood up and continued, "The physical evidence wasn't in those boxes but is being kept in a very secure location. If you want to write me up, do it. If you want to take me off this case, then do it. I doubt you will find anyone else in this office who has the time, the patience, or the intelligence to work through the complexities of this case. And for your information, I will be ready to present this case to the grand jury by next Monday." She tossed her head and threw out, "Oh, and thanks for checking to see if I was hurt in the explosion. I'm fine, thank you." Staci prepared to walk out, but Max stopped her.

"Sit down. No one is getting written up. And I'm certainly not going to take you off the case," Max said. "I should have known you would have everything backed up, that you would have planned for the unexpected. I apologize." He waited for Staci to sit down before he continued, "I put you on this case because I believed in your abilities. But you bring up an interesting point." He took a breath then continued, "Given that your safety has been compromised twice now, maybe you should have some protection, security, until this case comes to its conclusion."

Staci's eyes flashed, and her eyebrows knitted together. "Max, I don't need a security detail. I really don't think that's necessary."

Max waved her off. "Of course, it is. I would hate for anything to actually happen to you because of this assignment."

Slade spoke up at that point. He had been watching the exchange between Staci and Max, and he was bothered by it. There was something about how quickly Max was ready to crucify her in front of them all then how he switched to wanting her to keep the case that didn't sit right. He stood up and announced, "I will take

TO DIE FOR HER

care of the security detail. I know some people in the marshal's office that can handle something like this. I'll make some calls."

Max turned his attention to Slade, his eyes darkening for a moment before he nodded his head and agreed, "That's a good idea. I will leave you to do that then."

"Is this meeting over?" Staci asked. "I have things to do. I feel confident that I will have this case ready to take to the grand jury in a couple of weeks." She snatched the flash drive off the table.

"Yes, yes, please continue. I like that timeline," Max told her and stood up himself. He looked at the rest of the men and said, "Well, gentlemen, this meeting is concluded."

Staci stomped back to her office but not before smiling at Dana as she passed her desk to say, "Well, that went great."

A short time later, another knock at her office door made her snap her head up in annoyance. "What?" she asked shortly.

Slade stuck his head in. "We didn't come to his office until he summoned us up here. I don't know how he found out about your car, but he already knew about it when we got here. He questioned all of us about what we knew, and I pretty much told him what you told him," Slade told her.

"It doesn't matter." Staci sighed and leaned back in her chair a little. "I'm just ready to get this in front of the grand jury so we can get it to trial."

"I'll meet you at your house after work with a guy who will be your bodyguard in the evenings. I think you'll like him," Slade said.

Staci's eyes widened then narrowed. "I don't need a babysitter!"

Slade just laughed and replied, "Yeah, you do." He pulled the door shut as he left.

CHAPTER 10

When Staci pulled up into her driveway at the end of the day, she saw two black government issued SUVs parked along the curb of her street. As she pulled into her garage, she watched in her driver's side mirror as Slade got out of one. Shaking her head and rolling her eyes, she put the door down and got out of her car. Walking into her condo through the door that connected the foyer and the garage, she heard her doorbell ring. Looking through the peephole, she saw Slade and another man standing on her small front porch. Sighing, she opened the door. Glaring at Slade, he walked in without an invitation and motioned the other man, a man shorter than Slade who was balding and probably in his late forties, to enter as well. After Staci shut the door behind them, Slade introduced the second man.

"This is Bill. He works for the marshal's service. He will be here in the evenings and stay with you through the night. When you leave for work, he will follow you to work, and then you won't see him again until you get home each night." Slade gestured toward Bill. "I wanted to introduce you tonight so you will know he is who he is."

Staci reached out and offered her hand to Bill. "Nice to meet you, Bill. You can call me Staci. And just so you know, I don't think you are needed here, but this guy," she tossed her head in Slade's direction, "thinks you are."

"Pleasure to meet you," Bill responded and shook her hand.

"Great, so I will just leave you two to get acquainted." Slade seemed in a hurry to leave. He walked to the door and turned to address Staci. "Be nice. He doesn't want to be here anymore than you want him here." With that, Slade let himself out of the front door.

Staci locked the dead bolt behind him and turned to Bill.

"Have you eaten?" she asked.

TO DIE FOR HER

Bill nodded his head and stated, "Yes, ma'am. You won't have to feed me."

"Well, then, let me show you around," Staci responded.

She walked Bill through the layout of the downstairs, and then they climbed the stairs so she could let him get an idea of what the floor plan was there. After they returned to the first floor, she announced, "I haven't eaten, so I'm going to order something. Sure I can't order you something?"

"No, ma'am, you can't order anything to be delivered," Bill told her.

Staci paused, cell phone in hand. "What do you mean I can't order anything?"

"From a safety standpoint, if you order something, there is nothing stopping a bad guy from taking what you ordered from the delivery person and pretending to be that delivery person in order for you to open the door, thereby giving him an opportunity to make entry. Or put something dangerous in a box or bag being delivered," Bill explained.

Staci thought about what he said. He had a point. However, she just went from being inconvenienced to being annoyed. She didn't even know what food she had in the refrigerator. She huffed and put down her phone. Walking over to the refrigerator, she offered Bill a beer, which he turned down. He accepted the bottled water. Looking at the shelves of the refrigerator, Staci opened a couple of the to-go boxes and chose a half-eaten hamburger and french fries from two nights ago. She popped it in the microwave and told Bill she was going upstairs to change clothes. He merely nodded at her.

When she came back downstairs a few minutes later, he was standing in the exact same spot she had left him when she went upstairs to change.

"Bill, you can sit on the sofa, you know. I want you to make yourself at home." She walked over and picked up the television remote control. "Here, find something you want to watch. I have work I have to do, so I don't care what you choose."

Bill took the remote and turned on the television. Staci poured herself a hearty glass of wine and took her food out of the microwave.

She carried both to the sectional and placed them on the coffee table. She considered each piece of evidence and the questions to ask to get it admitted. She immersed herself totally in her work until her cell phone went off. Looking at the caller ID, she saw it was her sister, Allison.

"Hello?" she answered.

"Hey, sis! Guess what?" Allison's voice came over the receiver. "It's our shopping weekend!"

Every year, some combination of Staci's sisters came to St. Louis for the weekend. They spent the time shopping, dining in a popular restaurant that was predetermined, and then spent the night at Staci's place, staying up gossiping, snacking, and watching some cheesy movie.

"Who's coming?" Staci asked.

"Just me and Cassidy this year. Izzy is saving up her vacation days for Thanksgiving and Christmas, and Casey can't get away until Jeff's bye week. Meredith is being Meredith," Allison told her.

Meredith's husband had passed away in a car wreck three years ago. He had left her with two small children, and sometimes, Meredith had trouble coping with the responsibilities of being both mother and father, a trauma surgeon, and a grieving widow.

"Well, I don't think I can go shopping or eat lunch this year, but I can sure have an amazing array of snacks and wine for our sleepover," Staci informed her sister.

"What? Why not?" Allison's voice did not hide her dismay.

Staci quickly caught her up on what was happening at work, complete with the security detail and her car being blown up. She saw Bill watching her as she was divulging the information, and she paused to tell him, "This is my sister." Nodding, he went back to watching TV.

"You live an exciting life, my love," Allison sighed. She was an accountant and was convinced that everyone except herself lived an exciting life.

"It's not what it's cracked up to be." Staci laughed. "But like I said, I can have everything we need for our sleepover here, and we can still have a great time. You and Cassidy can model the clothes you all bought for me!"

"Can you have a bottle of that delicious buttery Chardonnay you introduced us to last year?"

"Absolutely, and some sweet treats from this adorable little bakery I discovered a few months ago. I've been looking for an excuse to go buy more," Staci vowed.

"Sounds like a plan! Gotta run for now! See you this weekend," Allison promised before she hung up.

Staci smiled. At least this weekend promised to be fun. She went back to her work until it was time to go to bed. Bringing Bill a couple of blankets and a pillow when he insisted he had to sleep on the sofa, she handed them over and then climbed the stairs. Today had been mentally exhausting, and she needed the rest.

Staci and Bill fell into a routine. It wasn't exactly comfortable, but it worked. He picked up food for himself, and she picked up food for herself, except on the evenings when she called him ahead of time and offered to get him something as well. She kept her refrigerator stocked with bottled water and orange juice since Bill had mentioned that he enjoyed ice-cold orange juice first thing in the morning. She would work on meaningless things at the office during the day, but at night, at home, she threw herself into preparing for the grand jury. She knew she wouldn't get much done when her sisters arrived, so she wanted everything to be ready before the weekend, other than preparing Slade for his testimony.

One night, as she was working on her case, her mind started to wander. She glanced over at Bill, who was sitting in his usual spot on the couch watching some documentary about some war, and she asked, "How do you know Agent Slade?"

Bill turned his head and looked at her. "Mike? We've had a few assignments together. When his investigations are over, I'm usually there to help make arrests, or I help him locate a suspect during an active investigation. Help execute warrants, that sort of thing." He chose his words deliberately.

Staci took in what he was saying. She probed further, "How long have you known him?"

He straightened up and looked directly at her when he replied, "Since he joined the DEA."

Nodding, she pretended to go back to reading what was displayed on her laptop. After a few moments, Bill turned back to what he was watching on the television. More silence until she asked as nonchalantly as she could manage, "So you married with kids?"

Sighing, Bill replied, "Yes, married for over twenty years. Two kids, youngest kid is in middle school, the oldest just started college."

"What does your wife think about you having to stay here at night with me?"

"It's part of the job. She doesn't ask a lot of questions," Bill told her pointedly.

Staci just smiled and returned to reading her laptop.

On Friday, when Staci pulled into her driveway, Bill's vehicle wasn't parked on her street. As she pulled into her garage, she wondered where he was. He wasn't the most talkative guy, getting information out of him was like pulling teeth, so she wasn't too surprised that he hadn't communicated any changes in the routine. She lowered the garage door and made her way inside. She had barely put her tote down when the doorbell rang. Looking through the peephole, she was surprised to see Slade standing in front of her door. Opening it, she noticed he was holding two grocery bags, a third was setting next to him on the right and a duffel bag was on the left. As soon as she opened the door, he walked in and put the two bags he was holding onto the granite countertop of the island.

"No, really, come in," Staci murmured.

He grinned at her and retrieved the duffel bag and the third grocery bag. "Where do I put my stuff?" He placed the third grocery bag next to the first two bags.

"What do you mean where do you put your stuff? Where's Bill?" She walked behind him as he walked around the kitchen island and started unpacking the grocery bags.

"I figured I would give him the weekend off. His youngest son has a ball game tonight, and his wife misses him." Slade shrugged his shoulders. Looking up, he grinned at her, that dimple deeply piercing his cheek. "Did you miss me?"

"What is all this?" Staci asked, gesturing at the groceries and ignoring his question,

"Bacon, eggs, milk, rib eye steaks, salad fixings, steak fries, beer, and coffee," he answered, putting the groceries into her refrigerator. "I remembered you don't keep a lot of food in the place."

"I also don't own a coffee maker, so what's with the coffee?"

Pulling a coffee maker out of one of the grocery bags, Slade's grin got even wider. "You do now."

Throwing up her hands in mock disgust, Staci just laughed and told him, "I'm going upstairs to change my clothes. I guess you've already made yourself at home."

She jogged up the stairs, both amused and annoyed at Slade's assumed welcome. When she had thrown on some fleece jogging pants, flip-flops, and a T-shirt, she returned downstairs to find Slade rummaging through her cabinets.

"What are you looking for?" she asked, walking over to where he was bent over, peering into a lower cabinet.

"Well, you don't have a grill, so I'm looking for a pan I can cook these steaks on and a baking sheet to put the fries on," he replied without looking at her.

She reached in next to him and pulled both out and set them on the counter. Straightening, his face somber, he said, "I have a serious question to ask you."

Her eyes widening, she replied, "What?"

"Are you wearing a bra because I really don't need that kind of distraction while I'm cooking." Slade's grin returned. He laughed when she threw the dish towel at him.

She stormed out of the kitchen into the living room. She could hear Slade's laugh follow her. He was the most maddening man she had ever met and yet charming at the same time. He had followed her from the kitchen, and when she turned in his direction, she saw he was holding a glass of wine.

"I bought you a couple of bottles of that wine you keep in the refrigerator. I figured that if your week was as stressful as mine, you could use it." He offered her the glass as a peace offering.

Taking it, Staci smelled it. It smelled like the kind she liked. She sipped it. He had really remembered what kind of wine she drank?

"Thank you." She smiled back at him.

He nodded slightly and returned to the kitchen to finish dinner. Staci switched on the television and found a movie revolving around the paranormal and drank her wine. They both watched each other, Slade cooking and Staci pretending to watch the movie, through side-eye looks.

When dinner was cooked, Staci ventured to the kitchen where they silently filled their plates. Slade put the steak on her plate, telling her, "I hope you like it medium rare. That's the only way I know how to cook it."

Staci cut into the steak. It was perfectly warm but dark pink. She sampled it. He had topped it with a garlic butter, and it melted in her mouth.

"This is amazing," she told him when she had swallowed her bite. "I usually eat mine more rare than medium, but this is perfect!"

Slade smiled at the compliment. He usually didn't care about impressing people, but for some reason, the fact she liked his cooking made his chest puff out a little more than normal.

Carrying their plates to the living room, he glanced at the movie she chose. "Is this a genre you like?" he asked, finding a neutral topic.

"Oh yeah, I love a great ghost story!" Staci was enthusiastic in her response. She plopped down on the sectional a little closer to him than she should.

He put his plate on the coffee table and sat on the edge of the sofa, close enough to his plate to be able to cut his steak.

"Do you believe in that stuff?" He put a bite of the steak in his mouth and chewed it, watching her.

"Absolutely. Don't you?"

He shook his head. "Nah. They're just stories."

"Do you believe in God?" she countered.

"I was raised Catholic," he answered.

"That's not what I asked. Do you believe in God?" Staci put a fry in her mouth and waited for him to answer,

TO DIE FOR HER

He shrugged. "I believe in what I see. I want to believe, but when my mom was sick, I prayed for her to get better. She didn't. I guess I lost my faith after that."

Staci mulled over what he said. She didn't know how to answer that. Changing the topic, she told him, "You can put your stuff in the guest room upstairs. My sisters are coming tomorrow for their annual shopping trip, and they will be staying here tomorrow night. I can share my bed with one of them, but I might have you move to the couch for the other one."

Slade nodded his head. This was a development he hadn't counted on. The silence grew awkward. Slade cleared his throat and broke it.

"So I brought dirty laundry with me. I thought I could use your washer and dryer?" He looked at Staci somewhat sheepishly.

"Of course. After we clean up the dishes, go get it, and I'll show you where the laundry room is. It's not much, but it has the basics," she replied.

After the movie and after the dishes were cleaned up, Slade went to his car and brought in a large white canvas bag. She let him in the door and looked at the bag.

She laughed softly and asked, "When was the last time you did laundry?"

"It's only been a couple of weeks. I've been a little busy," he pointed out.

"Follow me," she told him. She walked past the kitchen to a small hallway. She opened a single door and gestured inside. "You know how to work these?"

He peered inside. The room was small. The washer and dryer were basic, and the shelves above them held the detergent, dryer sheets, and a variety of items, including an iron. He nodded and put the bag on top of the washer. "Yeah, I can handle it."

Staci yawned. "I'm headed upstairs. It's been a long day. Just lock up and turn off the lights when you head up," she stated as she began climbing the stairs.

Slade watched her until she disappeared from sight, and then he heard her door shut softly. He sighed. He could have gotten a

103

second marshal to pull the security detail. It probably would have been smarter if he had. Something inside him, however, forced him to decide to do this himself. All the nights Bill was here, Slade had still worried about Staci even though he knew Bill was capable of doing the job. He had lain awake into the wee hours of every morning, worrying about her safety and remembering the last time he had stayed all night. He couldn't get her out of his head. This just seemed to be the most logical solution to the problem.

The next morning, Slade was awakened by the sound of Staci running on her treadmill and her damn heavy metal. This time, he knew what the noise was. He looked at his watch through sleepy, unfocused eyes, 5:00 a.m. Damn, that girl needed to learn how to sleep in. He lay in the dark, listening to the rhythmic *ka-thunks*, hoping to fall back asleep. After a few minutes, however, he realized it was going to be impossible to do so. Sighing, he rifled through his duffel bag and pulled out a clean pair of underwear and some toiletries. Walking silently to the guest bathroom, he shut and locked the door and turned on the shower. If he timed it right, he could be in and out of the shower and back in the bedroom before she finished her run.

Stepping into the shower, he let the hot water pour over him, washing away his fatigue. It did not cleanse him of his thoughts. As soon as he could make time, he was headed to the various locations where his witnesses were being held to do a photographic lineup this week. Before long, he would know who this mysterious "Zorro" was. With luck, the indictment would be returned, and he could get an arrest warrant for Ayala. He had feelers out, and he believed they were close to locating him. He had never been as ready to close out a case as he was this one.

After drying off, he slipped on his clean underwear and brushed his teeth. He ran his fingers through his shaggy hair that was still damp. He looked at himself in the mirror. He probably should shave, but the stubble wasn't too thick, and he didn't feel like shaving anyway. Gathering up his belongings, he listened at the door to make sure he could still hear Staci running. He could. The coast was clear. He made his way down the short hall to the bedroom and shut that door. He pulled on jeans, a thick belt, and an oatmeal-colored Henley. After pulling on socks and his usual work boots, he looked over at his gun belt. He didn't think he needed the whole apparatus, so he took his Glock out of the holster and tucked it into his waistband at the small of his back. He grabbed the towel and his dirty clothes and descended the stairs. Just as he hit the bottom landing, he heard the door where her treadmill was located open and shut softly. He smiled. His timing was perfect.

When Staci came downstairs about a half an hour later, she smelled coffee. She was surprised that Slade was up. She looked over at the kitchen and saw him standing behind the island/bar pouring a cup of coffee. He had put the coffee maker on the countertop behind him, and as he turned to return the pot back onto the heating element, he looked up, saw her, and smiled.

"Ah, there she is. The woman who can't sleep past five o'clock. Want some coffee?" he offered.

"Did you buy sweetener and heavy cream? Maybe one of those flavored syrups?" she inquired. When she saw him shake his head, she commented, "No thanks. I like girly coffee."

Slade saw that she wore gray sweatpants and a sweatshirt. Her hair was up in her ever-present messy bun, and she had sneakers on her feet.

"What's the plan for this morning?" he asked, pretty sure he knew the answer.

"Kickboxing class at eight. Then I have to go get some groceries for my sisters' visit." She reached behind him into the refrigerator and pulled out a bottle of water. "Did I wake you up?"

"Don't worry about it. I'm just not used to the sound of your treadmill yet or your choice of music." He sipped his coffee. It was thick and black and kicked in quickly.

Staci strolled into the living room and flipped on the television to catch the early news. Slade finished his cup of coffee and then started the first load of laundry in the washer. He joined her in the living room with his second cup of java. Soon enough, Staci stood up and started putting objects into her tote. She carried that tote everywhere. It was one of her favorite purchases made during one of her sisters' shopping trips; it was brown leather, large enough to pack a laptop, a wallet, a bottle of water, shoes, and whatever she needed for the day. Today, she threw a clean shirt into it. She jingled her keys, and Slade stood up.

"You leaving to go to class?" he asked while he emptied his cup into the sink in the kitchen.

"Yep, see ya in a couple of hours," she told him and headed to the garage.

"Hold up. You aren't driving around alone. It defeats the purpose of having a security detail. I'll drive. We can take my car," he told her. He retrieved his keys out of his pocket as Staci rolled her eyes.

He drove her to her kickboxing class, escorting her inside. He waited outside in the car, watching the door diligently. He made a few calls, answered some emails, and texted some people. His dad called while he was waiting.

"Hey, Dad," Slade answered his phone.

"Hey, son, whatcha doing this morning?" His dad's rough voice sounded in Slade's ear.

"Just pulling a security detail this weekend," Slade answered.

There was silence on the other end for a few moments. Then his dad observed, "You don't have security detail as part of your job description. That's for another agency. What's going on?"

Dammit, Slade thought. His dad was still one of the smartest men he knew. He saw right through his answer. So Slade briefed his father on the case.

"What's this prosecutor look like?" Slade could hear his father smile into the phone.

"She's pretty. Small, blonde, big green eyes. But this is professional, Dad, not personal," Slade told his father.

His father laughed and responded, "Keep telling yourself that. You aren't driving her around on her errands and using her washer because it's professional. You don't get this invested when it's professional."

"Sure, Dad," Slade retorted. He didn't feel like arguing with the old man.

TO DIE FOR HER

"Just remember, I'm not getting any younger, and I need grandchildren. Your brother and sister aren't cooperating either," his father mentioned.

"Dad, stop. I told you—" Slade started to reply, but his father cut him off with, "It's just professional. Yeah, whatever, kid."

Slade saw Staci exit the building and walk toward his car. "Hey, here she comes. I gotta go, Dad," Slade told his father. "And, Dad, I love you. Be safe."

Staci got into Slade's car. She was hot and sweaty. Her cheeks were flushed. Blonde curls were escaping her bun. Slade thought she was the most beautiful woman he had ever seen. Clearing his throat, he asked, "Where to?"

She directed him to a grocery store whose prices were higher than he was ever willing to pay. She roamed the deli and got a variety of meats and five types of cheeses whose names he couldn't pronounce. They cruised the produce section for grapes and carrots and something called capers. Smoked salmon went into the basket next. Finally, she loaded three bottles of a Chardonnay that Slade had never heard of into the cart and strolled to the checkout line. Staci then had him take her to a bakery closer to her condo. While he took in the vanilla and lemony smells that immediately struck him when he walked in the door, Staci picked out croissants and baguettes, petit fours, and a dozen fancy cupcakes decorated with pink and green frosting.

Loading the boxes and bags into the trunk of his car, Slade remarked, "I guess the government pays you more than they pay me."

Staci laughed. "You've seen my refrigerator. I rarely buy this stuff. Usually just for holiday gatherings or my sisters' big weekend. It's nice to be able to splurge once in a while."

They drove back to Staci's condo in semi-silence, listening to the radio. At one point, Staci asked if she could change the station, and Slade nodded his head. She turned the tuning button until a song with a screeching electric guitar and heavy bass line came on. Staci sat back, smiling, bouncing her head to the beat. Surprised, Slade turned to look at her for a second.

"Really?" he asked.

"What? I love this group, Velvet Revolver," she told him.

"You always have classic playing at your condo. You were digging electric dance music at that club. I didn't peg you for someone who listened to heavy metal," he commented.

"I listen to all kinds of genres. I run to heavy metal. I also enjoy hair bands, big band, and ska," she informed him.

Slade just smiled. This woman was an enigma, always surprising him.

"What kind of music do you like?" she asked.

Slade shrugged. "I work out to heavy metal, and I'll listen to just about anything, including country music." Staci made a face. "What, you don't like country music?" he asked.

"Some. Not much," she replied.

They pulled up in her driveway. Slade had her get out and follow him to the front door. After she unlocked it, he entered and made sure everything was safe and then had her wait for him on the other side of the closed door while he unloaded the groceries from the car. He set everything on the island and watched her slip off her sweatshirt to expose her sports bra.

Staci noticed he had one eyebrow raised, so she offered, "I need a shower and a change of clothes before I do anything else. Just put the wine in the refrigerator. I won't be long." She bounded up the stairs before shedding any more clothing.

She was correct: it didn't take her long. When she descended the stairs half an hour later, she was put together nicely. Low-riding jeans and a pink sweater that didn't quite meet the waistband of her jeans so that shiny belly bar was visible. Slade was obsessed with that bar. He remembered running his tongue over it a couple of weeks back, and the memory was playing havoc with his libido.

Her hair was still damp and twisted in the back up off her neck. Enormous hoop earrings were her only jewelry. She had a touch of bronzer and mascara on her face, far less than she wore to work, and on her feet, she had fuzzy brown moccasins. Slade's eyes darkened as he watched her walk over to where he was standing behind the island. She reached up into a cabinet to pull out two large wooden trays, and her sweater rode up. Slade had to shut his eyes and think of

TO DIE FOR HER

something besides her to keep from embarrassing himself. Once she had the wooden trays, his focus shifted to watching her arrange the meats and cheeses on the boards in a very precise manner. She placed the grapes and capers and celery sticks and carrots expertly among the meats and cheeses. Then she wrapped both boards tightly with cellophane wrap and set them in the refrigerator. She hauled out two multitiered serving stands and placed them on the island along with several wine glasses.

Finally, she stood back and said, "There. That's all I can do for now."

Slade remembered the laundry he had put in the washing machine before he drove her to her kickboxing class. He took off down the hallway and put it in the dryer. He put another load into the washing machine. He heard the doorbell ring and quickly made his way to the foyer. He pulled his firearm from the back of his waist with one hand and put the index finger of the other to his lips as he approached the door. Moving Staci behind him, he looked through the peephole and saw two women, one with straight blonde hair and one with the same wild curly hair as Staci standing on the other side of the door. Relaxing, he recognized them from the photographs Staci had hanging on the wall. He replaced his firearm to the small of his back and opened the door.

When he swung the door open, both women paused, their mouths slightly ajar. He smiled and said, "Welcome, ladies." He gestured at them to enter. They carried their many shopping bags across the threshold when Staci appeared from behind Slade and waved them in.

Allison was the first to speak. "Wow, where do I get a butler who looks like that?"

Cassidy didn't speak, but she was smiling and eyeing him up and down. Slade almost blushed.

"This is Agent Mike Slade. He's my security detail for the weekend. Come in! Tell me about your shopping. Where did you eat lunch?" Staci took a couple of the bags from Allison and set them next to the stairs.

"I'm Allison. This is Cassidy," Allison offered her hand to Slade, and he took it, shaking it.

"Nice to meet you both," he replied.

Staci went to the kitchen and poured wine into three of the wine glasses. She brought two of them to her sisters and handed a glass to each one.

Cassidy took a sip, smiled provocatively at Slade, and purred, "Once you're off this boring detail, I could use a little protection."

Before Slade could say anything, he felt a gentle pressure on his bicep. Staci's hand was gripping it, and she told her sister quite clearly, "Sorry, sis. He's not for rent. That isn't how it works. Maybe when someone blows up your car, you can get someone like him."

Slade smiled slyly. Staci was not taking kindly to her sister flirting with him. Cassidy also noticed, her eyes sparkling. Staci ushered both women to the living room and engaged them in family gossip and chatter about their shopping. They giggled and told stories about the sales clerks. They moaned over the delicious finger sandwiches and cocktails they had for lunch. Slade stood in the background, taking it in. He had never seen Staci in a social environment before, and he was surprised by how easily she interacted with her sisters. He heard the dryer buzz, and he excused himself to go get the laundry. As soon as he left the room, both sisters turned to her, their eyes big.

"Seriously, Staci, you have to tap that!" Cassidy whispered loudly.

"Cassidy! Stop!" Staci couldn't stop herself from blushing at the blatantly sexual demand her sister had made.

Allison smiled and told Cassidy, "Methinks she already has."

"Why do you two insist on talking about my personal life? We work together. He's in charge of that case I told you about. I can't mix personal and professional, at least not until this case is resolved," Staci told them. "And stop flirting with him, Cassidy. He already knows he's hot. You'll make his head so big it won't fit through the door!"

Cassidy giggled. "I'm only doing it to get under your skin."

Staci craned her head to see if he was still out of earshot. "Well, stop it. It's not funny."

TO DIE FOR HER

Slade strolled down the hallway carrying a pile of dry laundry. He tossed it on the end of the sectional where Staci was sitting. He grinned at the women and stated, "I don't mind the flirting as long as she knows I only have eyes for Staci."

The sisters gasped, and Staci groaned, wanting the floor to swallow her. He had heard everything. To lighten the moment, she said, "Did I mention there is nothing wrong with his ability to hear?"

"Well, I'm just saying, good-looking, tall, exudes sexual prowess, and he does laundry. He's a catch." Cassidy tossed her head at Staci and finished her wine.

Staci changed the subject back to family gossip, and Slade finished folding his laundry and packed it into the canvas bag he had brought. The women decided on a movie to watch later, and Allison mentioned she was starting to get hungry. They all moved into the kitchen. Slade followed but held back and watched. They worked together, independently of each other but yet as a team. Every woman had a job and didn't get in the way of the others. Staci pulled the wooden boards out of the refrigerator and cut the plastic wrap of them. She retrieved a raspberry jam, a blueberry jam, and honey and put each in a small ramekin and added a wooden spoon to each. Those she arranged within the boards among the meats, cheeses, and other delights. Cassidy skillfully cut pieces of baguette and arranged them on the center of the first tiered serving stand and placed croissant halves on the bottom. She pulled pita chips out of a drawer and poured them into a bowl which she placed next to the serving stand. Allison placed the cupcakes and petit fours on the second tiered serving stand and set it at the end of the island. Two bottles of the Chardonnay were brought out and opened and set next to the wine glasses. Plates, knives, and napkins were arranged. Slade was amazed at the organization of the task and how little time it took to prepare everything.

"Where did you all learn to do all that?" He had to know where this teamwork originated.

Allison laughed. "My dad was an officer in the Air Force. That meant we entertained other officers on a regular basis. My mom was a genius at coming up with themes, and since there were six of us girls, we all had to learn how to help out so it wasn't just on Mom."

Cassidy piped up with, "You should see us clean up."

Staci just shrugged. "Military brats learn how to do a lot of strange things in a very organized way."

They filled their plates with food and their glasses with wine and gathered once again in the living room. For hours, the women laughed and entertained Slade with stories of their misadventures growing up all over the world, particularly those stories involving Staci. It seemed she was fearless and reckless but never completely crossing the line set down by their parents. He laughed at the stories and was amazed by how completely normal they all seemed to have turned out. Their movie started, but they kept pausing it when one of them would say, "Hey remember that time…"

Finally, at midnight, they cleaned up the kitchen, again as a single moving unit, and then discussed the sleeping arrangements. Allison decided to bunk with Staci, Slade was moved to the couch, and Cassidy took the guest room. Doors were locked, windows were checked, and lights were dimmed. Finally, the condo fell into silence.

Slade lay on the couch, analyzing all the information he had learned tonight about Staci and her family. He understood more about where she came from and how grounded she really was. Their father had taught them how to shoot weapons, how to track, survival skills, and putting country first. Their mother had emphasized kindness, organization, and acceptance. She had made sure they attended church, school, and social events as a respectable family. His family wasn't that dissimilar, now that he compared them. Staci had made sure he was included tonight, and that made him smile. Her sisters, after their initial teasing of Staci, displayed their clear love for each other. They hadn't seen him as an outsider even though it was made clear that he was present as a bodyguard. Rolling over, he fell asleep easily and deeply.

Allison lay next to Staci, who was snoring softly. She had watched Staci and Slade tonight. She had seen how Slade looked at her. He did not look at Staci like someone who was there because they had to be. His eyes would soften or a soft smile would lift his lips. He kept a protective watch, but his whole demeanor when he was near her belied what he was feeling. Staci was just as obvious. She smiled brighter at him, and her eyes twinkled when she looked over at Slade. Small gestures, like a hand on his shoulder or when she refilled his plate, gave away the fact that Staci had feelings for Slade. Allison sighed in the dark. She hoped destiny would be kind to them. She didn't know Slade's story, but she knew when Staci and her boyfriend in law school broke up, even though she didn't know why they had broken up, Staci had pulled back. She didn't date, and she found fault with every man anyone tried to match her up with. Staci had thrown herself into her career and had foregone a social life that involved the opposite sex. Something about Slade was bringing her out of it, turning her back into the old Staci. Allison liked that.

Slade awakened at dawn the next morning. No *ka-thunk* of the treadmill. He remembered Staci didn't run on Sundays. He lay there, waiting to see if he could fall back to sleep, but it was useless. He listened carefully but didn't hear anyone stirring upstairs. He decided now was the safest time to shower before the women started waking up and moving around. He grabbed clean clothes out of the canvas bag that was laying on one side of the living room and quietly sneaked upstairs to the main bathroom in the hallway. He gently closed the door and turned on the shower, letting the water heat up. In moments, he was in the shower, letting the hot water flow over his body.

Cassidy heard the shower and slowly sat up. Was Allison already up and getting ready? She looked at her watch on the nightstand: 7:00 a.m. Not really that early. She heaved her body out of the bed and padded down the hall to Staci's room. She opened the door quietly, knocking very softly.

"Hey, you guys up already?" she asked.

Two bodies moved in the bed, and Allison slowly moved to a sitting position.

"No. What the hell?" Allison was known for being grumpy first thing in the morning.

"Someone's in the shower. I thought it was you," Cassidy told her. She entered the room, closing the door behind her. She walked over to the chaise lounge and sat on it, pulling her feet up and under her.

"It's gotta be Slade," Staci mumbled from the bed. She was still laying on her side, gently wiping her eyes.

"Totally didn't think of that," Cassidy said. "I like him. He sure likes you." She smiled in Staci's direction. Staci sat up and just looked at her sister.

Allison chimed in. "It's obvious that he is falling in love with you."

Staci growled. "Really, it's o-dark-thirty, and you want to discuss my love life? I'm not even awake yet."

Cassidy giggled. "That means you don't have time to think of reasons why we're wrong. Look, all I know—" She stopped suddenly, a panicked look on her face.

Allison and Staci both saw it. "What?" they asked in unison.

Cassidy pointed to a spot between the bed and the bathroom door. A large spider was just sitting there, not moving. When Cassidy attempted to stand, possibly to run or get a shoe to smash it, it moved in her direction. Allison, Cassidy, and Staci all screamed at the tops of their lungs.

Slade had just wrapped a towel around his waist and lathered up one side of his squared jaw when he heard the bloodcurdling screams. He threw open the door and ran to the guest room. Cassidy wasn't inside, but his gun belt was on the bureau. He slid his Glock out of its holster and bolted down the hallway to Staci's room. He threw open the door, his firearm pointed straight out in front of him.

When the bedroom door was thrown open, Staci and her sisters stopped screaming. They swiveled their heads to see Slade burst into the room. He stood there, glistening wet from his shower, wearing only a navy blue towel that hung dangerously low on his hips. His hair was dripping, and one side of his face had shaving cream on it. He wore the same expression one imagines a fierce warrior wears when he's headed to battle. Allison and Cassidy took in the muscled arms and torso, and their jaws dropped slightly. Staci's reaction was more sensual as she remembered the night she had run her hands up and down every inch of him.

TO DIE FOR HER

Slade relaxed when he saw that there wasn't an intruder. Although he was breathing heavily because of the adrenaline pulsing through him, he managed to sound calm when he asked, "What's with the screaming?"

Staci pointed at the spider. Slade followed her finger to the spot where she was pointing, and when he saw the spider, he lowered his weapon and rolled his eyes. He turned to leave, and Staci asked, "Aren't you going to kill it for us?"

"Nope," he replied over his shoulder as he marched back to the bathroom.

Cassidy's eyes were huge when she turned her gaze back to her sisters and declared, "He looks even better naked. He's even got that V in the front! Oh my god!"

Allison nodded and smiled. Staci couldn't dispute the statement.

When the women made it downstairs, dressed, carrying their luggage, Slade was in the kitchen. He had made them bacon and eggs and coffee and poured them juice so they could eat before they hit the road back to the western side of the state. Staci crossed her arms and smiled in approval as she watched her sisters taste their breakfast and then coo about Slade's cooking, declaring him to be a Renaissance man. He had dressed in jeans and a sweatshirt, feeling somewhat self-conscious after his sudden appearance in Staci's room earlier. He let them hug him when they said their goodbyes and helped them carry their belongings to Cassidy's late model sedan. When they were finally backing out of Staci's driveway, he shut and locked the door. When he turned to face Staci, he had a sheepish look on his face.

"Well, I'd say you are going to be the topic of conversation among my family for the next few days," Staci told him.

"Sorry about earlier," he replied as he walked to the kitchen to start cleaning it up.

Staci joined him, snagging a piece of bacon and lifting herself up to sit on the countertop. She laughed and chewed the bacon. When she swallowed, she commented, "No apology needed. You thought there was trouble. You were just doing your job. You just did it," she paused for effect, "spectacularly."

He chuckled softly. When he heard the screams, every instinct in his body kicked in. Not just the security aspect but a need to immediately protect her. Something that he hadn't experienced in a long time, maybe never. He gazed at her fresh face and easy smile. He could stare at her forever, he thought.

Staci jumped off the countertop and told him, "Let's prepare you for tomorrow."

CHAPTER 11

Monday morning came early. Staci and Slade had worked all day Sunday preparing his testimony, marking exhibits, and finalizing presentation slides. She packed everything up in her rental car and drove to the office followed by Slade. He helped her get everything to her office and then asked, "What time do I need to be at the courthouse?"

Turning away from the emails she was reading, she told him, "Ten. Sharp."

He nodded and left. Max wandered into her office shortly after Slade left.

"You're here early," he noted. He took in her navy pinstriped suit and white blouse. He looked around her office, waiting for her to reply.

Staci looked up from her computer once again. "I'm presenting to the grand jury today. I wanted to finalize some things."

Max nodded. "Do you want me to come with you, help with anything?" he offered.

"Nope. I got this," she replied, smiling at him although her smile did not reach her eyes. She was still ticked off at the stunt he pulled after her car got blown up.

He nodded again and told her, "Well, good luck."

"Thanks," Staci said, looking at him, waiting for him to leave. Finally, he turned and made his way across the lobby to his own office.

At nine forty-five, she turned the corner and headed down the long hallway toward the courtroom. She still marveled at the beautiful marble and carvings that marked the hallway. The stories these walls could tell if they could talk. She carried her belongings inside the courtroom and made her way to the prosecution's table. She fought back the nerves that were threatening to overwhelm her. As she was breathing in and out, trying to slow her pulse, she felt a hand on her shoulder. Glancing up, she was stunned. Slade stood there in his blue suit, white shirt, and red tie, which she had seen before, but now, he was completely clean-shaven, and he had gotten a haircut. Gone were the shaggy locks that curled over his ears and almost to his shoulders. Instead, he had what Staci's dad would have called a "high and tight." Close cut on the sides and in the back, and the top was only slightly longer.

"What have you done?" she asked, her mouth gaping.

"You don't like it?" He smiled at her.

"I mean, you're still unnaturally pretty, but I liked your hair like it was. It made you look like a pirate or something," she continued to stare at him.

He frowned. "I'm not sure I like being referred to as 'pretty,'" he told her. "I figured the grand jury might want me to look more like a respectable, believable witness."

"Lord, I don't know what to do with you," she muttered to herself.

Slade bent down and whispered in her ear, "Yeah, you do."

She blushed and pretended to read a document that lay in front of her on the table.

For the next three days, Staci presented evidence to the grand jury. Slade was the primary witness and testified for most of that time. In the evenings, she went home where Bill was waiting for her, and Slade went to his apartment. When the last piece of evidence was admitted and the last line of testimony was given, Staci breathed a sigh of relief. She was packing up her files for the last time when Slade came back into the courtroom.

"Now what?" he asked.

"Do you know where Ayala is? I mean if they indict him, he needs to be arrested when the indictment is unsealed," she asked.

"Yeah, I have a bead on him." He frowned at her.

She nodded. "Good. I don't know how long they will be out to decide the charges."

TO DIE FOR HER

He looked at his watch. "Do you have time to eat? I haven't seen you eat in the last three days."

"I've eaten. I eat when I get home," she lied to him.

"Mmhmm. Okay, well, do we have time to get something? I'm hungry." His face told her he wasn't buying her fib.

"Sure, let me get this stuff to my car." She went to lift her tote, but Slade took it from her. He escorted her out to his vehicle. "We'll take mine." He didn't wait for her to argue.

If she were being honest, she was exhausted. She hadn't been eating much, and she wasn't getting much sleep either. She couldn't get the adrenaline to slow down, even in the evenings, and she couldn't turn off her head when she tried to sleep. She got into the passenger side of Slade's SUV and laid her head back on the headrest. She closed her eyes, but before she got to sleep, the car stopped. Opening her eyes, she saw he had pulled into the parking lot next to the diner they had gone to the first time they had grabbed dinner.

The diner wasn't very busy. Slade chose a table away from the door and held her chair out for her. She sat. Slade ordered them both a glass of iced tea and studied her face. She looked tired.

"Not sleeping well?" he asked as he sipped his tea.

"Can't turn off my head. Now that this part is over, I should be back to normal." She smiled at him and picked up her glass to drink from it.

"What do you feel like eating?" He pretended to peruse the menu.

Staci shrugged. "The cheeseburger and fries, I guess."

Slade held his hand up for their server. He ordered them both cheeseburgers with fries.

"Feel like talking about it? How do you think it went?" He was curious. Always before, he came in, testified, and walked out. He didn't know what happened after that, except when he was subpoenaed to testify at trial if the defendant didn't take a plea deal.

"It's a pretty low burden for the government to prove. I did some things this time that I haven't done before, so it will be interesting," Staci answered.

"What did you do?"

Staci just smiled at him and said, "You'll see. Maybe."

Their dinners arrived, and they ate in relative silence. Staci's hunger had finally returned, and she eagerly ate the juicy burger. Slade smiled as he watched her eat. She had perked up. He tucked into his own food, enjoying just being in a relaxed environment with her for the first time in days.

When they had satisfied their hunger, Staci casually stated, "Your birthday is this weekend."

Slade started slightly but nodded. "Yes, Saturday."

"Big plans?"

He laughed. "Not hardly. At this point, birthdays are things I want to pretend don't exist."

"You're only what, thirty-five? Hardly old," she pointed out. "I guess in man years, it might be old. Want to know a fun fact?" When he raised an eyebrow, she continued, "Did you know that men reach their sexual peak at seventeen but women don't reach theirs until their mid-thirties?"

Slade leaned forward. "You don't say. So you haven't even reached your peak yet?" He grinned roguishly at her.

She smiled at him and replied, "Ah, but you have. Seventeen years ago."

He put his hand over his chest and pretended she had wounded him. They both laughed, and then Staci asked, "How much longer is Bill going to be at my house?"

"Depends. If you get an indictment, how fast can you get it to trial?"

"Well, if I get an indictment, the case has to be tried in ninety days unless there is an agreed continuance and the court allows it. Trial can take anywhere from a week to several months, depending on the number of charges, defendants, that sort of thing. Why does it matter?" Staci answered.

"Then I guess the answer to your question is depends on the number of charges and how long trial takes," Slade shrugged.

"That's ridiculous. Once you arrest Ayala, no one is coming after me to stop me." Staci's eyes flashed with irritation. She wanted her normal life back, and Slade was dragging his feet.

TO DIE FOR HER

"That's not true, and you know it. There is someone else out there who benefits from his relationship with Ayala. If Ayala gets put away, that benefit goes away. Whoever that person is, he is way more dangerous than Ayala, and he will do whatever he can to stop you from fracturing his parasitic relationship with Ayala," Slade pointed out.

"You haven't done a photo lineup yet with our three secret witnesses?" Staci asked, curious as to why Slade, who was usually so meticulous, would not have that done already.

"I'm waiting until I interrogate Ayala. I have a few things up my sleeve, but I have to wait until I get him into custody. We might be able to pull the detail after I do that." Slade shrugged.

Staci nodded, trying to figure out Slade's plan but not getting anywhere. Staci reached for the check that the server placed on their table. "I'll get it." Slade put his hands up in surrender.

Once the meal was paid for, Slade took Staci back to her vehicle and followed her home. He got out and assured himself that Bill was waiting and then told Staci, "Let me know when you find out something."

"I will. It could be days, you know." Slade nodded at her answer then left her in Bill's capable hands.

It took the grand jury until Friday afternoon to hand down an indictment. It was sealed until the following Monday, so Staci decided to spend her weekend doing things to distract her from the anticipation. She left work at noon on Friday to run errands, determined that neither Slade nor Bill follow her. After dropping off some purchases at her condo, she returned to work to find Max in her office.

"Well, I guess we won't know anything until Monday, but I wanted to congratulate you on a job well done," he told her.

"Thanks. I guess once we find out what charges they decided on, my next project is getting ready for trial." She shrugged and took a seat behind her desk.

"I imagine he might want a plea deal," Max suggested.

"Yeah, maybe. Of course, having an indictment is one thing, but actually getting him into custody is another," she reminded him.

Max leaned forward slightly. "Any idea where he is?"

Staci shook her head. "Nope, and that's really not my problem. I don't tell the investigation agency how to do their jobs, and they don't tell me how to do mine."

Max relaxed and leaned back into his chair once more. "True." He looked around her office. There was no sign of this case anywhere in the office. No diagrams, no paperwork, nothing. "Still keeping everything safe on that flash drive?"

"Why?" Staci countered.

"Because as you pointed out, the next step is trial. I don't want to have gone through the trouble of getting an indictment, making a public announcement to the media about the indictment, and then the case falling through because evidence disappeared," he told her.

Staci forced herself not to scowl at him. He was really the most misogynistic person she had ever met, or maybe it was just her that he didn't trust. Either way, he was getting on her nerves.

"It's safe. Don't worry about it," she assured him.

Max sauntered back to his office shortly after the exchange, and Staci spent the afternoon clearing out emails and messages and catching up on the work that had started to pile up while she had been in court. She looked forward to the end of the day, and the day seemed to drag on. She smiled when she thought about how Fridays meant Slade came to spend the weekend, and she had some surprises for him. When she finally shut off her light and locked her office door, she felt the heaviness that had plagued her all week lift.

Staci smiled when she pulled into her driveway. Slade was standing on her tiny front porch, his duffel next to him, and he was holding more grocery bags. She pulled into her garage, shut the door, then made her way into the condo. She unlocked the door before she set her tote down. Slade hustled in.

"Where's your laundry?" she asked, smiling.

Slade set the grocery bags down in the kitchen, reached out of the door, and snagged his duffel bag and then turned toward her. "In my car," he grinned. He left for a few moments then returned with the same canvas bag he had brought last weekend. He carried it to the laundry room while Staci pulled groceries out of the bags. Chicken breasts, salad, ground beef, tortilla chips, spicy tomatoes, and some fresh produce. No junk food. She was really hoping he had bought some ice cream, chips and dip, something that wasn't good for her.

When he reappeared, she commented on the lack of junk food. He watched her put up the groceries and told her, "You eat like a toddler. You need to add some fresh veggies and lean meat to your diet."

"Says the man who keeps driving me to that diner with the greasy burgers and fries," she shot back playfully. "Listen, I really want to take you to dinner tomorrow night. It's your birthday. I want to do something nice to say thank you for going the extra mile with this case and to show you how much I really enjoy your company."

"Wow, that's pretty platonic of you." He grimaced.

Staci sighed. "We had an agreement. Until this case is over, that is all this is." She gestured back and forth between them. "I'm trying my best to make it as bearable as possible."

"And what happens when the case comes to its conclusion?"

Staci looked directly at him. "I guess that depends on you. I honestly don't know what your expectations are."

Slade held her gaze. He wasn't completely sure what his expectations were either. He couldn't answer her. He knew he enjoyed spending time with her. He knew the sex had been amazing the one night they had let themselves indulge in their baser instincts. He knew that whenever he believed she was in danger, his first reaction was to protect her. But he didn't know what he ultimately wanted in the long run.

Staci noted his lack of an answer and nodded. "I guess that tells me what I needed to know," she remarked. She did an about-face and went upstairs to change her clothes.

"Dammit," Slade cursed under his breath. He pulled out pans and cooking utensils, slamming them down. He was blowing this. Then he caught himself. What the hell was he blowing? What is "this"? She had him so twisted around he didn't know if he was coming or going. He sure as hell didn't recognize himself anymore. He washed the chicken breasts and got them in the oven. He put the salad together and found the croissants that were left over from the previous weekend. He wrapped them in a damp dishtowel and popped them in the microwave for later. He pulled a beer out of the refrigerator and took a long drink. He reached for the wine Staci enjoyed, preparing to pour her a glass when he noticed a white box in the back of the refrigerator. Wondering what was inside, he reached in and started to pull it out when Staci's voice clearly and firmly said, "Put that back."

Startled, he pushed the box back inside and turned around, wine bottle in hand. "Just getting ready to pour you a little pre-dinner drink." He grinned.

"Mmmhmm. Quit nosing around in my refrigerator." She walked into the kitchen wearing black leggings and a long flannel shirt worn over a tight black T-shirt and no shoes. Slade thought she looked amazing.

"So listen, I know you like red meat, so I made us a reservation for tomorrow night at a steak house I've been to. I think you'll like it. I was going to surprise you for your birthday, but you don't like birthdays, and apparently, you don't like for people to do nice things for you. It's just a dinner that neither of us has to cook or clean up." She took the glass of wine from him and sipped it.

"I didn't bring any clothes for a nice restaurant," he pointed out.

"We can go by your place tomorrow and pick up something after I get out of my kickboxing class," she suggested.

"Yeah, I guess we can do that." Slade shrugged. He turned the chicken breasts over and put them back into the oven.

The evening was awkward. He did his laundry, she cleaned up the dinner dishes, neither of them really talking to the other after their earlier exchange about expectations. Staci knew she was falling in love with Slade, but she wasn't going to show her hand. If he didn't feel the same way, there was no way she was going to humiliate herself admitting that to him or anyone else. That way, when he walked away, she could mend her heart in private, and no one would be the wiser. Especially Slade.

Slade, on the other hand, was trying to analyze how he felt and what he wanted. These feelings were new. He didn't know what they were or what they meant. He didn't want to scare Staci away with the

TO DIE FOR HER

magnitude of what he felt, and he didn't want to hurt her by staying if he was eventually going to leave.

When he saw Staci yawn, he suggested that she turn in. "I'm going to stay up for a little while, check the perimeter, watch some TV. You're exhausted and need sleep. Go on up. Don't worry about having to entertain me," he told her.

She nodded and took him up on his suggestion. When her head hit the pillow, she fell into a deep, relaxing sleep for the first time that week.

*****

After Staci finished her kickboxing class, she climbed into Slade's car. She was sweaty and hot, but kicking that bag felt great. Slade had stayed in the car, keeping watch as usual. He noticed her red cheeks and saw the sweat had made the baby hairs surrounding her face wet and very curly.

"Let's go get me some clothes," he told her as she shut the door.

Driving for several minutes, Staci noticed he went through a number of outlying suburbs until he got to Ballwin, a moderately upper middle-class neighborhood. He pulled into a parking lot that was almost empty and parked his car. The apartments were standard on the outside, with a lower level and an upper lever that had a balcony. He entered a lower-level apartment. Staci followed him inside. There was the standard wool carpet in a neutral color, and the walls were beige. There was a couch and a recliner, both tan in color. There was a metal and wood coffee table and a couple of lamps. There was a fairly large television that took up most of the living room. The kitchen was small, and there was no place to eat. The place screamed "Bachelor!"

Staci waited in the living room while he strode quickly down a short hallway, presumably the bedroom. She looked around and saw some photographs in frames set on a table near the television. An older man and woman were in one. Clearly, these were his parents. Slade looked very much like the older man, but he got his coloring from the woman. She was smiling, and her eyes were squinted against what must have been a bright sun. The couple looked happy.

"That's my parents," a voice behind her made her jump. Still holding onto the photograph, Staci turned and smiled at Slade.

"They look happy. You look like both of your parents," she commented.

Slade strode over and took the photograph from her hand. He looked at it a minute and then said, "They were happy. This was a few months before my mom got her diagnosis, but even when she was sick, if my dad walked into the room, she would smile. Him too. No matter what kind of shit day he had, when he got home and saw her, he smiled. They brought out the best in each other." He set the photo back on the table. He pointed at the other photograph. "That's my brother and sister," he told her unnecessarily. They both looked amazingly like Slade.

"What are your parents' names?" she asked, curious.

"Ruby and David." He held up the suit he had brought out of the bedroom. "Will this do?"

"Is that the same suit you testified in all week?" Staci smiled at him. The only thing he had changed was the shirt and tie.

"Yeah, I don't have a large calling for wearing suits. Waste of money," Slade gruffly replied, slightly embarrassed.

"Well, you look pretty awesome in it, but the place we are going to isn't that fancy. Nice jeans and a nice shirt will suffice," she assured him.

He turned around and went back into the bedroom.

She took the opportunity to look on his kitchen cabinet where some mail lay. Some circulars, no bills. All made out to occupant. She heard him start down the hall and quickly stepped back into the living room. He was carrying cowboy boots and a hanger with clothes. He looked up when he got to the living room and asked, "All through snooping?"

Staci had the decency to blush a little. He just grinned at her and told her, "I'll tell you anything you want. All you have to do is ask."

TO DIE FOR HER

She opened the door for him, and he put the items he was carrying into the back seat of his car. They climbed in and he started the engine. Before he could pull out of the parking lot, Staci asked, "How many women have seen your apartment?"

He paused and thought a moment. "Including you?"

"Yes."

"One." He glanced over at her to see her reaction. None.

"Here's a better question," she said. "How many women have you brought to any place you've lived as an adult?"

"Three. You, my sister, and my mom," he told her, again glancing in her direction.

"Why?"

He shrugged. "I don't know. It felt like an invasion of privacy, I guess. Once you bring a woman back to your place, I feel like she might start thinking she's welcome to come over anytime she wants. If I was planning on hooking up with someone, it was going to happen at their place, not mine."

"But you brought me," Staci pointed out.

Slade laughed shortly. "First, not a lot of choice since I had to pick up something, and we were already out. Second, I don't see you as being as presumptuous as most women. I mean, we didn't have sex at my apartment now, did we?" He gave her a side-eye.

"Is that your furniture or did it come furnished?" Staci asked, ignoring his baiting.

"Mostly furnished. The television is mine. I don't own that much stuff. I'm only there to sleep mostly. I work a lot. Less stuff for people to steal too." He waited for the next question. She did not disappoint.

"Do you have friends? Do you socialize with people? I mean, when you aren't working, what do you do?" She pushed a little further, trying to get into his head and figure him out.

"Yes, I socialize but not that much. Until I started coming to your place to do weekend security, I had a weekly poker game at Rodriguez's house every Friday. I go to baseball games or hockey games. I watch TV. I work out every night after work. I do stuff," he defended himself.

127

"Ooh, you like hockey? I love hockey," Staci almost squealed. "I try to get to a Blues game at least a few times during the season."

"Really. What do you like about hockey?" Slade asked, surprised by that revelation.

"Are you kidding me? The fights! I love sports that are high contact and fast. I think that's why I like football too," she told him.

He smiled. It figured that she enjoyed the contact sports for their contact.

"Do you own a gun?" He switched topics.

"Yes, a nine millimeter. Why?" She turned to look at him.

"Let's drop off these clothes and get your gun, and I'll take you to the firing range," he suggested.

Staci grinned. She enjoyed shooting and it had been awhile since she'd been to the range.

"That sounds amazing!" she enthusiastically declared.

*****

Both were laughing when they pulled into Staci's driveway several hours later. They had dropped off his clothes and picked up her weapon and had gone to a private gun club on the outskirts of town. Slade was impressed that not only could she shoot fairly accurately but could also load her own magazine with the bullets. They had decided to have a friendly competition, and although Slade hit every single area they called for aim, Staci didn't lose by much. The activity also provided Slade knowledge about Staci's ability to protect herself with the weapon should she need to.

"So your dad took you and your sisters to the range a lot as a kid?" Slade repeated her statement that she had just made in the car as she let them both into the condo.

"Oh yeah. He was determined we would never be defenseless. The nine was a present from him when I first started at the US attorney's office," she responded. "I'm going to need to buy more bullets after today." She started up the stairs. "I'm going to jump in the shower and get ready to go to dinner. Give me about ten minutes, and you can use the other shower," she told him over her shoulder.

TO DIE FOR HER

An hour later, Staci emerged from her bedroom and descended the stairs. She didn't see Slade. She was adjusting her strappy heel when she heard him behind her in the foyer. She turned and smiled brightly. His jeans and boots were impressive enough, but he had picked out a dark gray button-up shirt with long sleeves that set off his eyes. He had let his stubble grow back some, and it cast just enough shadow to be dashing. She felt that longing deep inside her, and she fought to tamp it down. She had drawn a line in the sand with him, and her own sexual longings were threatening to move that line.

When Slade saw Staci slightly bent over adjusting her heel, he had closed his eyes so he wouldn't have to look at her tempting little ass, but when she had turned around, he felt as if all the air had been knocked out of him. Wearing tight-fitting black pants with the heels; she paired them with a silky red blouse that plunged to the middle of her cleavage. The heart-shaped birthmark on the side of her left breast was peeking at him. She wore large silver hoops in her ears that touched her shoulders, and she had worn her hair down. It was curly and wild, and instantly, Slade wanted to run his hands through it.

"Wow," he said when he could breathe again. "You look stunning."

"Yeah, I clean up pretty good. You look pretty tasty yourself," she informed him.

"Grab your purse and let's go before I completely disregard that agreement we made about no sex," he told her, his voice rough.

She grabbed a black wristlet off the kitchen island along with the white box in the refrigerator that had piqued Slade's interest earlier, and they went outside to his car. She gave him directions as he drove, and soon, they were pulling into a parking spot downtown outside of a popular steak house that had menus without prices. Because she had made reservations, they did not have to wait and were shown to a table that was lit by a candle near a fireplace that had a small fire burning in it. Slade took a minute to look around the restaurant, partly for security reasons and partly to soak in the environment.

"Is this a place you go to often?" he asked when he returned his focus back to Staci.

She snorted rather inelegantly. "Hardly. I can't afford this place on the regular. But since it is a special occasion, I thought it would be a nice treat."

"My birthday isn't a special occasion," Slade corrected her.

"Of course, it is! Growing up, birthdays were always a special occasion. It was the one day that was all your own. Of course, Casey and Cassidy had to share, but," she shrugged, "my mom found a way to individualize it for each one of them. Birthdays are a celebration of your life!" Staci was emphatic.

They ordered a cocktail and then dinner. When the server had left with their order, Staci moved the white box in Slade's direction. "Here, nosy. This is for you."

Slade looked at Staci for a moment then carefully lifted the lid, not knowing what to expect. Inside was a small cake. It was simply decorated with plain white icing, and all it said was "Happy Birthday" in green letters. He looked back up at Staci. He didn't know how to react. It wasn't a large gesture, just something that was thoughtful.

"I hope you like white velvet cake and butter cream frosting." She excused the cake. He hadn't reacted at all, and she wasn't sure what to make of that.

"It's great. Really," he said. "I just wasn't expecting all of this." His throat felt a little full, like he was about to choke.

"Not to overwhelm you, but here." She pushed a green envelope at him across the table.

"More birthday?" Slade opened the envelope and read the card inside. Closing it, he smiled. "Thank you. This was nice." The card wasn't mushy or dreamy. It simply wished him a happy birthday, and she had written her name inside.

"I had a present for you, but in light of our conversation last night, I decided not to give it to you," she informed him.

"What conversation?" Slade was confused.

Their food arrived at that moment, and they immediately dug into the perfectly cooked steaks, baked potatoes, and seasonal vegetables. She sipped her cocktail, a dirty martini, as she ate. Slade had ordered a craft brew, and he was clearly enjoying it. Their server appeared when they were almost through eating and asked if they needed anything else. Staci asked for two clean dessert plates and a butter knife. The server nodded his head and turned to retrieve the requested items.

"That was delicious," Slade told her. "Great choice."

"Thanks. I've heard nothing but good things about this place, so I figured we would try it out." She smiled at his compliment.

The server returned with the plates and the knife, and Staci expertly cut the cake and placed the two pieces on the plates. She handed Slade's over to him. As he was taking it out of her hand, he looked at her quizzically and asked, "What conversation did we have that made you change your mind about giving me a present?"

"Oh, you know, about expectations." She tasted a tiny amount of cake that was on her fork.

"Oh," was all Slade said. He took a more generous bite of the cake. Perfectly moist, exactly the right amount of sweetness. After swallowing the bite, he pushed a little. "Well, what were you going to give me?"

Staci glared at him for a second. The reasoning behind the gift really didn't have anything to do with their relationship, but when he was so noncommittal about how he viewed the relationship after the case was resolved, she panicked a little. She didn't want him to think that she was trying to push anything at him. Making a decision, she slammed her napkin down onto the table.

"Fine," she said. She dug around in the wristlet and produced a key. She handed it to him. "Take it. Happy Birthday."

Taking the key, Slade felt both panic and relief. He wasn't sure what this meant. "What is this?" he asked slowly.

"A key to my condo. I see you outside waiting on me on Fridays with all your stuff. I figured if you had a key, you could let yourself in and wouldn't have to wait on me." Staci carefully chose her words.

Slade turned the key every which way and appeared to be studying it. This was unexpected. He had half-hoped and half-feared it was the key to her place, but when she explained the reason behind giving it to him, it was so logical it made him angry. Did he really want it to mean something else? He had some self-reflection to do.

Instead of voicing any of his thoughts, he asked her, "How many men have you given keys to?" drawing on her earlier questions about his apartment.

She burst out laughing. "None. When I lived with the guy in law school, I moved into his place, not the other way around, and he never had a key to my apartment."

Slade nodded. He took out his key chain and added the key to the others on his key chain. "I won't abuse this, you know that, right?"

Staci smiled and took another bite of the frosting from the cake. "If I thought that, I wouldn't have given you a key."

CHAPTER 12

Monday morning arrived with a cold front and orange skies. Staci descended her stairs dressed for success, ready for whatever the grand jury would throw at her. She patiently waited on Slade to finish dressing and join her. She made him coffee in the coffee maker he had bought, carefully measuring out the coffee and water according to the instructions he had given her. She checked her image in the mirror in the foyer several times, a nervous habit she had picked up as a law student: her makeup was on point, her hair carefully pulled back into a single french braid, and her navy pencil skirt and white blouse fit her like a glove. She carefully pulled on the matching blazer. The smell of the brewing coffee made her stomach lurch a bit. She enjoyed coffee whenever she picked it up at the local coffeehouse, but she never liked the smell of it being prepared. She was tired, but she had carefully applied her concealer to hide the circles under her eyes. The stress she had been dealing with these last few weeks was starting to take its toll.

"Let me fill my cup with that coffee," Slade's voice came down the stairs before his body. He emerged with his large travel cup and filled it with the freshly brewed liquid then shut off the coffee maker.

As their routine on Mondays, he left through the front door to go to his vehicle and do a quick scan of the neighborhood then started his car while he waited for Staci to raise the garage door. He backed out and then waited in the street for her to back out and shut the garage door. Following her to work, he parked near her in the parking garage and escorted her to the elevators. His stop was two floors below hers, but there was no sign of danger, and he smiled and told her "Good luck" before he exited the elevator.

Staci got off on her floor, unlocked her office, changed into her heels, and waited. The press conference was at ten, and until then, the indictment remained sealed. She nervously checked her emails and voicemails. She walked around the office, trying to make the time go faster. When 10:00 a.m. was finally approaching, she entered the press room and stood by the podium where Max would stand when he read the indictment to the press. Max arrived with it in his hand. The usual method was that he would read it before the press conference to himself and then make the announcement when the press had gathered. Today was no different. He opened it and read through it. His face was a conglomeration of several emotions. He frowned, smiled, and nodded his head. He was difficult to read.

He turned to Staci as the press entered the room and told her, "You knocked it out of the park, Staci. I knew you were the right prosecutor for this case."

As the press conference opened, Max began to read, "United States v. Miguel Antonio Ayala and an individual known as 'Zorro' and others known and unknown are hereby charged with…"

Staci listened, keeping her face straight, but her heart was soaring as the grand jury indicted Ayala, Zorro, and anyone else connected to them with seventy-six counts, ranging from all the murders, drug trafficking, money laundering, bank and wire fraud, and more.

When Max finished reading the indictment, he focused on the office's dedication to taking each of the charges to jury trial to achieve law and order and justice for the families of the people killed. He didn't take any questions, and the press conference ended. Staci knew he would not introduce her to the press. He never introduced any of his prosecutors to the press. He had a protocol that he followed, and he followed it today. When he was ready to go back to his office, he handed the indictment to Staci.

"You need to get a trial date and get on this. You will be busy for a while," he warned her.

She nodded. She had a hearing on it later in the afternoon, and she was certain the trial date would be determined at that hearing. The trial would be set for some time in the next ninety days, and

TO DIE FOR HER

Slade still had to do the photo lineups and finish the investigation. She needed to call her sister to get the coordinates for the transmitters they had found in the silver crosses as well.

She made her way back to her office, and to her surprise, Slade was waiting on her inside. He was grinning from ear to ear.

"Seventy-six counts! And you got that Zorro and anyone else involved indicted!" He picked her up and twirled her around. "How did you even think to do that?"

Staci just shrugged. "No big deal. It just made sense to include him and everyone else that was giving orders. You still have work to do to finish this," she reminded him. "We have to be able to ID Zorro and any others, and my burden of proof just rose to beyond a reasonable doubt."

"No worries. I can get everything tied up in a bow for you. Just tell me when you need it by."

"I'll find out this afternoon at my hearing. The court will set a trial date," she stated. She looked at him and asked, "Do you think you can take the security detail off now?"

He stared at her for a moment, considering the possibility. "I want to wait. It's possible that you are in more danger now that you included the others. Let's see how things go. Maybe we can pull the detail in a couple of weeks."

Staci sighed. "Fine."

Slade plopped down in a chair opposite from Staci's desk. "It's not that bad, is it? I mean Bill pretty much stays to himself, and you and I get along okay."

Staci quirked an eyebrow at him. "We get along okay? Is that how you characterize it?"

"How do you characterize it?" Slade was interested to know her take on the time they spent together.

"I think we have fun. I think you are interesting to talk to, you watch football with me, you think of interesting things to do, like going to the range." She measured her words carefully. She wasn't sure what he wanted to hear.

He nodded. "Okay, that's fair. We more than get along. I think it's safe to say that we've become friends and that we enjoy each other's company." His gaze held hers, daring her to expound on what he threw out.

Staci wasn't taking the bait. "I think I definitely would say we've become friends. Spending time with you isn't awful. I'm just so used to having my private life separate from my professional life. My home was always somewhere I could go to escape, you know?"

Slade wasn't sure how he felt about Staci agreeing with him that they were friends. He didn't know what he wanted her to say, but "friends" seemed anticlimactic and sterile. He stood. "Well, I better get back to work. I just wanted to tell you congratulations." He wanted to leave before the conversation got any more awkward.

Smiling up at him, Staci told him, "Thank you." She watched him leave. When he shut the door, her smile left her face. She didn't want to be his friend. She could at least admit that. She wasn't going to push him into anything either. At least she had the trial to focus on now.

*****

The gentleman glanced at his cell phone that was buzzing and blinking, letting him know he was getting a call. He wiped his mouth with his cloth napkin and took a sip of the wine. When the phone kept blinking, he sighed and pushed the answer button.

"Hello?" he answered.

"That bitch indicted me!" The angry voice caused him to wince and pull the phone away from his ear.

"Calm down. It's just an indictment. She doesn't even know your name or it would have appeared on the indictment," the gentleman reasoned.

"In case you missed it, she indicted you, too, Mr. Others Known and Unknown," the man on the other end of the conversation pointed out sarcastically.

"Again, just an indictment. She has to prove everything at trial." The gentleman took another sip of his wine.

"What are we going to do about it?" the man on the other end demanded.

TO DIE FOR HER

"I'm not going to do anything. She can't prove anything."

"Right, because you never showed your face. You left me to do the dirty work. DC can help, right?"

The gentleman paused a moment before answering. "Actually, it's more of a 'if you get caught, we don't know you' sort of thing. If you make a mess, nobody is going to clean it up."

"Dammit! So I have to freakin' clean this up. What do you suggest?" The irritation on the other end of the phone was starting to leak into the gentleman's patience.

"Find whoever can identify you. Neutralize or nullify the ID. It's actually pretty simple," the gentleman pointed out.

"I don't know where they are!" the man on the other end of the conversation screamed in frustration.

"How can you not know? They're in federal custody. You have the databases at your fingertips." The gentleman's food was getting cold, and he wanted to end the conversation and finish his dinner.

"They keep getting moved around. They're being held in places other than federal facilities, and he's playing a shell game with them," the man on the other end calmed somewhat.

"Then you might need to be creative. I suggest you figure it out," the gentleman coldly told the man on the other end of the phone.

He hung up and placed the cell phone back onto the table. Picking up his knife and fork, he cut a piece of his filet mignon and brought it to his mouth, savoring the rich seasonings and perfectly cooked meat. He didn't smile as he thought about what a jumbled-up situation this had become.

*****

For the next two weeks, Staci, Bill, and Slade continued their routine. Staci worked on pretrial motions, witness lists, and cataloging exhibits, mostly in the evening after she left the office. Bill was at her condo Monday evening to Thursday evening. Slade took over on the weekends. Staci needed Slade to conduct the photo lineups, but he said he was still missing a couple of photographs of the potential

"Zorro." They hadn't arrested Ayala yet, but Slade promised her he was getting closer to locating him. One evening, her personal cell phone rang.

"Hello?" She knew who it was when her sister, Isabella's, picture popped up on the screen.

"Hey, sis," Isabella responded. "How you doing?"

"Not bad. I got that indictment I was seeking. Trial is in a few weeks, so I'm pretty busy, but other than that, not much going on here. How are you?"

"How's that hotty that's playing bodyguard? Allison and Cassidy told me all about him," Isabella asked.

Staci rolled her eyes. "He's fine. Also working a lot of hours tying up the loose ends. I can only imagine what they told you."

Isabella chuckled. "Well, I know what he looks like wearing just a towel."

Staci laughed at the memory of Slade barging into her bedroom, gun ready, only to be met by three stunned women staring at his mostly naked body. "Yeah, well, I'm sure their description doesn't do him justice."

"So listen. Remember when you sent me that cross with the transmitter?"

"Yes," Staci refocused on the turn in the conversation.

"I ran it. I have coordinates for you."

"Okay. So if I want to use those coordinates as testimony, what do I need to know in order to ask the right questions?" Staci grabbed a legal pad and pen from the coffee table.

Bill was trying to look as if he wasn't listening, but she could tell that he was.

"So it's pretty basic. It is a GPS type of system. It doesn't collect any data or images, just sends code signals from a constellation of satellites so that the receiver can calculate its position accurately," Isabella began explaining. "The receiver might create a data stream that can be used by other devices. An example is that it can be used to connect ship's autopilots, radio, GPS, radar, etc. Information in that stream includes latitude, longitude, elevation, time, signal quality, and speed."

TO DIE FOR HER

Staci was writing as fast as she could. "Slow down a second," she told Isabella. Isabella waited until Staci signaled she was ready to continue.

"The transmitter in these crosses collects geospatial data, represented either in longitude and latitude or X, Y, and Z form. Either way, it locates certain position on earth. This particular device can provide continuous points calling it tracks to capture movement of device. Ergo, it is a tracking system," Isabella told her. "Some GPS devices also embed cameras to take pictures and can match the position to the image, or they can provide memory and an imagery download option so that points are visualized as in global surface. This one doesn't do that. It is a more simplistic version, so literally, all I have for you are coordinates of where the receiver is located most of the time in terms of longitude and latitude. If you can figure out where that location is, you can narrow down who is receiving the information."

"In other words, you are going to give me the coordinates and I have to have an investigator or someone familiar with cyber tracking to figure out where that location is?" Staci clarified.

"Correct. Then you have to figure out who is at the location during the periods of time that I will also be giving you," Isabella confirmed.

"Okay, I can do that. Fortunately, as you well know, the federal government has an awesome cyber division in its investigative pocket." Staci smiled. "Okay, give me the coordinates and times."

Isabella told her the coordinates. "There's only two sets. The first set is the location used the majority of the time. The second set has only been used a few times." She delineated between the two sets by time for Staci. "The first location is usually used between 7:30 a.m. and 5:30 p.m. It has the most pings. The second set is after 5:30 p.m. or on a weekend."

Staci read back the coordinates. Isabella confirmed them. They chatted about the upcoming Thanksgiving holidays for a few minutes before telling each other goodbye. When Staci hung up the cell phone, she stared at the coordinates for a long few minutes. She needed to get these to Slade so he could get the cyber unit working on them. She texted him on the work cell he had provided to her. She wondered what kind of a cartel chief worked mostly nine to five. Obviously, someone who has a day job as a cover for the criminal activity he or she was dabbling in.

*****

Slade, Vaughn, and Rodriguez sat in Slade's SUV, allowing the US Marshals to go ahead of them on the gravel road where they had pulled off. The approach had to be precise or people could die. Their outer perimeter had been previously set up with men in camouflage and rifles circling around the house that sat on a five-acre plot. Because it was the first of November, the plan was to pass for deer hunters so they didn't raise suspicion. The men were careful to place themselves between the house and the outer buildings, which included a horse barn and a smaller building. They hid among the trees roughly a thousand feet away from the main house. The sun had not yet risen, and the moon had not yet set. The adrenaline pumping through their bodies kept them oblivious of the cold. They slowly approached the house. Before continuing forward to set up their inner perimeter, Slade turned the bill of his hat backward so his view above wasn't obscured. He ran an index finger over the newly grown mustache on his lip. It had grown down each side of his mouth, almost to his chin. Slade smoothed it down in anticipation of their approach.

Slade took the one/four corner so he had a clear view of the front of the house and one side of the house. Vaughn took the two/three corner with a view of the back of the house and the opposite side of the house that Slade had eyes on. Rodriguez joined up with the entry team which was sneaking up to the house behind Vaughn. The arrest team, comprised solely of US Marshals, was cautiously approaching the back of the house near Slade. The arrest warrant allowed them to make entry without knocking and announcing because announcing their presence would create an imminent threat of physical violence to the agents, given the violent history of Ayala and cartels in general.

TO DIE FOR HER

As everyone settled into their previously decided locations, Slade waited impatiently for the call over his earpiece to make entry. They had scouted the area prior to this morning, locating cameras that had been set up in the trees, along the gravel drive, and around the house. The men had carefully avoided them up so as not to tip off anyone who might be tasked with watching the surveillance video. The rifle Slade held was getting heavy, and he resisted the temptation to shift its weight. He could feel his heart pounding. This had been his goal for a very long time, finding and arresting Ayala, a major mover of narcotics, and he prayed that none of his team or the marshals would be injured during this operation. He also figuratively crossed his fingers that Ayala was inside and hadn't given them the slip again.

The call to move forward finally came through, and Slade held his breath, waiting. He heard the marshals kick in the front door, and he pulled his rifle up, holding it in such a way that should someone come out a door or window, he had a bead on them. He heard a lot of yelling then silence. No gunfire. He waited until "Clear" was called, meaning the entry team had gone room to room, clearing each room of any danger or people who were hiding. After what seemed an eternity, the clear call came through. He slung his rifle onto his back and walked to the front of the house. He had purposely kept the rest of his team in the dark about the operation this morning. He knew one of them was involved with Ayala, but he just didn't know who. He had no choice but to keep Carmichael, Westbrook, and Saenz out of the know. By allowing Vaughn to be part of the takedown, he would know if Vaughn was involved if anything went sideways. If not, then he would start eliminating each of the other three to find out who the mole was.

As he approached the now wide-open front door, he watched as the marshals began bringing people out. All were handcuffed. Slade counted five men. He waited. After a few minutes, Rodriguez and Vaughn emerged with Ayala in tow. He nodded at them, knowing they would be placing Ayala in Slade's SUV for transport. Ayala glared at Slade but didn't say anything. Slade entered the house and looked around. The federal agents who were still inside were executing their own search warrant, looking in every nook and cranny. Large amounts of money and guns had already been discovered. Slade figured they would find narcotics in the small outbuilding, maybe even in the horse barn. He was looking for something entirely different. He was searching for the silver crosses that Ayala's men wore. That would indicate Ayala was the one who was tracking them. If it wasn't Ayala, that was one more indicator that a third party was involved in the planning and probably the execution of the murders of the men his team had found at each location they had believed they could catch Ayala in the act last summer. No crosses were recovered.

Staci had texted him coordinates pulled from the GPS data of the transmitters a few nights ago, and he had immediately made a request with the cyber team to identify the locations, but they hadn't gotten back to him yet. Now he was certain it would come back to a third party.

For the next few hours, Slade and the rest of the investigators and marshals scoured the property, took photos, cataloged evidence, and cleared the location. When he hiked back to his vehicle parked up by the highway, the air was still chilly but not as cold as it had been at 5:00 a.m. this morning. Ayala, Vaughn, and Rodriguez were all still waiting in the vehicle. Sighing, Slade climbed in. He had to get Ayala booked and then transported to one of the hiding spots where he had been keeping Gestado, the accountant, and the third man. He and Rodriguez would interview Ayala, test the waters on how accommodating he would be to identify the outside party or give information that would be incriminating. Pulling onto the highway, Slade knew this day was going to be a long one.

*****

Staci stared at her computer. She was in the middle of writer's block as she struggled to find the right words to complete her pretrial motion brief. She was exhausted and hungry, and it wasn't even noon yet. A knock on her office door drew her gaze upward. Slade stood in her doorway, leaning against one side of the trim. He had a huge grin on his face. Staci raised her eyebrows at his Fu Manchu moustache.

"That's new," she commented.

TO DIE FOR HER

Slade stroked it and grinned even wider. "Sexy, right?"

Staci snorted and replied, "I'm not sure I would use that word."

"You have lunch plans?" he asked as he sauntered into her office.

"No, and I'm starving." She started gathering her tote and changed her shoes to flats.

"Let's go. I have an update for you."

When they arrived at his favorite diner, Slade held the door for Staci. She automatically walked to the booth where they usually sat and slid in. Slade joined her, sitting across from her. He studied her face, concern showing on his own.

"Are you feeling alright?" he asked.

"Tired. Stressed. Ready for this case to be over." Staci gave her order to the server and turned her attention fully to Slade. "What's the update?"

"We arrested Ayala yesterday." He leaned back and waited for her reaction.

Her face lit up, and she smiled. "Really?"

"Yep. No shots fired either. We found a ton of money, several kilos of methamphetamine, fentanyl, and cocaine and a stash of guns. I guess that makes your job a little easier, huh?" Slade bragged slightly.

Staci nodded enthusiastically. "Absolutely. Did you interview him? Did he say anything?"

Slade paused while the server set down their plates. Staci tore into her cheeseburger with vigor. It was juicy and cooked to perfection. She shoved a couple of french fries into her mouth. Slade watched with some amusement. Since he had first taken her to eat, he had been amazed at the amount of food she could put away.

He swallowed the bite he had taken of his own burger, then answered, "He's not talking. I have a plan to maybe change that, but we'll see how it plays out. You don't really need a confession considering everything we found."

Swallowing, Staci took a healthy gulp of her iced tea then responded, "For the drug trafficking and money laundering, no, but I have a few murders thrown in that I have to prove."

"Ah, yes, well, that's where my three witnesses come in. I'll get their statements in a few days, along with the photo lineup. You'll have what you need," he assured her.

She nodded, her mouth full again. They ate in silence for a few minutes, and when they had cleaned their plates, Staci leaned back and smiled.

"I needed that. Thanks." She looked a little sheepish and asked, "You mind if I have a piece of that chocolate pie? I've admired their pies every time we've come here, but I was too embarrassed to eat a piece. It's bad enough I can go toe to toe with you on the burgers."

Slade chuckled and told her, "Go ahead. You've earned it."

Staci signaled for the server and requested the pie. While she was waiting for it, she asked Slade, "Does this mean Bill doesn't have to babysit me anymore?"

Slade watched the server set the enormous piece of chocolate pie in front of Staci. She took her fork and filled it with the rich, smooth dark chocolate and creamy meringue. Sliding it into her mouth, she closed her eyes in delight.

"Good?" Slade smiled at her obvious pleasure with the pie.

"Amazing," Staci replied. "You want to try it?"

Slade took his own fork and took a chunk of it. He rolled the bite around in his mouth. Staci was right. The pie was delicious. Creamy and thick. When his mouth was empty, he answered her question.

"I think to be safe, let's give it a week. If no problems, then I will call off Bill. Fair?"

Staci grimaced slightly but conceded. "Fine. I can handle it a little longer."

"If Ayala wasn't the one calling the shots on the murders, you aren't safe. I have to make sure we know who was in charge. It shouldn't take that much longer, I promise." He smiled at her.

"Does that mean you'll be at my condo this weekend?" Staci took another bite of the pie.

"Yeah, just one more weekend." Slade finished his iced tea and signaled for the check.

TO DIE FOR HER

"I have a project I need your help with." Staci grinned devilishly at him.

"Uh-oh, what?"

"You'll see." She tossed her head and put her tote over her shoulder, sliding out of the booth.

*****

When Staci pulled into her driveway on Friday evening, Slade's car was parked in the street. She smiled to herself. She liked coming home to him even if she couldn't admit it to him or herself. Closing the garage door, she opened the door to the foyer and was instantly hit with the aroma of chili. She wasn't a fan of chili, but she could boil some spaghetti noodles and be able to stomach three-way chili. Slade was stirring the chili in the pot and looked up to smile at her when she entered the condo. He had shaved off the enormous moustache and just sported his usual five o'clock stubble.

"I made chili," he announced unnecessarily.

"So I smell. Can you throw on some spaghetti noodles to go with it?" Staci strolled into the kitchen and peered into the pot. She frowned. "There's no beans in here," she observed.

"Um, no, because chili doesn't have beans," Slade told her.

"Then two-way chili it is for me." She shrugged and headed to the stairs.

"You don't like chili?" Slade sounded shocked.

"Eh, it's okay. I can put it over spaghetti, and it will be fine," she informed him as she strode up the stairs.

"What kind of psycho doesn't like chili on a cold day?" Slade called up the stairs. He then proceeded to make the spaghetti noodles, muttering to himself the whole time.

The next morning, after Staci ran her five miles and returned from her kickboxing class, she kicked her shoes off in the hallway and reminded him that she had a project she needed help with. Slade had believed it was work related, but instead, Staci led him to the garage and pointed into the corner.

"I need those three large tubs brought into the house, and there is a Christmas tree in a box leaning against this wall." She pointed to the opposite corner near the door that entered into the house.

"Um, we just completed the first week of November. You're a little early, aren't you?" Slade put his hands on his hips and stared at her.

"Christmas decorations make me happy. Plus, I'm going to be busy trying this complex seventy-six count case you might have heard about right before Christmas. I won't have time to decorate then." Staci started carrying large plastic bags into the house while Slade just stood and watched. "Chop, chop, Agent," Staci shot over her shoulder.

Slade began toting everything into the house, and under Staci's close micromanaging supervision, he began assembling the tree, hanging decorations that were too far up for Staci to reach and generally helping her unpack the decorations. He didn't really mind helping her, but he was befuddled by all the fuss. She lived here by herself. The only person she was decorating for was herself.

Staci programmed the music on the surround sound to Christmas music, and Slade was suddenly immersed in a cacophony of both old and new carols. He watched as Staci flitted around the condo, hanging ornaments and wreaths and valances. She carefully set out crystal and ceramic candy dishes and nutcrackers. He watched as she stood back and reviewed her work, only to rearrange or straighten as needed. Her mood was bright, and she hummed along with the music. He was content on just watching her. Still wearing her sweats from her kickboxing class, her hair falling out of that ever-present bun, she was the most exquisite creature Slade had ever seen.

Finally, she stood back and announced, "Okay, I think that will do it."

She turned to Slade, her face glowing, and said, "Thank you so much for your help. I usually have to do this by myself every year. It went by faster than normal with your help."

Slade just shrugged. He began putting the lids back on the tubs. "I guess these all go back where I got them?"

TO DIE FOR HER

"Yes, please. Hey, I have an idea. How about I cook dinner for you tonight instead of you cooking?"

Slade stopped in his tracks and stared at Staci. Finding his words, he asked, "Do you have anything here to cook?"

"Sure, I can find something to whip up. I know how to cook, I just don't like cooking for one," she explained.

Slade nodded and told her, "Sounds great." He was still skeptical.

After the decoration containers were put up, Slade's laundry was well on its way to being completed, and they had exhausted themselves on college football, Staci went to the kitchen to start dinner. Slade followed. He wanted to watch this happen since he couldn't remember a time when he had actually seen Staci cook. In less than an hour, she produced perfectly baked salmon, rice pilaf, and roasted asparagus. She plated their food, and with a flourish, placed it on the island with a "Voilà!" Slade tasted the food on his plate and nodded his head.

"Taste okay?" Staci asked him.

"Mm, yes, wow. This is really tasty," he complimented her. It was another hidden talent he had discovered in this woman.

They carried their plates to the coffee table and found a movie to watch. They both agreed they disliked romantic comedies, but after that, their tastes were vastly different. She enjoyed horror movies or quirky movies with very dry humor. He enjoyed movies where things blew up. They compromised and found a movie that had the humor she liked and the occasional explosion. Every so often, they exchanged a remark about the movie or a character, never sitting close to each other. Both noticed the distance they placed away from each other, but neither brought it up. Instead, they would sneak glances at each other. Staci noticed how Slade's eyes would darken when he looked at her, and Slade noticed the flush on Staci's cheeks when she looked at him, but they had an agreement. Both wanted desperately to break that agreement, but neither wanted to be the one who did it.

*****

Monday dawned cold and wet. Glancing outside, Staci was worried about the weather turning icy. She had pulled out her winter coat and gloves and was putting them on when Slade came downstairs. He poured a healthy amount of the coffee Staci had made for him in a tall, insulated cup to go. He was wearing his usual khakis and a thick coat. He had a beanie on his head and looked as rugged as any lumberjack ever did. Staci stood admiring him until his voice broke into her thoughts.

"Ready?" he asked.

She nodded and left through the garage door. Slade followed and went to his car. He followed her to work and rode up in the elevator with her. He noticed she smelled really good, the scent of some new perfume permeating the elevator.

"What is that perfume you're wearing? Is it new?" Slade made idle conversation.

Staci beamed. He had paid attention to her new perfume. "Yes, it's by Jessica McClintock."

"It's nice." The elevator door opened at his floor. "Have a great week," he told her before exiting.

Staci pouted a little. His departure was rather anticlimactic. She was getting more and more used to him being around, and unless he came by her office during the week, she found herself missing him. That scared her.

*****

On Thursday, Staci's week was almost up. This should be the last night Bill was at her house. No sign of trouble, no interference with her case. Staci was both elated at the idea of having her privacy back but also miserable at the idea of not having Slade spend the weekend. He hadn't been to visit her all week, so she had no idea what the plan was. She texted him on the burner phone he had provided to ask. He responded after a few minutes that confirmed this was Bill's last night. He didn't give any feedback on her question about the plan going forward. When she pulled into her garage that evening, she let Bill into the house. She had picked up some barbe-

TO DIE FOR HER

que from a local joint because she knew that Bill really enjoyed good barbeque. Staci could tell Bill was glad this assignment was almost over, and they talked and laughed freely when Bill started telling stories about his two sons and their misadventures. Before long, both were yawning, and Staci bid Bill good night and walked up the stairs. She took a long soaking bath that relaxed her. She climbed into bed, exhausted, and fell asleep almost immediately.

She was awakened by the sound of voices. She glanced at her phone. The bright light told her it was midnight. She recognized Bill's voice but not the second voice. She listened for a minute and then climbed out of bed. She was just about to open her bedroom door when she heard what sounded like a gunshot. She yanked open her door. It was pitch-dark with some light on downstairs that barely lit the hallway and stairs. She saw a dark figure at the bottom of the stairs. When the figure stepped on the first stair, she hit the panic button on the alarm extension. The house was immediately filled with a deafening siren and strobe lighting. She slammed her door shut and locked it. She grabbed her cell phone and ran to her closet. Locking it, she dug her 9mm out of the drawer where she kept it and immediately called the only person she could think of.

*****

Slade was deep asleep. He was jerked awake by the sound of his phone blaring the sound he had assigned to Staci's personal cell number. He sat up like a shot and grabbed his phone. "Yes?" He was holding his breath.

The only sound that came across the phone was a panicked Staci who whimpered, "Michael."

"On my way," he told her, jumping out of bed.

Slade drove like a madman, breaking most of the traffic laws he knew. When he pulled up to her condo, four patrol cars and three SUVs he identified as government cars were outside. The patrol cars still had their emergency lights flashing. He went into full panic mode; he couldn't breathe, he couldn't think. He slammed on his brakes and threw his car into park, talking to himself the entire time. "Fuck. Fuck, no, no. Let her be alright, please, God."

He ran to her front door, which was wide open and burst through it, yelling, "Staci!"

Staci was sitting on the sectional, and when she heard Slade yell her name, she whipped her head around. Relief washed through her. She jumped over the back of the sofa and ran to him. He caught her in his open, outstretched arms and wrapped her tightly against him. She suddenly started crying hysterically, shaking.

Slade kissed the top of her head and repeatedly told her, "It's okay. I'm here. It's going to be alright."

Neither of them paid attention to the three men standing around the island in Staci's kitchen, watching them intently. One narrowed his eyes. The other two seemed surprised and slightly embarrassed by the embrace.

Slade watched over the top of Staci's head as several police were making notes, taking pictures of Bill's body which was lying half in and half out of the sliding glass door leading out to the patio. A bullet hole marred his forehead, his eyes open. Blood surrounded his head.

Slade suddenly took notice of the three men in the kitchen. He looked at them pointedly, and all three of them turned their gaze to the floor. He also noticed at the same time that Staci was only wearing a deep green baby doll nightgown made out of some slick, satiny material. Slade took Staci by the elbow and led her to the laundry room. Once they got into the room, Slade shut the door and held Staci away from him.

"Calm down. I need you to tell me what happened," he sternly commanded Staci, hoping to get her to think straight.

Taking a deep breath, Staci's chest rose and fell rapidly. She sucked air in through her nose and breathed it out through her mouth until she calmed down significantly. Once Staci appeared to have regained her composure, Slade asked her again, "What happened?"

"I was asleep upstairs. I was woken up by Bill and some other man talking. They weren't yelling, but they were talking. Then I heard a gunshot. I opened the door and looked downstairs. There was a person at the bottom of the stairs, and he started coming up

TO DIE FOR HER

the stairs. That's when I hit the panic button by the bedroom door. I locked myself in the closet with my gun and my phone. I called you, then the alarm company called me, and I told them to send police. I waited inside until the police announced their presence. That's when I came downstairs and saw Bill." She started tearing up again. "Oh, god, poor Bill!"

She sobbed into Slade's chest. He stroked her back and her hair and tried soothing her again by reminding her he was there and she was okay.

When Staci calmed down again, he started interrogating her again. "Was anything taken?"

"What?" Staci was trying to clear her head.

"Was anything taken?"

She thought for a moment and replied, "Yes. I had three flash drives on the coffee table. They're all gone."

"Was the blue one there? Were any of them the flash drive with the case on it?" Slade put both hands on her shoulders.

Staci shook her head. "No, they were all decoys. I always set them out when I go to bed. I also hide decoys around the house. All of them blue."

"Where is the actual flash drive?" Slade pushed.

"Somewhere safe. And I made backups," Staci told him. Slade almost smiled. She was a smart cookie. He admired her brilliance.

"Who got here first?"

"What do you mean?" She sniffled.

"After the police got here, who was here first, Carmichael, Vaughn, or Rodriguez?"

"They were all three here when I came downstairs. I don't know who was here first," she told him.

He just nodded. He waited until she stopped sniffling and told her, "Go upstairs. Put on a robe or something and get warm. I have some of my own questions to ask, then I will lock up and come upstairs. Deal?"

He leaned back to look in her eyes. Even puffy and red from crying, her deep green eyes mesmerized him. He had felt like he had been gut-pinched when she had called. She hadn't said anything but

151

his name, but he knew she needed him, and when he got to her place and saw all the police lights and cars, he couldn't breathe until he had seen she was alive and, although upset, uninjured. He gave her one last tight squeeze and kissed her full pouty lips soundly before opening the door and leading her back into the main room.

"Hey, guys," he called to the police. "Do you need anything else from Ms. Everly or can she go upstairs and get out of your hair?"

The coroner's office was there and had loaded Bill's body onto a stretcher, wheeling him toward the front door. An officer wearing a suit, a homicide detective Slade guessed, looked over at them both and replied, "Nah, we got everything we need from here. She can leave if she wants."

Slade nodded and gave Staci a gentle nudge in the small of her back. She sprinted upstairs without any more encouragement. Slade ran a hand through his hair, which was starting to grow out, and went to her refrigerator. He got himself a beer that he had previously stocked up and took a long gulp from the bottle. Vaughn, Carmichael, and Rodriguez just watched.

Finally, Slade looked at the trio and asked, "How did you all know to come here? That there was trouble here?"

Carmichael started. "I was dropping off a date in the neighborhood and saw all the cop cars racing in this direction. I turned on the scanner to see what was up and heard the address, and dispatch mentioned her name. I followed the police and called Vaughn."

Vaughn nodded. "Carmichael called me, and I called Rodriguez."

"Carmichael, you got here first before Vaughn or Rodriguez?"

"Like I said, I was in the neighborhood," he replied.

"How did you know this was her address?"

"I didn't until dispatch used her name and stated it was an assistant US attorney. I put two and two together," he explained.

"City cops were already here when you got here?"

"Yeah, they had already made entry."

"Why didn't anyone think to call me?" Slade's eyebrows knitted together into a scowl.

No one had an answer. They just stared at Slade. Slade grunted and finished the beer. He tossed it into the trash can under the sink.

His three coworkers watched as he moved around the condo, clearly familiar with it. He walked over to where Bill's body had lain and stared. Then he checked the sliding glass door, placing the metal bar in position to keep the door from being opened. He turned around and announced that someone was going to have to tell Bill's family what happened.

"We can all do it," Vaughn volunteered himself and his two colleagues.

Slade nodded. He sent them Bill's address over their phones. "Let the boss know I may not make it in tomorrow, or if I do, I'll be late. I'm going to help arrange for the mess to be cleaned up, and I'm going to go to the police station to get copies of reports." He sighed. "I'm going to go by Bill's in the morning and see how I can help the family get through this too."

Vaughn, Carmichael, and Rodriguez just nodded. They made their way to the door, and Slade stood at the threshold, watching each get into his car. He watched them drive away before he shut the door and bolted the lock. He checked the lock on the garage door as well. He went around the first floor, shutting off lights. He was suddenly tired down to his soul. He slowly mounted the stairs and walked to the guest room. He took off his holster and put it on the dresser then sat on the end of the bed and began unlacing his boots. He had one boot off when he heard a noise. Looking up from where he was sitting, he saw Staci. She was standing in the doorway of her bedroom looking forlorn. Her eyes were still puffy. She hadn't put on a robe as he had instructed her to do. Instead she wore just the green baby doll nightgown. She put one hand onto the doorway trim and slightly leaned into it. She looked at him and simply said, "Michael."

He took off his remaining boot then stood. He slowly walked down the hallway toward Staci, unbuckling his belt and unbuttoning his jeans as he approached. He reached her, and she turned her face up to look in his eyes. He put his hands in her hair to frame her face and leaned down. Instead of kissing her, as Staci had anticipated, he told her in his deep, sexy voice, "If we do this, I'm never sleeping in that goddamn guest room again, understand?"

Knowing he wanted her as much as she wanted him gave Staci the courage to tell him, "I don't want to be just your friend."

Slade's heart nearly exploded inside his chest. His lips descended onto hers, moving them apart to slip his tongue inside her mouth. He kissed her long and deep. When he raised his head back up, he told her, "And I don't want to be just your booty call."

He lowered his head and kissed her again, this time more urgently. Staci began kissing him back, frantically, letting him know that she wanted him. Groaning, he slid his hands under her nightgown to cup her bottom. His hands hit flesh, and with a sweep of his thumbs, he discovered she was wearing a thong under the gown. The thought and the picture that suddenly popped into his head were too much. His breath left him, and he rained kisses on her cheeks. He picked her up by her butt, a cheek in each hand. He raised her up and pushed her against the wall just inside the door of her bedroom.

"Your ass fits perfectly in my hands, darlin'." His baritone voice was husky and sensual, his drawl pronounced.

He set her down long enough to pull the nightgown over her head. She was as beautiful and perfect as he remembered. He had to close his eyes to regain control. Staci leaned into him and placed light butterfly kisses on his muscular chest while she ran her hands lightly down his stomach. When they reached the open waistband, she hesitated.

Slade's eyes snapped open, and he saw her eyes were dilated, and the smile she had on her face was mischievous. She licked her lips as she ran a finger over the tip of his penis that was hard and throbbing and protruding out of the top of his boxer briefs. Slade jerked at the touch.

Staci whispered, "Do you want me?"

Pushing her away slightly, he ran his thumbs along the waistband of the thong. "If you don't take this off, I'll have to tear it off you," he told her softly.

Staci slid the waistband down to her thighs where it floated to the floor on its own. She quickly stepped out of it and reached for Slade again. He grabbed her by her butt again, lifting her up and against the wall. Her nipples were almost at eye level, and he used

TO DIE FOR HER

his lips to snag one, causing Staci to squeal and thrust her chest at him. He switched nipples, gently sucking, listening to the sounds of pleasure coming from Staci. The more pleasure he brought her, the more excited he became. He lowered her down long enough to slip a condom onto himself and push his own pants lower. He reached between her legs to find that she was wet and ready for him. Lifting her up again, he used the wall as a brace. She wrapped her legs around his waist, and he thrust himself inside of her in one move. He held himself there, not moving, letting himself adjust to the heat and tightness of her.

Staci began to squirm and she begged him, "Please, Michael."

The sound of his name on her lips made the fire already raging inside of him burn hotter. He began thrusting. Staci matched every stroke. Her moans began a crescendo, getting louder and higher.

"Baby, if you don't slow down, this isn't going to last very long," he warned her.

She paid no heed to his warning and instead began pushing him to go faster. He became lost in the feeling, oblivious to everything, seeking only to bring them both to a climax. When it came, it came hard. He felt her tighten around him, and then the vibrations began inside her, and he knew she was ready for him to reach the pinnacle with her. Staci threw back her head and opened her mouth in a silent scream. With three long, slow, hard strokes, grunting as he thrust, he climaxed. It raced through him, causing him to shudder. Finally, he found the strength to lower her so her feet could touch the floor.

Staci's breathing returned to normal before she looked at him and grinned. "Wow," she said.

"Wow, indeed." He grinned back at her.

She led him to the bed. He slipped off his pants and briefs and socks and climbed in next to her. He pulled her close to him, her arm across his chest, his arm wrapped around her shoulder.

"I'm taking over all babysitting responsibilities until this case is over," he told her softly.

She nodded.

"I mean it," he said. "I'm not leaving you alone again or with anyone else."

"I guess you need to bring some clothes and stuff over here then," she mused. "So you aren't driving back and forth."

"Yeah."

"I guess this means I should probably make an appointment to get on birth control, huh?" she thought out loud.

The memory of their first sexual encounter, when he had gotten so bewitched by Staci's spell that he had forgotten to put on a condom, flooded his mind. The thought of being flesh on flesh with her started to arouse him.

"Yeah, that would be a good idea," he agreed with her hoarsely, concentrating on keeping himself in control.

Staci lightly ran her fingers down his chest, down his belly, and under the covers. She touched his erection, and Slade knew he was lost. She raised herself up and smiled a naughty smile at him.

"Hmm, wonder what that is," she said to no one in particular. She began placing gentle kisses down the same path her fingers had just taken.

Slade realized he was holding his breath as she kissed him lower and lower. When her mouth finally enveloped him, he let out the air he had been holding in, and it left his body with a slow hiss. His hands were tangled in her wild mane. She stopped briefly and brought her eyes up to meet his.

"Say my name," she demanded, using the same line he had used on her.

"Staci," he whispered.

Once again, her mouth surrounded him, and he forgot everything except the pleasure she was giving him.

CHAPTER 13

Slade strolled into the office the next afternoon. The morning had started off fantastically, including an early morning lovemaking session and a hot shower. It quickly went downhill after he made a visit to Bill's widow. Several marshals were there, as he had expected, and Bill's wife and two boys greeted him generously. However, their grief was palatable, and Slade was flooded with guilt for asking Bill to help him protect Staci these last few weeks. When he left, he swung by a fast-food place and got some lunch to take with him to the office. Now he tossed the bag onto the desk he used and sat down, rifling through paperwork and reading through a report.

Carmichael came over and pulled a chair up to the front of the desk. He sat in the chair, putting his feet on Slade's desk. He was chewing on a toothpick and grinning.

"So how long have you been banging little miss prosecutor?" Carmichael asked.

Slade stopped reading. He raised his head slowly, keeping his face emotionless.

"What the hell did you just ask me?" Slade quietly asked, a warning in his tone. He looked around and saw that every one of his team was watching and waiting.

Carmichael snorted. "Oh, come on! We were there. We saw that sweet little embrace, how she ran to you, used 'Michael' when she addressed you. You had a good hold on her, nice and tight. You even had your brand of beer in her fridge."

"You have no idea what you're talking about," Slade calmly told him, the warning again in his tone.

"We know what we saw," Carmichael insisted, making a circling motion with one hand, including the others in the conversation.

Slade took a few breaths so he wouldn't explode. Maintaining an even voice and stoic face, he told Carmichael, "What you saw was a terrified woman. Someone had just broken into her home and killed a man. She was horrified and in a panic. When I came inside, I didn't see one of you offering her any sort of sympathy or comfort." Slade looked each member of his team in the eye as he continued, "What you saw was me providing that empathy, that comfort. And, yes, I know where things are in her home, and, yes, I brought beer over there since I've been spending my weekends guarding her. Something I didn't ask any one of you to do. I didn't ask any of you to give up family time or date night or any off-time activities. I did it myself so you wouldn't have to." Slade took another deep breath, still maintaining control over his emotions. "Because I spend those weekends guarding her, yeah, she trusts me to keep her safe."

One by one, each team member looked away from Slade's gaze and downward at imaginary paperwork on their desks or at their computers. All except Carmichael who held Slade's gaze. "And just so you are aware, since Bill was murdered last night, I will be guarding her full time until this case goes to trial," Slade shot at Carmichael.

He shoved Carmichael's feet off his desk and snatched up the bag that still held his lunch. "I'm going to go eat this in peace." He stomped out of the room before he said or did anything that would tip off his men about his feelings toward Staci.

*****

The tattooed man's cell phone rang.

"Yeah," he answered.

"I'm going to need you to step up your game for a while. Keep her in your view at all times. Report in," the voice on the other end told Manny.

"I heard about the marshal," Manny commented.

"Yeah. Don't let her out of your sight. That includes her home and car," the voice demanded.

TO DIE FOR HER

"On it," Manny reassured the caller. He disconnected his phone and revved the engine on his motorcycle, pulling into traffic.

*****

Staci was busy formulating the discovery motion she intended to file when a sound at her doorway drew her attention away from the computer. Glancing over, she saw Max standing there.

"May I?" he asked and moved into the office without waiting for a reply. He sat in one of her chairs and stared intently at Staci.

"Sure, come on in," Staci belatedly told him. She couldn't really disguise the sarcasm.

"I heard about that marshal that was providing security for you. I'm surprised you made it into the office today," he told her. No emotion on his face, he leaned forward slightly.

Staci shrugged and turned in her chair to face him. "The trial is coming up. I don't have the luxury of taking time off, and besides, if I'm at home, I'd just dwell on everything." She sighed. "This keeps my mind off it."

Max nodded and leaned back in the chair, toying with his fingers, not looking at her. "Terrible, what happened."

"Yeah. I feel horrible for his family." Staci almost teared up again, feeling a sob catch in her throat.

"What will you do about security?"

"Slade is taking over those duties full time until the trial is over." Staci studied Max, looking for a hint about where this topic was going.

Max nodded vigorously. "Good, good. He's quite capable of keeping you safe." He looked at her somewhat curiously. "Is there more to your relationship that I should know about?"

Staci squinted at him. "Why would you ask me that?" She avoided answering his question.

"I know what my eyes tell me, Staci." He smiled softly at her.

"I don't know what your eyes are telling you," Staci countered. "All I know is that we've sort of been thrown together because of this case, and we're just making the best of it. Once it's over, who knows what will happen."

Max nodded, noting that she didn't deny a more personal relationship. That was dangerous. He pulled himself out of the chair. "Do you want me to reassign this case? You've been looking very tired and thin. Have you been losing weight?"

"I've been eating, don't worry. And I just have a hard time turning off my head at night when I go to bed. I'll be alright." Staci reassured Max. "Oh, the Friday before Thanksgiving, I need to take the afternoon off. I have a doctor's appointment."

Max smiled and told her, "Yeah, sure. No problem. Just put it on the calendar." He referred to the online shared calendar that the office utilized.

Staci nodded and watched him leave her office. *How curious*, she thought to herself.

*****

Slade sighed and pretended to be interested in the dancer on stage. She was wrapped around the steel pole and going through the usual motions. Three of his team members were there with him. They were pretending to be construction guys on a break, enjoying the girls and beer flowing at the club, and his teammates were certainly living the part. They were whooping and making catcalls and flashing money at the dancers, elbowing each other and laughing. Slade pasted a smile on his face and sat back, watching. Another case had been opened, and rumor had it that drugs were being trafficked out of this strip club. The point was to get in good with the dancers and get them to talk. He checked his watch. They'd only been here under an hour. Three scantily clad dancers approached their group and chatted up his team. Handing them money, they let the dancers do their thing, a chair dance that would eventually turn into lap dances. Slade continued watching until he felt a light touch on one of his shoulders. Looking up, he saw a pretty redhead smiling at him.

TO DIE FOR HER

Wearing only a teal thong and matching bikini top with her high heels, she leaned down and whispered into his ear, "You don't talk much, do you?"

Slade grinned up at her, playing his part. "I like to watch."

"Ooh, kinky!" the redhead squealed softly. She helped herself to Slade's lap, turning to face him, straddling him. "Maybe I can arrange for you to watch more than that," she said, tossing her head in the direction of his team and the other women. "Would you like that?" She leaned down and nuzzled his neck.

"That sounds like a party," he replied softly, fighting back the urge to shove her off his lap.

Back in his youth, this would have been fun. He had visited his share of strip clubs in Dallas, but he was younger and dumber and single. Slade jerked, stunned. When had he stopped thinking of himself as single? When had he become monogamous? Staci's face flashed into his mind, and he knew. The moment he laid eyes on her—so intense, so determined to bust the Ayala case out of the park, chewing on a fingernail and looking at photographs strewn over her office floor—that was the moment he was no longer in charge of his own destiny. She held his heart in her hand and didn't even know it.

"Baby, you still with me?" the redhead asked him breathlessly.

Slade snapped out of his thoughts and murmured, "Right here." The redhead dropped her top and rubbed her ample bosom on his chest. "Would you like a little dance to get things started?"

He felt nothing. No twinge of excitement, no anticipation. Nothing.

"You know what would make this party even better?" he asked, running his hands along her thighs. "Blow. You got any?"

"Not at the moment. But," she leaned in and whispered, "I'll have some in a couple of days."

"Yeah?" he whispered right back.

She nodded coyly. "I can get some for you." She proceeded to tell him what body part she would snort it off and offered up a body part for him to use as well. He handed her a fake card, with a fake name, but the real number on his government issued work cell.

TARA BRITT

"I have to go back to work, but call me." He gently set her on her feet and stood up. He yelled over at his teammates, "Break's over! Get back to the job site!"

He kissed the back of her hand as if she were a princess, making her giggle. He grinned and winked at her then made his way to the door.

Once everyone got into the fake work truck, they commented on Slade's encounter with the redhead.

"How do you always get the finest women on these jobs?" Rodriguez asked.

"She was all over you!" Westbrook commented. "Was it worth it?"

"Yeah, they have a shipment of coke coming in between now and two days from now. She's going to call when she has some. Once we arrest her for possession, maybe she'll tell us who she bought it from. If not, we can still keep working that angle." He turned to look at Carmicheal. "You're going to stake out this place for the next two days. If you see anything, call it in. We'll be there."

Carmichael frowned but nodded. He snarkily asked, "Wonder what Ms. Everly will think about you being in a strip club with a hot redhead hanging on you?"

"Not a damn thing," Slade shot back. He was wrong.

When Staci walked through her door at the end of the day, Slade was just pulling into the driveway. She waited by the door for him. When he walked by her, she sniffed the air. She frowned. She didn't say anything. She watched as Slade went to the fridge and pulled out a beer. He took a long drink and noticed her looking at him. He grinned at her and sauntered over to where she was still standing in the foyer staring at him. He put a hand around her waist and pulled her close to him. When he leaned down to nibble on her neck, she put a hand up and stopped him.

"What is that smell?" she asked.

"What are you talking about?" Slade was puzzled.

"A combination of smoke and perfume," she clarified.

Slade thought for a moment how he was going to explain how he had spent his afternoon.

162

TO DIE FOR HER

"It's not my perfume," she pointed out. "Look, I know we haven't defined our relationship beyond I am not just your friend and you're not my booty call. What you do on your own time is not my business, but out of respect, you can't bed me when you smell like another woman. If you want to get laid tonight, you need to shower off her smell."

Slade explained how he had been on assignment with a new case, how the redhead approached him, and some general details. Staci didn't look skeptical, but she didn't look relieved either.

"How often do your assignments take you to places like that?" she asked.

"Sometimes. Not a lot, but a lot of dope gets bought and sold out of those establishments. They're mostly owned by motorcycle gangs, and that's how they launder their money. A lot of business happens in the back rooms of those places," Slade told her.

She nodded. After a few minutes, she asked, "Does that sort of thing turn you on?"

"No. Back in the day, it was fun to go with friends once in a while, but turn me on? No." He thought how turned off he was today, how he didn't even want the woman sitting on his lap or touching him. "You know what does turn me on?"

"What?"

"You." He moved in to nibble her neck again, and she stopped him again.

"Not until you take a shower and get that smell off," Staci told him.

Slade looked into her wide green eyes and saw determination. She wasn't changing her mind about that shower. He dropped his arms, put the beer on the island, and surrendered with a gentle "Fine."

Hours later, after dinner and another incredible round of sex, they lay in Staci's bed, naked and sweaty and thoroughly satiated. As Slade held Staci in the afterglow, Staci told him, "My sister Meredith will be here the Friday before Thanksgiving. She's doing a floating round at Barnes-Jewish Hospital. I want to go have lunch with her on that Saturday. Will you be joining us or just following me to and from the restaurant?"

Slade stared at the ceiling and thought about it. He pulled Staci a little closer. "I would join you, but I would kind of be the third wheel," he reasoned. "I'm sure you have sister stuff you want to talk about, and I really don't have anything to contribute."

"You mean other than being eye candy and a continuing topic of gossip among my sisters?" She laughed.

"Right." He rolled over to face her. He gently outlined her lips with his thumb. "I'll take you and sit outside if you're okay with that." Leaning up to place a light kiss on his lips, Staci nodded. Slade kissed her back, harder, eager. Their conversation was over.

The next day, Staci's personal cell phone buzzed. She looked down and saw it was her brother-in-law, Jeff. He was married to her sister, Casey. Puzzled as to why he would be calling, Staci answered. "Hello?"

"Hey, sister-in-law, how you doing?" Jeff's deep voice, always full of mischief, came across the connection.

"I'm good. What about yourself?"

"Great, listen, do you have lunch plans today?"

More than a little confused, Staci answered, "No. Why?"

"I'm in town on a promotional junket. I'll only be here a few hours, but I thought I might take you to lunch," Jeff offered.

"Don't you have a game this weekend?"

"Ouch, is that no? I don't have practice today because of this junket. It's part of my contract," he told her.

Staci looked at her watch. It was close to lunchtime. "I don't have plans, and I would love for you to buy me food."

"Cool. I'm in the lobby." Jeff hung up.

Staci stood up, shoved her phone and other items in her tote, and opened her office door. Sure enough, Jeff stood there, all six feet six inches of him, all muscle, his dark hair flowing to his shoulders. Staci squealed and ran to hug him. He laughed and twirled her around and planted a big kiss on her forehead.

"You are a sight for sore eyes!" she told him. She noticed a lot of other people in the lobby just staring at them. "Yes," she announced loudly. "This is Jeff Cummings, linebacker." She turned to face Jeff.

"These people are so nosy. They'll be googling you before we're out of the building."

She led him to the elevators and pushed the button to the parking garage. He leaned over and pushed the button to the ground floor.

"We're taking my car," he told her. "I rented an awesome Italian sports car, and I love driving it. But," he grinned when he shrugged, "I have to turn it back in when I board that plane tonight."

Staci smiled and nodded at him. When the elevator door opened at the ground floor, he walked her outside and to his rental car. He was right; it was awesome. Shiny, small, and cherry red.

"Too bad it's too cold to take the roof off," she commented.

Jeff opened the passenger door and let Staci inside.

As Jeff rounded the back end to get to the driver's side, Slade watched from across the parking lot. He was pulling in and saw Staci and this large good-looking man exit the building, so he turned his SUV around and parked in the visitor's parking lot. He watched as the man held the door of his expensive sports car for Staci who was beaming from ear to ear. He waited until they pulled out then impulsively followed them to a restaurant that he had never eaten at before in large part because it was well beyond his means. He watched as they entered the restaurant and debated what he wanted to do next. *Screw it*, he thought as he put his own vehicle in park and stomped to the front door. Surprisingly, they let him sit at the elegant bar. He was close enough to be able to spy on Staci and the big man but far enough away that their vision would be blocked by the multitude of crystal glasses and mirrors that hung behind the bar. He watched as they laughed and talked, and he felt a sudden rage. It built slowly. He ordered a water and an appetizer and continued to watch.

Staci and Jeff were laughing over the antics of her nephew, Jeff's son, who just turned four. Their server silently slipped up to the table and patiently waited.

Jeff looked at Staci and asked, "What would you like? You're looking a little on the thin side. You should eat something hearty."

Pretending to be insulted, Staci pouted her lips and declared, "Most men like their women to be thin."

"Your sister is as big as a house these days," he commented. "That's why we won't be making it to Thanksgiving. Doctor says she's too pregnant to fly, plus you know, I have a game that day."

Staci ordered pasta, and Jeff ordered red meat and a salad. After giving the menus back to their server, Jeff asked, "So your sisters told Casey that some gorgeous man is living at your house. Security. What's up?"

Staci briefly explained the reason for the security but glossed over the actual dangers that had befallen her. Jeff listened intently and at one point reached out and snagged her hand, holding it. "If I didn't have to be on the East Coast for work, I would gladly provide protection for you, you know that, right?"

Staci smiled at him, squeezing his hand. "Your job when you aren't playing football is protecting my sister and my nephew. Besides, my bodyguard isn't that bad." She took a sip of her iced tea.

"Yeah? Your eyes tell me you kind of like this guy," Jeff said. He looked at her, waiting for her to deny it.

"Well, we haven't really defined our relationship. He said he has no expectations. So I've kind of adopted the same philosophy." She shrugged.

Their food was served, and Jeff commented, "I don't think you have. I think you have feelings for him, but are too scared to admit it."

"Well, he's here, watching us. I saw him when he walked in." She smiled mischievously. "He thinks we can't see him."

"Hmm, a man doesn't follow and spy on a woman if he doesn't have feelings for her," Jeff observed. Then he grimaced. "That sounds a bit creepy. Stalker-like."

Staci laughed and took a bite of her own food. "I know what you meant. He's probably wondering who you are and why we're together."

"We should make him furious," Jeff suggested. "If he's jealous, that just confirms what I was trying to say a few minutes ago."

Staci shook her head. "I don't play games. As tempting as it sounds, and he certainly deserves it, I can't do that."

TO DIE FOR HER

"God, you are too nice." Jeff finished his steak and leaned back. "This was great, getting to see you! Once the season is over, we'll fly you and the rest of the family to our place in the islands. It'll be fun to get you sisters all together!"

Their place in the islands was in the Bahamas. It was seaside, had a pool, and they had full access to a boat. The sisters had spent more than one vacation there and always left happy and relaxed.

"That sounds wonderful!" Staci exclaimed. "I hear you just signed a new contract, so you won't be moving this year."

"Yeah, maybe we can actually buy a house instead of renting one. I know Casey will feel better if we are more settled."

They chatted a little while longer, then Jeff paid the bill. Someone recognized him and approached their table for an autograph. Jeff obliged him.

Slade took all this in. Who was this bonehead? Signing autographs? When Slade saw him take Staci's hand in his, Slade thought he was going to come across the bar, but he made himself sit silently. Brooding. He watched as the man helped Staci out of her chair and walk to the door. He waited a few moments then walked outside. He jumped into his SUV and followed the sports car back to the visitor's lot. He parked a few spaces away and watched as the man helped Staci out of the car and then envelope her in a hug. She placed a kiss on the man's cheek and hugged his neck. She then turned and walked back into the building, and the sports car took off.

Slade sat in his own vehicle, his eyes narrowed, tamping down the rage that continued to burn inside of him. The guy had his hands all over her. Obviously, he was trying to impress her, and damn it, it looked like she was soaking it up. Clearly, she had a type, given that the man was similar to his own build, just a bit bigger, bulkier, he mused. Growling, he threw the SUV into reverse and drove to the employees' parking underground. He was determined to find out who that man was and why Staci was drooling all over him.

When he arrived at Staci's condo, she was in the kitchen, chopping vegetables. She had already changed her clothes and now wore sweatpants that were low slung and hanging on her hips and a top that barely came to her navel. She was chopping furiously, and Slade

167

thought she'd never looked sexier. He had sat in his car in the driveway for several minutes, thinking about how he was going to broach the subject of her lunch date, but when he walked in and saw her, everything he planned flew out the window.

"Hey," he said.

Staci looked up from her chopping and smiled. "Hey back," she said.

"Whatcha doing?" Slade walked over to the island and started dismantling his gun belt.

"Well, I got this idea that we should have vegetable soup for dinner," Staci explained. "But I don't think it will cook in time to eat it tonight."

He put his gun belt on the cabinet behind him and then stood behind her. He looked over her shoulder and saw that most of the vegetables looked like they were mashed rather than chopped.

"That's an interesting chopping method," he observed, his voice in her ear.

"Yeah, I need to practice," she conceded.

Slade slid his hands around her waist then slowly moved them up and under her shirt. He was pleasantly surprised that she wasn't wearing bra. Given that information, he moved his hands up to cup her breasts and flicked her nipples with his thumbs. Even though they instantly hardened into points, she flinched slightly.

Slade frowned and asked, "Did that hurt? I'm sorry, that wasn't at all what I was going for."

"A little. They're just sore today. I gotta lay off the caffeine," she told him.

Gentler, her touched her nipples again and smiled to himself when she sucked in a deep breath of air. "Mmm, I missed you today," he softly whispered in her ear.

He moved against her to let her feel his excitement. She moved back against him, very lightly. She could feel him pulsing against her. Slade closed his eyes and let the feeling wash over him. He slid his hands into the waistband of her sweats and slowly worked his way down. Even through her panties, he could feel that she was already wet. The memory of how she smelled and tasted drove him wild. He

TO DIE FOR HER

lowered her pants and panties and then moved his hands back up to touch her again. Hearing her moan, he quickly unbuttoned his own pants and pushed them down with one hand.

Slade whispered in her ear, "I intend to make you forget about every other man in the world." When Staci whimpered back "You already have," he lifted her slightly, aligning their bodies.

Stacy bent over the island just enough to grant him access, and Slade took it. Sliding into her, they moved together until they were both reeling from the powerful climax that seized them.

When Slade came back to earth, he jerked out of her and apologized. "Staci, I'm so sorry. Damn you're intoxicating. It's my fault, I'm sorry."

Staci snapped out of the glow she was feeling and pulled her pants up. "What are you talking about?"

Slade hugged her, held her head against his chest. "I forgot to use protection again."

Staci sighed and then suddenly started sobbing. Slade felt like crap. He held her and tried to soothe her. "I know we're playing with fire, baby. But once you go to your doctor tomorrow and get your birth control, this won't be an issue any longer. I just can't reign it in around you."

Staci continued to cry. She had a secret. She hated secrets. Slade wasn't helping at all.

"I just saw you with that guy at lunch. I was going to come in here, demanding that you explain who he was and what he meant to you, but then I touched you and breathed you in, and I couldn't think anymore, about him, about anything, just us," Slade babbled, feeling helpless.

Staci suddenly quit crying. She stepped back, her face furious.

"That is what this is all about? Because you were jealous?" She put her hands on her hips, and her voice raised almost an octave. "First of all, no expectations, remember? That's your rule. Second of all, instead of jumping to conclusions, having a little trust and asking me what the deal was would have been more rational."

"I don't want other men touching you," Slade confessed to her in the heat of the argument, raising his voice to match hers.

"Um, he didn't. We hugged a couple of times, he held my hand, and the only kisses were one on my forehead and one on his cheek. But then you saw all of that since you decided to stalk me at the restaurant," she informed him and went back to demolishing the vegetables. This man absolutely infuriated her. He wanted his cake and to eat it too. She stopped chopping and turned to face him, knife in hand.

"For your information, that other guy is married to my sister, Casey, who is eight months pregnant. Her doctor wouldn't let her fly too far away from her hospital, so Jeff had to come by himself on this promotional thing he has to do for the NFL. She also won't be able to be here for Thanksgiving for the same reason," she told Slade, who had the decency to look embarrassed. He also kept one eye on the knife in Staci's hand.

"I'm sorry. I was an idiot. I just saw him pawing you, and I lost my mind," Slade admitted.

Staci studied him for a minute then turned back to the vegetables. "So it really worked you up to see another man pay attention to me?" She gave him a side-eye, smiling slightly, her mood shifting again.

Slade kissed the top of her head. "I don't know what made me madder, him paying attention to you or you looking like you were eating it up."

"If you saw my sister, when she isn't pregnant, you would understand why I wouldn't have a chance with him. She's absolutely stunning. Beauty queen beautiful," Staci told him. "And she's kind and fun.'"

"Aren't she and Cassidy twins? Cassidy is pretty, but beauty queen?" Slade tilted his head.

"Yes, identical. However, how a woman preserves herself can make a difference. How they carry themselves too. Cassidy is a flirt, she's had a boob job, just a completely different personality."

"Cassidy has had a boob job?" Slade's eyebrows shot up.

"Yeah, but don't tell her you know or that I told you." Staci laughed. She threw the knife onto the counter. "These vegetables need a funeral. No soup today or tomorrow. Can we just go get something?"

"Sure, let me change." Slade grabbed his gun belt and holster off the counter and bolted upstairs.

Staci watched him go then let out a deep breath. Damn, she hated secrets.

CHAPTER 14

As Staci and Slade lay entangled in bed that night, they listened to the soft noises coming from outside. Neither could sleep. Staci was thinking about her doctor's appointment the next day. Slade was thinking about his assignment the next day. He would be traveling to the facilities where his witnesses were being held and asking them to look at the photo lineup he had finally decided on. He was certain "Zorro" was among the pictures, and although he suspected he knew who he was, he dreaded hearing the reality of the truth. A thought came to him.

"Darlin', are your phones up here?" he softly asked Staci. He knew she wasn't asleep. Whenever she slept, her breathing was rhythmic and deep. Laying close to her, he could feel her pauses in breathing and hear her gentle sighs.

"Yeah, they're on the dresser, charging," she told him. She turned her head to look at him. "Why?"

"Go get them. Both of them," he instructed her.

She moved out of the bed and returned a few seconds later, turning on the lamp and pulling the sheet up over her naked chest. Slade sat up and asked her to sign in to her personal cell and then give it to him. He scrolled and pushed the side button and then waited, staring at the screen. He then did the same with the burner phone she handed him. He gave them both to her then did something on his phone. Staci plugged the phones back in and then joined him in bed once again. She looked at him curiously.

"What was that about?' she asked.

"I put a tracking app on both of your phones and added you to mine," he responded.

172

TO DIE FOR HER

"Why?" Staci didn't know if she should be mad that he was going to track her or be grateful.

"We're getting close to trial. It just makes me more comfortable to know that should you need help or something happens, if you have your phones, I can find you," he told her.

He didn't tell her that some instinct compelled him to add the tracking app. Some niggling in the back of his mind was telling him that he needed to do this. He didn't want to worry her, and if she got mad about it, he could handle that if he knew she was safe.

"Leave the app on the phones until after the trial. Then you can take them off if you want."

She nodded. She wasn't mad. She didn't think he was the type who was so controlling that he needed to know where she was every minute of the day. She was more paranoid now than ever, and she liked the idea that he could find her if necessary. She reached over and shut off the lamp and settled down in the crook of his arm once more. She trusted him more than anyone other than her dad, and he was a close second to her dad.

"Can I ask you a question?" Staci whispered.

"Yeah, sure, what?"

"That tattoo on your back, near your shoulder, what is that?"

"It's a Comanche war shield." Slade rolled away from Staci and turned on the lamp next to him. "If you look closely, you see that?" He pointed to an area near the center where the skin was puckered. "I got shot. It's above where the Kevlar covers. Fortunately, it's also in an area where there is a lot of muscle. It missed the bone."

Staci looked closely. She touched it gently.

"After I healed up, I decided to get the tattoo."

"Do you have Comanche in your heritage?"

Slade rolled back to the other side and took Staci in his arm. "Not that I know of, but I like the idea of a war shield. The Comanche carried them. They believed their shields protected them."

"Did it hurt? When you got shot?"

"Like a bitch." Slade chuckled. "But I proved I was tougher."

Staci nodded and cuddled closer to Slade. Sleep eventually found them although it was fitful and brief.

*****

Staci was sitting in her gynecologist's office, waiting for them to call her name when her personal cell phone buzzed. She looked at it and saw that her friend Monica was calling. "Hey, Monica," she answered.

"Sorry it's taken me so long to get back to you about those pictures you gave me. I checked and double-checked and wanted to make sure I had accurate info before I called you." Her friend's voice was somber. "You were right. One of them isn't like the other. Number five is CIA. He's rumored to have gone deep, but he has a handler, someone in charge of him, who should be keeping him on task."

"Who would that be?" Staci stared out the window, a sense of urgency gripping her. She had to tell Slade this information as soon as possible.

"I don't know that. No one seems to know," Monica answered.

The receptionist called Staci's name to go back to the examination room. "Hey, if you find out, call me. I gotta go. They're calling my name." Staci ended the call and threw the phone in her tote.

A couple of hours later, Staci slid into her rental car. She sat behind the wheel, trying to organize all the thoughts and emotions that were overwhelming her. She definitely had a secret, and she hated secrets. Leaning her head against the headrest, she closed her eyes and concentrated on her breathing. She heard the passenger door open and close. She opened her eyes and turned her head to see Carmichael in the passenger seat with an evil smile on his face. She glanced down and saw he had a gun held low, near his lap, pointed at her. Number five.

"Well, hello, Ms. Everly. Fancy meeting you here." He chuckled.

Staci fought with everything she had to stay calm. "What do you want?" she asked as calmly as she could.

TO DIE FOR HER

"We are going to go for a drive. When your boyfriend realizes I have you, he'll give me what I want, and your case will go down the toilet," he told her. He held her gaze.

Staci didn't flinch.

"I don't know who you are talking about," Staci lied.

"Yes, you do. Agent Slade. He has some information I need. He'll give it to me, and then we can all walk away. I'll use the information to trash your case, and you two can ride off in the sunset, a win-win." His left eye twitched as he explained his purpose.

He's lying, Staci acknowledged to herself. He intended to kill both her and Slade. She looked around to see if there was any way she could jump out of the car safely, but like a responsible driver, she had already fastened her seat belt.

"Don't worry about trying to escape. It isn't going to happen." Carmichael watched her intently.

Focusing on keeping her breathing steady, Staci asked, "What is it you want me to do?"

"To start with, just drive. I'll give you directions as we go. And you can give me your cell phone. We want to make sure our hero knows where to meet us." Carmichael kept his gaze on Staci.

She nodded. Carefully, slowly, she moved her hand to her tote that was on the center console.

"I'm reaching in here to get my phone," she told him, assuring him that she wasn't trying to trick him. He nodded. She rooted around in the tote and pulled out the burner phone, hiding her personal cell phone under all the other stuff she kept in her tote. She pulled it out and handed it to Carmichael. He took it from her with his free hand, the gun hand never wavering.

"Now drive," he told her.

Staci started the car and backed out of the parking spot. She turned the car in the direction he told her.

"Make sure you don't speed. You follow all the traffic laws. Don't do anything that would cause a cop to want to pull you over, and don't try warning any other drivers," Carmichael demanded.

175

Staci nodded and gently accelerated her car.

*****

Slade was speeding down I-44. He had just left the last of his witnesses, and all of them had immediately identified Carmichael as the person they knew as Zorro. He should have known. He wasn't one of the members of his team he had handpicked, and he'd always been, well, off. The fact he had recently started to show an interest in his and Staci's relationship, hell, the fact he had seen how Staci had run to him the night Bill was killed and Slade's response to the crisis, gave Carmichael plenty of ammo. He pulled out his burner phone and was getting ready to punch in her number when his personal phone buzzed. He looked at it. *Dammit.* He had to answer it.

"What?" he all but shouted.

"Carmichael has your chick," the voice on the other end told him.

Slade couldn't breathe. He couldn't think. His heart was pounding so hard that he could hear it. Panic washed over him even though Slade kept telling himself to stay calm. He was well past that point.

"Thanks." He hung up the phone and pushed Staci's number in the burner phone.

Two rings, and Carmichael's voice answered. "Hello, Mike."

Slade could picture the wicked smile on that son of a bitch's face.

"Let me talk to Staci," Slade demanded.

"I don't think so, at least not yet," Carmichael responded. "If you want to see her again, at least in one piece and alive, I suggest you follow my instructions."

"Give 'em to me," Slade slowed his voice. *Carmichael cannot, under any circumstances, know this is my only button to push*, Slade told himself.

"Remember where it all started? Meet me there. Come alone. If I see anyone with you, she dies," Carmichael told him.

"Before I do, let me talk to her, make sure you haven't already killed her," Slade shot back.

TO DIE FOR HER

Carmichael held the phone up to Staci who was driving as slowly as she could get away with. "Lover boy wants to talk to you," Carmichael sneered.

"Michael?" Staci was careful to keep her voice monotone.

"Are you alright?" Slade held his breath.

"I'm fine," she answered. She wasn't going to say any more than she had to. *Never volunteer information, answer only what is asked*, she reminded herself.

"Has he hurt you?" Slade asked.

"Not yet," she told him, hoping he understood what she was trying to tell him. *He's going to*, the voice in her head screamed. *He's going to hurt us both*.

"I'm coming for you," Slade assured her, his panic gone for the moment. He was formulating a plan. His panic had turned into anger, and he always worked best when he was pissed off.

"We certainly hope you are coming for her," Carmichael's voice came back on the phone. "Follow the rules, Slade, so we can all walk away from this."

He threw the burner phone out of the car window. He turned to Staci and grinned an evil, distorted grin. "Good job. We'll get where we need to be and wait for lover boy to show up."

*****

When the phone went dead, Slade immediately checked the tracker on his phone. He saw Staci's burner phone wasn't moving. He switched to her personal cell. It was moving. Good, Carmichael didn't know about it, or he would have thrown it out as well. He made two phone calls while he drove in the direction Staci was driving. He knew exactly where she was headed. He would have liked to have beaten them there, but that wasn't going to happen. He told the others about his plan, then hung up, keeping the tracker on the screen. He worked on regulating his breathing, slowing his heart rate. He knew what would happen if his plan didn't work.

*****

Staci focused on the road. Because of the recent time change, it was starting to get dark earlier. She drove well under the speed limit and pretended to relax, leaning back in the seat.

"Drive faster," Carmichael ordered.

"Can't. You told me not to draw attention to us. We're getting ready to cross the county line, and small-town cops just wait for city folks to make a traffic mistake so they can stop them," Staci reasoned with him. "If you want to get where we're going, let me drive."

"Bitch, you're not in charge," Carmichael snapped at her. "It's your fault any of this is happening, so you better get humble fast."

Staci was soon driving across the St. Louis County line into Franklin County and into the city of Pacific, Missouri. Some thirty miles southwest of St. Louis, Pacific had roughly 7,210 residents and only 5.93 square miles. Known for Bigfoot 4×4 Inc., the Black Madonna Shrine, and Greensfelder Park, it was a sleepy little town. The Union Pacific railroad, BNSF Railway, and Route 66 all ran through Pacific, Missouri. It was surrounded by farmland on all sides. When the federal agents invaded the town several months ago because of several bodies found in an old, run-down barn several miles outside of town, the townspeople gossiped endlessly about it for weeks. It was probably the most exciting thing that had happened there since the flood of 1982. No one really knew what happened, but for several days, government vehicles drove through the town. People in dark suits asked a lot of questions of the townspeople, and other people in regular clothes but wearing guns on their hips followed the men in suits with their own questions. No one really told them what was being investigated or why those dead people were killed. Everyone had their own theory. Things has calmed down substantially since then. The inhabitants of Pacific went back to their everyday lives, and no one mentioned the bodies anymore.

It was completely dark when Staci entered the town. Streetlights shone, and some of the vintage shops and restaurants were still open, the lights from the inside illuminating the sidewalks. Very few people were out. The night was very cool, almost freezing, so they were most likely inside their own cozy homes or the establishments that were still open. There was no one to see them drive by, no one for Staci to make a face at or signal. Carmichael had her drive straight, through the town, and down the main highway until she reached a four-way stop. She turned left at his direction, and approximately three miles later, Carmichael had her pull onto a road that was half paved and half gravel. She slowed the car considerably as potholes and bumps in the road appeared in front of the car, and there was no light other than her headlights to show what lay ahead. Staci continued to drive until the road ended in front of the most dilapidated barn Staci had ever seen.

"Get out," Carmichael told her.

He kept the gun leveled at her as he opened his own door and backed out of the passenger side, his eyes on her the whole time. Staci opened her door after she shut off the car. She left the keys in the ignition in case she was able to get away from her abductor. She opened her door and slid out carefully. She hadn't worn a coat today. She was so focused on her doctor's appointment she had left her condo wearing only the blue floral cotton maxi skirt and blue cable-knit sweater. At least she had worn sensible shoes, she thought, looking down at her brown flat-heeled ankle boots. She knew she could run in these.

Carmichael used his firearm to gesture her to proceed to the barn. When they got right outside the door, Carmichael shoved the door aside. He grabbed Staci by her bicep with his free hand and dragged her inside. Amazingly, the barn had electricity. He hit the light switch, and a single bulb in the middle of the barn lit up. Staci stood at the door, shivering, looking around. She didn't see any other exit. The floor was dirt. There was a table under the light and several wooden chairs. The slats that made up the barn had been red once upon a time. Now they were gray, and the paint was peeling. There were gaps between the boards as they had shrunk with age. A couple of windows on either end of the barn were boarded over. It had a strange smell. Musky and something else, something Staci couldn't put her finger on. There was hay strewn about randomly as if it had fallen out of bales as they were being moved.

Carmichael left the wide door open. He told Staci, "Go sit in that chair by the table, the one on the right."

Staci complied. So far, he hadn't tied her up, and she didn't want to remind him.

He stood by her, pacing. He whipped out his cell phone and called someone.

"I have Staci Everly. Slade's on his way. I'll get the information I need soon," he told the person on the other end of the phone.

Staci couldn't hear what was being said to Carmichael, but his entire demeanor changed. While he had been calm before, he seemed enraged now. He started yelling into the phone.

"I don't give a fuck what you think! It's not your ass on the line! You told me to fix this, and dammit, this is how I'm fixing it. You know what?" He switched the phone to his other ear after he put his gun in his waistband. "Stop. Just stop ordering me around. Nothing you have done has worked, and I can promise you, I will take you down after I deal with this shit!"

He threw the phone at one of the barn walls. Staci watched it hit the wall and fall to the floor. Staci remained silent. The less attention she drew to herself the better.

"You!" he screamed at her. "This is all your fault!" He advanced on her, stopping short just in front of where she was sitting.

"I don't know what you're talking about," Staci calmly replied, much more calm than she felt inside. She was terrified. Carmichael seemed to be completely out of control and unpredictable, calm one minute and like a wild animal the next.

He leaned down over her, still yelling, "You indicted me, you little twit! You should have just gone after Ayala, but now you sucked me into it!"

As he leaned over, Staci got a peek at silver around his neck, the same kind of silver in the chains that held the crosses of the murdered men. Carmichael noticed where her attention was drawn and he stood up.

"What are you looking at?"

"You have a silver cross around your neck," she told him. "Did you know they have transmitters in them? Whoever is receiving the data can keep track of your every move."

TO DIE FOR HER

Carmichael's eyes widened for a second, just long enough for Staci to figure out he didn't know about the transmitter. That meant he wasn't the one tracking everybody. She pushed him a little further.

"Whoever gave you that has been tracking you since they gave it to you. Kind of an invasion of your privacy, wouldn't you agree?"

Carmichael immediately started to scroll his phone, but he had broken it when he threw it, and now he couldn't call out. This infuriated him even more.

"Goddammit, I knew I was being double-crossed! That son of a bitch!" Carmichael stomped around, looking around somewhat desperately, apparently at a loss about what to do. He advanced on Staci once again. "Where is Slade keeping Gestado and the other two witnesses?"

Staci shrugged and softly answered, "I don't know."

Carmichael backhanded her across the face and screamed, "Don't lie to me! You're screwing him! I know he has told you everything about this case!"

Staci's face had jerked to the right when Carmichael struck her. It dazed her slightly, and she felt blood on her lip. She turned her head to look at Carmichael again. She licked the blood off her lip and replied, "We don't talk about the case. He didn't tell me very much about any of the witnesses, and I don't know where they are."

As Carmichael approached her again with his fist starting to draw back, Staci jumped out of the chair and kicked him as hard as she could between the legs. When he doubled over, she took her chance to run. She knew she could outrun him once she got out of the barn. Just as she reached the door, she felt a jerk on her hair. Carmichael had grabbed a handful of it and yanked her backward, throwing her into the table. Her temple hit the edge of the table. She fell to the floor, completely disoriented. Before she could get her bearings, Carmichael was on top of her, raining blows on her over and over. Staci fought as instinctively as she could, getting in her own strikes, but Carmichael was bigger and had her pinned down, not to mention she was still dizzy from her head hitting the table.

Carmichael stood up and continued his assault. He dragged her by her hair and kicked her in the ribs and the abdomen several times.

181

Staci felt something on her side move and knew he had broken a rib. The pain was intense and sharp. She tried to crawl away from him, but he followed, continuing to kick her anywhere he could land a blow. It was becoming harder to breathe. She could barely suck air into her lungs. Her left eye was completely swollen shut, and she could no longer see out of it. Blood ran into the other eye, obscuring her vision. Carmichael continued to yell at her to tell him where the witnesses were being held. Staci couldn't answer his questions because she had purposely made sure that Slade never told her. She also could no longer talk; she couldn't make her jaw work. More kicks landed on her back and her abdomen, and she quit moving. Carmichael rolled her over onto her back and straddled her. He reached behind him and snatched a handful of her skirt, yanking it up to her thighs.

"Maybe I should sample a little of what Slade's been feasting on." He leaned his face close to hers. "I bet you'll like it."

Ah, hell no, Staci thought to herself. He could beat her all day long, even kill her, but there was no way he was going to rape her. Gathering all her strength, she threw her head forward and head-butted Carmichael. He jerked his head back, wailing.

"You bitch! You broke my nose!" He put his hands around her throat and started to squeeze.

Staci was helpless to stop him. She could no longer move, and she couldn't breathe. Staci felt the intense cramping in her lower abdomen. Before she lost consciousness, she felt her secret, the one she had been hiding for over a week and only confirmed today, slip from her body.

*****

Slade pulled off the main road. He knew this area because of the amount of time they had spent at the crime scene so many months ago. Staci's phone had remained stationary for the last half hour. It was pitch-dark. Even the stars were muted by clouds. He was trying not to hyperventilate; his terror was so strong. As he slowed down to approach the barn, he kept telling himself that he had to pull it together. If he gave Carmichael any inkling that he was rattled,

TO DIE FOR HER

Carmichael would use it against him. He pulled his extra gun from underneath his seat and stuck it behind his back in his waistband. He still had on his Kevlar vest, and he left it on. If Carmichael was going to shoot him, he would have to shoot him in the head. As he drove closer and closer to the old barn, his resolve became solid; his fear was replaced by a fury he had never before experienced. His only mission tonight was to get Staci safely out of there. He could deal with Carmichael later if necessary. He checked with the rest of his team via text to make sure they were in place. They were.

He drove close enough to now see light pouring through the open door of the barn. He could see Staci laying on the ground, not moving, and Carmichael was on top of her, strangling her. The sight caused the terror to envelope him again, and Slade gulped, forcing himself to don a calm, reasonable demeanor. Carmichael was expecting him to react emotionally, but Slade wasn't giving him that. Slade planned to surprise Carmichael in a number of ways.

Slade opened the door to his car and stood behind it. He yelled at Carmichael, "Let her go! It's me you want!"

He waited behind the door, one firearm in his hand. Carmichael stopped and slowly got off Staci. He picked up the weapon that was next to her and pointed at Slade. He stood, never taking the gun off Slade.

"Come closer, Slade," Carmichael yelled. "I want us communicating like reasonable humans, not yelling like banshees."

Yeah, reasonable humans don't beat and strangle women, Slade thought. He kept glancing at Staci, hoping for some sign of life. She wasn't moving. Her face was turned in his direction, and he could see even from the distance he was from her that Carmichael had inflicted a lot of damage. Slade slowly backed away from the open door until he could no longer use it as a shield.

He kept his own weapon pointed at Carmichael. "What do you want?" he demanded.

Carmichael glanced back at Staci's lifeless body. "I tried getting the information out of your little girlfriend, but she didn't exactly cooperate," Carmichael calmly told Slade. "I just want to know where Gestado and the others are being held. That's it."

"She doesn't know where they are. That's why she couldn't tell you." Slade's eyes turned onyx with the rage he was controlling. "And you know I can't tell you that information."

"I'm pretty sure I can make you tell me anything. I've been trained by the best, you know," Carmichael bragged. "I will emotionally break you and then physically, and we can start with letting you watch me kill pretty Ms. Everly here." He laughed and glanced back at her again. "Although I guess she's not as pretty anymore, huh?"

I will kill him with my bare hands, Slade thought to himself. *I just have to get close enough to him.* Slade started to slowly walk toward Carmichael. Time was of the essence. He had to get to Staci.

"Nope, stop right there," Carmichael told Slade. "Throw me your weapon. Kick it to me."

"Why are you doing this? You're supposed to be one of the good guys," Slade stalled.

Carmichael snorted. "I am one of the good guys, you dumbass. Stop treating this like I'm a cartoon supervillain."

"Educate me. Make me understand why you need to know where the witnesses are," Slade reasoned with him.

"I'm CIA," Carmichael told him. Seeing the look of surprise and doubt on Slade's face, Carmichael laughed and continued. "All those intelligence reports that come in from the Middle East? Who do you think gathers that intelligence? We have agents throughout that region. Only problem, it costs money. How do you think the government funds black ops?"

"With the budget?" Slade answered.

Carmichael laughed even louder. "You really are stupid! All muscles and no brains!" He stopped laughing. "No, that doesn't cover nearly what we need, and there's not a congressional committee that would approve and fund some of the techniques we have to use to get the information this country needs to find terrorists and stop them before they strike again. This little operation of Ayala's funds some of our projects. It's simple. All I had to do was convince Ayala that for a price, I could protect him from people like you. All I had to do was keep him paranoid," Carmichael explained.

"What about all those murdered underbosses?" Slade asked.

TO DIE FOR HER

"I kept Ayala paranoid enough to convince him that they were passing information to the heads of the cartel in order to dethrone him. He bought it. All I had to do was arrange for the killings to prove I had his best interests at heart," Carmichael bragged. "The more I 'protected' him, the more he trusted me."

"Then you also started skimming his product," Slade guessed.

"Yeah, and there's a lot of money selling even the small amounts I was taking. It was so easy to convince him those underbosses were the ones skimming." Carmichael started filling in the holes. "I managed not only to make the agency the money it needed to fund some of the ventures it had going on, but I also built myself a nice little nest egg."

"So why target Staci Everly?" Slade still had his weapon aimed at Carmichael, but Carmichael had yet to take his eyes off Slade.

"Because she isn't as dumb as she looks. She was starting to put the pieces together. If the case could be compromised, then everyone walked away, and no one was the wiser." Carmichael shrugged. "But she didn't back off. Not when Gestado tried to attack her, not when her car blew up with all the evidence boxes in it. Not even when I had to kill Bill," Carmichael explained. "All Bill had to do was let me in her house to grab those flash drives. But, no, he refused and then threatened to call you, tell you I was there and ask you if you had sent me over. I had no choice."

Staci regained consciousness during the exchange. At first, she just heard Carmichael's voice and someone else, then she recognized it was Slade. She peered through the eye that wasn't swollen shut and saw him standing in front of Carmichael although she couldn't judge the distance. *Damn*, she thought. *It hurts so much to breathe.* She had to pant to get enough air. She very gently and slowly moved her fingers on her right hand into a fist and then released the fist. She was trying to let Slade know she wasn't unconscious and could hear everything.

Slade saw Staci's hand make a fist and then open again. He knew instinctively she was motioning to him.

"Then she indicted me, the slut. She couldn't just let it go with Ayala. She went after me and anyone else involved. I need to know where those witnesses are, Slade. I don't care what happens to Ayala. He's made his bed. But there is no way I can let anyone finger me as being involved." Carmichael's voice rose. "It's the patriotic thing to do, Slade."

"I won't give you that information, not even to save Staci," Slade informed Carmichael. "What you've done is not patriotic. It's criminal. What you have done to Staci is criminal. What you did to Bill is criminal. You aren't getting away with it." Slade's voice was firm and resolute.

"Now do what I told you to do. Kick your firearm over here." Carmichael's eyes narrowed and he matched Slade in determination.

Slade dropped his gun on the ground and kicked it as hard as he could in Staci's direction. It whizzed by Carmichael and came to rest near Staci's right hand. Staci heard it and then felt the gun as it hit her hand and rebounded slightly. She didn't dare move, knowing that Carmichael no doubt had turned his head to look where the gun lay.

She was right. He watched it go past him and within a foot of Staci. He turned back to Slade, grinning a malevolent smile. "She's not gonna save you, hero. Now give me your backup weapon."

Slade raised his pants leg up on both legs. "No backup. You know I don't wear a backup."

A stick snapped to the right of Slade. It was loud enough to draw Carmichael's attention. "Who's out there. Show your face or I shoot the girl right freakin' now."

Steve Vaughn came slowly into view from the right. He was wearing his tactical gear and had his firearm aimed at Carmichael.

"It's over, Carmichael. We have everything recorded. All Slade had to do was get you talking, and you're stupid and arrogant enough to do it." Vaughn smiled at Carmichael.

Without saying a word, Carmichael shot off two rounds. One hit Vaughn in the chest, and as he fell backward, the second shot hit Vaughn in the thigh. Vaughn hit the ground hard.

Carmichael turned his complete attention on Slade. "That one's on you. I told you to come alone."

At the sound of the shots, Staci almost panicked. She could see it wasn't Slade that was hit although she couldn't tell who it was.

TO DIE FOR HER

Laying on the ground, she could see someone else slowly moving in behind Slade. She couldn't warn him. Her jaw still wasn't working. She could hear her heart pounding in her chest as she watched a heavily tattooed man move in from the left, still out of Carmichael's sight. His weapon looked like it was pointed directly at Slade. Staci knew she had to save Slade even if it meant she had to sacrifice herself. She pulled the gun laying near her into her hand and raised it, pointing it in Carmichael's direction.

Carmichael heard the movement behind him. He took his eyes off Slade to look back and see Staci raise the gun. He turned slightly, pointing his own weapon directly at Staci. When Slade saw the scene unfold, he yelled, "Now!"

Before Carmichael could fire off a shot or turn back in Slade's direction, Manny Coronado, the heavily tattooed man who had been deep undercover DEA for the last three years and a close friend of Slade's, fired his gun. The bullet struck Carmichael on the left side of his head, just above his ear. Without a sound, Carmichael's eyes widened in realization of what just happened, then he hit the dirt floor of the old derelict barn with a thud.

Rodriguez emerged from the brush near the barn. Slade barked out orders. "Get to Vaughn, check him. Manny, call for two ambulances and get the rest of the team and the marshals out here."

He ran to Staci. He held her head in his hands and listened. He could hear gurgling coming from her chest. He saw the bruises to her face and her swollen eye, and he almost burst into tears. She blinked at him a couple of times. He saw that there was something wrong with her jaw, probably broken. She had bruises everywhere he could see. There was blood on her head, blood coming out of her nose and mouth, blood on her legs where her skirt was hiked up. *Oh, god*, Slade thought. *Did that savage rape her?*

Staci was suddenly very tired. Slade was safe. She could rest. She closed her eyes and concentrated on getting air. Slade saw her close her eyes, and he howled. "No, baby, stay with me. Please, wake up. Look at me. I'm here, look at me!" he told her over and over. He began to rock her gently.

Rodriguez had tied off Vaughn's leg with the tourniquet from the medical kit, and Vaughn was talking. His vest had taken the brunt of the first bullet, but the breath was knocked out of him.

Manny walked over to where Carmichael's body lay and commented, "Wow, she sure gave him as good as she got. It looks like she put up a fight."

None of this registered with Slade. All his focus was on Staci, brushing her hair back from her face, rocking her, talking to her, telling her to look at him. When the ambulances arrived and the paramedics came in to get her, they had to tell him multiple times to let go of Staci so they could get her loaded up. Finally, their commands brought Slade back to earth. He turned numbly to look up at the paramedic and nodded. He let go of Staci's head and scooted backward on the floor. After the paramedics had her on the stretcher, he snapped back to action. He holstered the gun he had kicked to Staci after he stood up and began barking orders.

"Take them both to Barnes-Jewish Hospital. Her sister is a visiting trauma surgeon there this weekend. Meredith…" He paused. He didn't know Meredith's last name. He ran to Staci's car and grabbed her tote. He rifled through it, pulling out a notebook, sonogram pictures, her wallet, and finally he found her cell phone. Remembering her password he had memorized when she wasn't paying attention, he scrolled through her contacts and found Meredith's name. He yelled out, "Dr. Meredith Dickey!"

The paramedics nodded and closed the doors. The medics in the second ambulance containing Vaughn followed suit. With a roar of the sirens, the ambulances sped toward St. Louis.

Slade stuffed everything back into Staci's tote and threw the tote into his own car. He turned to Manny and said, "When they're through asking you questions, get it towed. I'm following the ambulances."

Manny nodded.

Slade walked over to where Carmichael's body lay. He moved Carmichael's collar to the side and saw the cross. Leaning over, Slade yanked the cross off. He searched around the body and found Carmichael's cell phone laying on the ground. He put both in a pocket of his cargo pants. He studied Carmichael and saw the injuries Staci had inflicted on him when she was fighting for her life. If he hadn't been as worried as he was, he would have smiled at the damage. He hurried to his vehicle and started it up.

Slade caught up to the ambulances and followed them. His breathing was frantic and labored. He alternated between praying and cursing. He had to keep rubbing his eyes because of the tears that threatened to pour out of him. The drive seemed to take forever, and his patience was gone. If Carmichael wasn't already dead, he would kill him again and again. *Goddamn animal!*

CHAPTER 15

Slade pulled into emergency parking at the hospital. He ran to the doors as the paramedics rolled Staci and Vaughn inside. They were met by a medical team that had been notified of the situation by the ambulance crew, and the trauma rooms had been prepped. A tall dark-haired woman in scrubs was waiting in the room Vaughn was rolled into, and a medium-build balding man was waiting in the room where they took Staci. Slade didn't know which room to go to, so he chose the one Vaughn was in. As a team leader, he was required to put his team first, which was frustrating. He stood by the door as the tall dark woman quickly removed Vaughn's vest and the nurses cut Vaughn's pants off him. He watched as the trauma team evaluated him, and the dark-haired woman barked orders which were obeyed immediately. The dark-haired doctor walked over to where Slade was leaning against the wall.

"I'm Dr. Meredith Dickey. Who are you?" she curtly introduced herself.

"Mike Slade, his team leader. You're Staci's sister," Slade answered.

Meredith's eyes widened slightly, then she smiled. "Yes, I am. She's in the next room. Dr. Pritchett is working on her. I can't since I'm a close relation. Ethics, you know," she told him.

Slade nodded. "How is he?" Slade asked. Vaughn was conscious but softly moaning in pain.

"Well, lucky for him he had on his vest. Just a bruise there. His leg is another matter." She sighed. "It looks like a through and through, and another two centimeters to the outside and his femoral artery would have been at least nicked if not severed," she answered.

190

TO DIE FOR HER

"We're going to clean the wounds but leave them open so they can drain."

Slade nodded. "Meredith, may I call you that?" When she nodded, he continued, "I need to notify your family. They might want to be here."

"Stay here," she commanded, and Slade obeyed.

She left the room and was gone for several minutes. When she came back, her face was drawn and sober. She pulled her cell phone out of her scrubs pocket and dialed.

"Dad, yeah, it's Meredith. You and mom need to come to Barnes-Jewish Hospital here in St. Louis. It's Staci. She was attacked and it's pretty serious. She's critical," she told the person on the other end.

A sob caught in Slade's throat. When a doctor tells someone it's "pretty serious," it's never good. Then she followed with "critical." He covered his face with his hands and drew in a ragged breath. He internally prayed, begging God to heal Staci. He was filled with guilt. His job was to protect her, and he had failed miserably. He promised God that if he would heal Staci, he would make sure that she was protected for the rest of her life. That he would do everything in his power to make sure she was always safe. A hand on his shoulder snapped him out of his prayer. Meredith was watching him with empathy.

"Go wash your hands. You have blood all over them. You're getting it on your face," she told him.

He looked down at his hands. She was right. Blood was on his hands, under his fingernails, and in the creases where his knuckles were. Staci's blood. He nodded and left the room in search of a restroom. Finding one, he coated his hands in soap. He scrubbed his hands over and over under the hot water. The blood had started to dry and was stubborn. When he finally got it off his hands, he looked in the mirror. He had smeared blood on his cheeks and around his eyes, so he got busy scrubbing his face. When he was satisfied that most of the blood was off his face, he splashed cold water on his face. He needed to focus.

When he walked back down the hallway to Vaughn's room, he looked in and saw Vaughn appeared to be fully awake. He was smiling at Meredith, and it sounded and looked like he was flirting with her. Slade rolled his eyes. At least he would be okay. Clearing his throat, Slade watched Meredith jump back as if she had been doing something naughty. Vaughn just grinned at him.

"Hey, I think the pain meds are working," he told Slade, his words slurring.

"Yeah, I think they are." Slade smiled at him. "Dr. Meredith here says you were lucky and you should be okay."

Vaughn nodded, sighing, laying his head back. "She's pretty, isn't she? And smart!"

Slade was slightly uncomfortable with Vaughn's assessment. Rodriguez burst into the room at that moment, relieving Slade from having to comment.

"How's Vaughn?" he asked a little too loudly.

"He'll live," Slade answered.

"I've got this. Go to Staci," Rodriguez told him.

Slade immediately started for the door. Meredith's voice stopped him.

"They've taken her to surgery. You'll need to go to the fourth floor surgery waiting area," she told him.

Not pausing or looking back, Slade left the room and found the elevators. Instead of getting off on the fourth floor, he made a pit stop. The chapel was on the second floor, and he found his way inside.

Slade had not been inside a church since his mother's funeral. He had quit relying on something he couldn't see. No matter how hard he had prayed, his mother had died. For the last five years, he had held a grudge against God. Tonight, Staci's fate was not in his hands. He had not been there when Carmichael snatched her, no matter that he had her followed everywhere, that he had put eyes on her in all the ways he could. It still had not been enough to keep her safe. He needed help. He needed to believe again. So he sat in the back of the chapel, praying. He had no idea how long he had been

TO DIE FOR HER

there when he finally stood up to leave. He paused and went to the front of the chapel and lit a candle.

"Mom, I need your help. If you can hear me, please ask whoever's in charge to help Staci. I need you now, Mom, more than ever." Slade fell to his knees and sobbed. He sobbed like he had never sobbed when his mother died. He felt a grief that he didn't recognize. Despite all of his experience, he had never felt this helpless. A hand touched him on his shoulder, and he jerked his head up and around. No one was there.

Slade wiped his eyes. He rubbed his nose on his sleeve. He needed to pull it together. He walked down the aisle between the seats and left the chapel. Outside the chapel doors, he drew in several breaths to control his panic and to clear his head. When he felt like he was calmer, he walked to the elevators to go upstairs to the surgery waiting area.

Slade stepped off the elevator and found the waiting room. He sat in a chair for a while then paced around the room like a nervous animal. Then he sat again. He kept checking his watch, but the time wasn't registering. Finally, after what seemed an eternity, a nurse poked her head in.

"You here for Anastasia Everly?" she asked.

His throat suddenly dry, Slade merely nodded.

"They've taken her to ICU. There's a waiting room there, and the doctor will be in soon to update you on her condition. It's on the sixth floor," the nurse told him.

Slade quickly made his way back to the elevators to go up the two floors. When the door opened, he was met by a small crowd of people. He immediately recognized Cassidy and Allison, Staci's sisters. A tall silver-haired man with deep green eyes that had wrinkles on the outside corners was there, along with a small older woman with dark curly hair. Cassidy gasped and went to hug Slade but pulled back, looking at his chest. He still had on his vest, and Slade looked down to see what had repelled her. Blood. Staci's blood.

"It's Staci's," he somberly told her, and his eyes teared up again.

"Are you alright, Mike?" Allison asked, her eyes filled with empathy.

193

"I'm fine. It's Staci," he choked out.

They all nodded, and the older man said, "I'm Ken Everly, and this," indicating the older woman, "is my wife, Marie. We're Staci's parents. Get into the elevator, son. We're on our way up to the ICU waiting room."

The authority in his voice compelled Slade into the elevator. In silence, they rode up and found the waiting room. When they got to the waiting room, they dispersed around the room. Slade flopped into a chair, his hand covering his face, trying to get his emotions under control. Staci's parents sat on a faux leather love seat that was perpendicular to Slade's chair. They held hands. Cassidy and Allison walked around the room, looking out of the windows and at the charts hanging on the walls.

Eventually, Ken Everly looked over at Slade and asked, "What happened?"

Slade explained the case they had been working on, how the team and Staci had been double-crossed, how he had put a security detail on her. "When the marshal was murdered, I moved in and took over the detail myself. Even when I couldn't be with her, I had eyes on her. I don't know how Carmichael was able to get to her," he looked Staci's father in the eye. "I failed her, sir. I should have insisted that I go with her to her appointment, but I was trying to get the case tied up so she could put the case in front of a jury the week after Thanksgiving. I'm so sorry." Slade's voice caught ever so slightly.

"You didn't fail her. This isn't your fault." Marie patted his knee. "You did what you could, and that's all anyone could ask."

"No, when she insisted I go get those IDs made, I should have waited until she was safely back at the office. I could have waited," Slade insisted.

From across the room, one of her sisters snorted.

"Nope, Staci's a little dictator. You weren't going to change her mind about going," Cassidy told him.

"Then I should have insisted on going with her on her errand," Slade muttered. He didn't want to have to tell her father that she went to the doctor to get birth control because he was bedding his daughter.

TO DIE FOR HER

"Again, if Staci didn't want you going, you weren't going," Cassidy retorted.

Allison joined in, "Mike, she's hardheaded. Seriously."

"You can say what you want. It's my fault," Slade repeated.

He stood up and stretched. The anxiety was beginning to take its toll on him, and the lack of information by any medical staff was starting to worry him. At about that time, a man in scrubs entered the waiting area. He still had the scrub hat on, and he was holding a chart. Slade recognized him as the trauma doctor from downstairs.

"Are you all here for Anastasia Everly?" he asked.

"Yes." Ken Everly stood.

"Okay. I'm Dr. Pritchett. I'm the trauma surgeon who treated her in the ER and then took her into surgery." He looked at the chart. "We'll start at the top and work our way down. She has a concussion. It's mild, but it's still a concussion. Probably from hitting her head on something. We didn't put stitches on the cut on her head. We used glue to lessen the scarring," he read from the chart. "Her jaw was broken, so we set it and wired it. She'll be on a liquid diet for a few weeks." He paused and looked around at the family. Seeing no questions, he continued, "She has a non-displaced fracture of her orbital bone. That's this bone," he pointed to the bone under his eye socket and traced around his own eye. "Non-displaced means it was broken but hadn't moved from its location. We left it alone to heal by itself. Her left eye. Which is why it was swollen shut and her face looked so disfigured. As it heals, she will start to look more like herself. Her nose was broken, but we were able to fix that as well."

Dr. Pritchett looked up again and then sat in a chair. "Next, she was strangled. She has petechia in the right eye and some on her face. You know what petechia is?" Everyone nodded. "Great, okay, you will be able to see the bruising on her neck, but the hyoid bone was not broken. She has several broken ribs. One of them punctured her lung. That's the cause of the rasping sound when she breathed. We moved the ribs back into place, and she has a chest tube in. Several organs were bruised but not lacerated. That's the good news. Her hands tell us she put up quite a fight." He smiled slightly.

TARA BRITT

Slade walked slowly over to the window and gazed out. He had to ask the question, but he didn't want to look at anyone when he did.

"Was she sexually assaulted?" His baritone voice was barely audible.

"No, there's no sign of sexual assault, but I'm sorry to have to tell you, she lost the baby she was carrying," Dr. Pritchett replied.

Slade's throat constricted. The blood drained from his face. Everything became dizzy, and his knees buckled. He caught himself as he started to slide down by grabbing onto the sides of the window ledge. He rested his forehead on the window.

Staci had been pregnant. He tried to grasp what the doctor had said.

"There's no permanent damage to her reproductive organs that we can see. And she was only about eight weeks along, so she may not have known she was pregnant." The doctor tried to be reassuring, but it didn't register with Slade.

Eight weeks. Slade did the math. The night her car blew up. The exhaustion, sore breasts, the constant hunger, and the mood swings she was starting to have. It all made sense now.

He turned around after he steadied himself. The fury he felt at this very moment was so tangible he no longer wanted to control it. The family, her parents, and sisters, looked at him. They were as in shock as he was. Firming his jaw and gritting his teeth, his eyes dark and stormy, Slade stomped out of the waiting area at a quick pace. He pushed the button on the elevator and waited, clenching and unclenching his hands into fists. He heard one of the sisters call his name as he stepped onto the elevator, but he ignored her. When the elevator opened on the main floor, he walked purposefully to his vehicle. Staci's tote was in the passenger seat. He vaguely remembered seeing photos. Jerking open the door of the car, he rifled through the tote until he found what he was looking for. Sonogram photos. He had assumed they were her sister's, Casey's, who was pregnant. He looked at them closely. Everly was the name typed across the top of each and today's, he looked at his watch and saw it was after midnight and corrected himself, yesterday's date. Very clearly,

TO DIE FOR HER

he could see the shape of a small human. He couldn't tell you where an eye was or even a face, but he could clearly see it was a baby. His rage was now joined by a grief that was completely unexpected. If she had told him three days ago that she thought she was pregnant, Slade knew he would have panicked. He might even have been angry. Now he wanted to cry for a child he had never known. That son of a bitch not only almost killed Staci, but he had also killed her baby. *His* baby. Slade wished Carmichael was alive just so he could kill him with his bare hands. A bullet to his brain had been too humane.

He threw the photos back into the tote and slammed the door. He needed to hit something. The first thing he saw was a metal trash can by the sidewalk. He punched it as hard as he could. His hand immediately hurt, but the pain only fueled him to continue to assault the trash can. He punched and kicked the trash can over and over. The tears flowed, and with every punch he threw, he screamed curse words until he was almost hoarse. He wanted to go to the toughest bar in town and pick a fight with the biggest man there and hit and be hit.

Ken Everly leaned his shoulder against the brick wall outside of the ER doors, watching Slade. He understood how Slade was feeling, but time and experience had taught him how to control his emotions. He let Slade beat up the trash can for a while, letting him get it out of his system. Finally, Ken pushed himself off the wall and took a few steps toward Slade.

"Son, take off that bloody vest and let's go for a ride," Ken calmly commanded Slade.

Slade paused and looked at Ken. He heard the calmness in his voice. He also heard the authority. Slade stood there for a minute, his fists clenched and bloodied, panting. Finally, he unclenched his fists and nodded. He stormed over to his car, opened the back passenger door and began taking off his vest. The Velcro peeling off sounded loud in the cold silent air. Slade didn't feel the cold. The fire burning in his gut was keeping him warm. He threw the vest into the back seat and closed the door. Ken motioned him over to a discreet gray sedan and climbed behind the wheel. Slade let himself into the passenger side. In silence, Ken Everly drove out of the parking lot.

"Where's the quietest bar in the area?" Ken asked.

"Three blocks. Turn left at the next light," Slade answered.

Ken nodded and followed Slade's directions, and soon, he pulled into a parking lot of an establishment that had been designed to look like an old English pub, complete with Tudor architecture. The two men left the car and entered the bar. A handful of people were still there. Ken chose a table in the back. Both men sat where they could watch the exit. A plump woman in her forties wearing jeans and a T-shirt with the bar's logo on it came over to take their orders.

"Two Scotches. Neat," Ken ordered.

"I don't drink Scotch," Slade told him.

"You do tonight," Ken responded.

When their drinks were delivered, Ken took a sip and let the liquid slide down his throat, burning it. Slade took his own sip, trying not to grimace as the amber liquid burned his own throat.

"Was it yours?" Ken asked. He took another sip.

Morosely, Slade looked into the glass holding the spirit he was being forced to drink. "Yeah," he replied finally.

"Did you know?" Ken asked another question and took another sip.

"No." Slade's voice held regret.

"Do you love her?" Another question, another sip.

"Yeah." Slade sighed. There was no use lying to Ken or himself about how he felt about Staci.

"Are you willing to die for her?"

Slade never hesitated. "Yes." He hissed and swallowed a larger amount of the Scotch.

Ken nodded. He mulled the information around for a minute then said, "I'm gonna tell you a story. Just between you and me."

Slade sipped his Scotch again. After the first three sips, it wasn't too bad. He just looked at Ken and waited.

"I guess you know I was in the Air Force," Ken began. When Slade nodded, Ken continued, "I flew fighter missions, Desert Storm, other small missions. But after 9/11, that changed. We were stationed in Italy. I was approached by another government agency. They were

TO DIE FOR HER

recruiting people who were already attached to the government in some way, particularly military personnel, to gather intelligence."

"CIA," Slade inserted.

Ken nodded. "It made sense. The physical training was already documented. The other training, well, we just didn't need as much as someone fresh out of college or off the street. Our loyalty to the United States was also already established. We had positions that we could use to hide our real missions. A plausible cover."

"Carmichael claimed he was CIA. That the whole double-cross was just a cover so that the government could sell the narcotics and use the money to pay for the operations in the Middle East that Congress wouldn't let into the budget. He said he would take part of the money the traffickers made to pay for the operations in exchange for protecting them from my agency," Slade confided in Ken. "The problem with Carmichael was that he got greedy, starting skimming for himself and having the money sent to his personal bank account overseas. When Staci took over this case and was actually using due diligence, it threatened his own personal interests. Then she indicted him, unknowingly, but still." Slade shrugged.

Ken nodded. "We call that 'going rogue.' It happens sometimes. And sometimes, other government agencies get in the way of what we are supposed to be accomplishing. That complicates things." He took the last sip from his glass. "Usually, we just stay out of the way and let the natural course of events happen, but occasionally, some-one either lets something happen that should have never happened because they don't want to blow their own cover or they become too immersed in their cover. They lose sight of what their assignment is."

Slade remained silent, processing what Ken was telling him.

"Carmichael had a handler. Someone who was supposed to keep him on task, bring him out if things got out of control. His handler either let him do the things he did because of negligence or some benefit the handler was receiving or the handler was actually giving the orders. There is someone else out there that needs to be brought in," Ken summed it up.

Slade thought furiously. *Who would that be? Surely not someone else on his team?*

"Son, you need to understand something. When I was first recruited, no one in my family knew. They weren't allowed to know. Then we had to move to the States, Hawaii, so they could be on US soil in case things got really dangerous. Terrorists have a way of finding out things, and it would be harder to retaliate on a US air base in the States than an air base in some other country. So I had to tell Marie. The older girls, even though they knew military personnel moved around because of reassignment, were devastated at the move. So little by little, we let them in on things, but they were sworn to secrecy. They couldn't tell their friends, other family members. It was just something they knew, and it stayed in our home. Staci in particular hated the secrecy. She yelled at us once that when she was grown-up and in charge of her own life, there would be no more secrets." Ken smiled wryly. "I guess, judging by the fact you didn't know she was carrying your baby, that didn't work out quite like she planned."

"Yeah, she mentioned one time that she grew up in a house of secrets. I didn't know what she was talking about." Slade chose to ignore the last statement. The pain was still too acute.

"I'd like to find out who this guy's handler was," Ken told him softly.

"Why?"

Ken's face darkened. "For one thing, as long as he's out there, Staci is in danger. Whether she knows anything or not about him, he will assume she does. Dead people don't tell secrets. For another thing, I have my own reasons."

Slade paled at the realization that Staci was still in danger. He moved to stand, but Ken put a hand on his arm. "Sit. We need to figure out who this person could be."

Slade sat, but he wasn't sure how he was going to figure it out. He remembered the cross he yanked off Carmichael's body and the cell phone he snatched off the floor of the barn. He pulled them out of the pocket in his cargo pants and stared at them. His eyes brightened suddenly.

TO DIE FOR HER

"Staci sent one of these crosses to Isabella. They all have transmitters in them. Isabella managed to find a series of coordinates and times that matched all of the crosses we recovered," Slade told Ken.

"And?"

"I sent them off for analysis," Slade explained. He looked at the text that Staci had sent him. "Here's her text. I have the coordinates and times, but I don't know where the coordinates go."

Ken pulled his cell phone out, picked an app, and requested the coordinates at the most used location. After a few seconds, he showed Slade the map. Slade's eyes narrowed.

"That's the same building Staci and I work out of." His mind raced. The time frames were largely between 8:00 a.m. and 5:30 p.m. "It's somebody that works regular hours."

Ken nodded. "Give me the next regular set of coordinates."

Slade obliged, and again, only a few seconds later, Ken showed a map to Slade. He slid his fingers across the screen, zooming in on the area where the pinpoint sat. "Figure out who lives at this address and works in your building during those hours," Ken stated. "And you most likely have the handler."

Slade took a picture with his own phone. He looked at Carmichael's phone. The screen was shattered. He wasn't sure he could get anything to come up. He played with it for a few minutes, and suddenly it lit up. It demanded a passcode. Slade tried several things, using the knowledge he had gained from Carmichael in the time he had worked with him. Nothing worked.

"If you can find out who he called last, you might have an answer. Or maybe someone he called that you wouldn't think he would call," Ken commented.

Slade just nodded as he typed in idea after idea for a password. Then a thought came to him. *Surely Carmichael wasn't so arrogant as to use something that obvious*, Slade told himself. He typed in ZORRO. Magically, the screen switched to the user screen. Slade smiled. He went to the screen where he could view calls made. There were several to a number Slade didn't recognize the area code, including the last call made. He called it with Carmichael's phone. A voice answered on the other end. Slade hung up immediately. His eyes widened slightly and only for a moment. He knew that voice.

"You know who answered?" Ken guessed.

Slade nodded. Ken's eyes smiled but not his mouth. "You realize that there's not even probable cause based solely on someone answering a call from that asshole's phone?"

"True, but it's a place to start," Slade conceded.

"I can have someone locate that address. Then we can organize. Formulate a plan. How good of an actor are you?" Ken sat back and motioned for the check.

"I mean I've been trained to interrogate. There's different methods," Slade offered.

Ken nodded. "We should get back to the hospital. Think you can keep it together if we go?"

Slade stood up and took a deep breath. "Yeah, I got it." He didn't even try to explain his earlier behavior.

Ken nodded. "Good. Son, I'm about to teach you the most basic lesson of life. The difference between the woman you love and your child is that you would die for your woman. You would kill for your child." He strode toward the exit, leaving Slade wondering what he meant.

CHAPTER 16

When they returned to the hospital, they first went to the ICU waiting area. No one was there. Next, they went to the nurses' station to find out if anyone knew where the family had gone. A chubby dark-haired nurse looked up from the computer she was entering data into and told them Staci's room number.

"They are outside of the room. Only one at a time can go in," she informed them.

Ken and Slade walked around the corner and down the hall. They saw Marie and Cassidy standing along the wall.

"There you are." Marie smiled slightly. Her eyes didn't reflect the smile, and Slade thought he detected some sadness in them.

"How's she doing?" Ken asked as he hugged his wife.

"The doctor will be along in a minute, but I think there's a problem," Marie answered.

Slade swallowed and braced himself for whatever news the doctor might have. He couldn't let himself get out of control again. Allison exited the room. She sighed and saw Slade. She walked over and hugged him. Neither spoke because neither knew what to say.

They all stood in the hallway, watching nurses and orderlies enter and exit rooms. They could hear the various machines with the beeping and chirping. Every sound became magnified as they all stayed silent. Finally, Dr. Pritchett came around the corner. He looked tired.

"So she has good brain activity. No sign of internal bleeding. Her numbers are actually pretty good. The only problem we have is that she isn't waking up. She's not in a coma," he told them before one of them asked. "She's literally asleep. Not in a vegetative state, as I told you. She has good brain activity. Sometimes, when someone suffers an incredibly traumatic emotional experience, the brain has to take time to process it. Allow the person to deal with it from the inside out. Ms. Everly has suffered quite a traumatic experience, and we are operating under the theory that as of now, she isn't waking up because her brain isn't prepared to handle what has happened to her."

"How long will it last?" Cassidy asked. Her face and the tone of her voice exhibited the worry everyone had.

"I can't tell you that. What she needs right now is rest and a chance to handle the emotional trauma she's suffered," Dr. Pritchett replied. "I suggest that you all go get some rest and let her do the same."

"I'm putting someone outside her room, police protection," Slade told the doctor. "We need a chair placed outside the door."

The doctor nodded and turned to leave. Staci's sisters turned to Slade, obvious concern and confusion on their faces.

"We thought the person who did this to Staci wasn't a threat anymore?" Cassidy voiced what Allison and Marie were thinking.

Ken nodded and pulled Marie tight against him.

"Yeah, that guy's dead, but this is just a precaution in case he wasn't working alone." Slade wasn't about to go into the conversation he and Ken had earlier, and he certainly wasn't going to tell them about the "handler" that existed.

"I think that's a good idea." Ken looked at Slade, silently communicating his approval of the explanation. He turned to look at his wife. "Well, Marie, I think we need to find a hotel so we can get some sleep."

Slade spoke up. "Why don't you all just stay at Staci's condo? There are plenty of beds. Staci would hate it if you stayed at a hotel." He pulled out his keys and peeled the key to the condo off it. "Here's the key. Just let yourself in. I'm going to make the arrangements for the security detail, and I'll come over after that. I need a shower and some sleep myself."

"Where will you sleep?" Ken looked at him pointedly.

"On the couch. I'll swing by my own place and grab some clothes." Slade stared back at Ken, who nodded.

TO DIE FOR HER

Even though Slade had moved a lot of his belongings to Staci's condo over the last few weeks, he still had toiletries and a few clothes remaining at his apartment. Something had made him hesitate to completely move in with her. By keeping his apartment, he had allowed himself a backup plan, his fear of commitment still holding him back.

He watched as Staci's family walked down the hall and around the corner. He pulled out his cell phone and called Manny.

"Hey, it's me," Slade told Manny unnecessarily.

"How's she doing?" Manny asked. It was obvious he had been sleeping.

"Not great, but she could be worse. Listen, I need a favor, and you're the only one I trust right now to do it." Slade told him briefly about the possible handler and the possibility of Staci still being in danger. "I hate to ask you, but like I said, you're the only one I trust to do this right."

"Can you give me an hour to get there?" Manny looked over at the woman sleeping next to him. He had to shower and get rid of her without a lot of explanation.

"Sure, no problem. I'll brief you when you get here. And, hey," Slade's anxiety lessened, knowing Manny was coming, "thank you for earlier." Manny had literally saved both his and Staci's lives.

"Yeah. We're even now, right?"

"Yeah." Slade hung up his phone and waited outside Staci's room for Manny to arrive.

*****

Once Slade got Manny situated outside Staci's room, he headed for her condo. It looked dark from the street. He tried the door and found that someone had left it open for him. He tiptoed in as quietly as he could and shut and locked the door behind him. There was a lamp on in the living room. and it gave him just enough light to make his way to the kitchen bar. He took off his holster and gun belt and laid them on the bar. He saw that someone had lain his key on the bar. He smiled to himself and put it back onto his key ring, which

205

he set down next to his gun belt. He looked down at himself. *Damn*, he thought. *I'm a mess.* He walked quietly to the laundry room and shed his shirt and threw it in the washer. He checked the dryer. Nope. No clean clothes. He had forgotten to go by his apartment and pick up clothes, so that meant that he was going to eventually have to go upstairs and get clothes out of the main bedroom. Not tonight.

He walked back into the living room and sat down on the sectional to remove his shoes. He had one boot off when he heard a noise behind him. He slowly turned his head without raising up. Allison was standing by the bar.

"It's just me," Slade told her softly.

She nodded and walked toward him. He finished taking off his second boot and glanced up to see her standing behind the sectional. "What?" he asked.

"She's in love with you, you know," Allison whispered.

Slade just nodded. Allison came around the sectional and dug around in a stylish trunk by the fireplace. She pulled out a fleece blanket and handed it to Slade.

"You're probably the only person who can bring her out of whatever she's wrestling with right now," Allison confided. "I'm really scared for her."

Slade took the blanket from Allison. He thought about his words for a minute then said, "I'm in love with your sister, Allison. None of this is a game for me."

"Have you told her?"

"Told her what?"

"That you love her," Allison clarified.

"No." Slade sighed. "Hell, until recently, I didn't know what I felt. I couldn't put a name to it. Couldn't define it. I wasn't sure if what I was feeling was love or something else. I've never been in love with anyone before, so I didn't have anything to compare it to."

"You need to tell her," Allison insisted. "She needs to know."

Slade rubbed his face with his hand. "I know."

Allison nodded and left the room, leaving Slade alone in the near-darkness. He pulled his bloody pants off and laid them next to the sectional and laid down, covering himself with the blanket

TO DIE FOR HER

Allison had given him. He thought he would have a hard time falling asleep after everything that had happened in the last nine hours, but the next thing he knew, he was waking up to noises coming from the kitchen, and the sun was shining in through the patio blinds. Looking at his watch, he was surprised to see that he had slept for several hours. Popping his head up, he saw the Everly women bustling around the kitchen cooking food. He smelled coffee. He lay back down, wondering how he was going to be able to put his pants back on without anyone seeing him. He shouldn't have worried about that as Cassidy came rushing up to the back of the sectional.

"Good, you're awake. You need to get a shower and get dressed so we can go back to the hospital and check on Staci," she ordered. She glanced at the floor where his pants lay and snorted. "Don't worry, some of us have seen you wearing just a towel. Just wrap the blanket around you and get going."

Slade felt his face grow hot, and he knew he was blushing.

Marie looked over to where Slade was now sitting and joined in. "They tell me you look quite spectacular in a towel." She smiled at him, and Slade noticed it was exactly like Staci's smile.

Ken walked in from the hallway where the laundry room was located holding a cup of what Slade assumed was coffee. "You heard her, get going," he commented.

Slade wrapped the blanket around his waist and strolled as quickly as he could to the stairs. As he went up, he heard Cassidy sigh and say, "Why is it that whenever Staci walks into a room, only the most handsome men are immediately attracted to her like moths to a flame? What's her secret?"

Slade could have listed the dozens of reasons why Staci was so attractive and very few of those reasons had anything to do with her looks.

A few minutes later, Slade came back downstairs, showered and wearing clean jeans and a cable-knit sweater. His hair was still damp, and because it had started growing back, the curl around his ears and the back of his neck were visible. He walked over to the sectional to get his boots. Ken was sitting on it, flipping through the news and eating a piece of toast. His coffee cup was on the coffee table. He looked over at Slade as he approached.

"Never met a security detail that kept their clothes and toiletries in the client's own closet and bathroom," he commented dryly.

"Well, it's not a secret that I've been sleeping with her. Not anymore anyway," Slade shot back.

Ken laughed and finished his toast. He looked around at the decorated condo and commented, "I see you've been introduced to Staci's love of everything Christmas."

"Yeah, she had me help her decorate a couple of weeks ago right after Halloween." Slade looked around at their handiwork.

"Well, get used to it. If Staci had her way, she would leave Christmas decorations up year-round," Allison joined the conversation.

Slade finished putting on his boots and stood. He grabbed a jacket out of the closet in the small hallway and announced to all of them, "I put my key back on my key ring, so you'll have to leave when I do. I'd like to get to the hospital now."

Everyone paused to look at him. Marie gently but firmly told him, "Not until we eat a good breakfast. It's going to be a long day for everyone, and it doesn't do Staci any good for us to starve ourselves." She handed him a plate with bacon and eggs and toast. Cassidy passed him a cup of coffee.

Slade, feeling fully chastised, sat without comment and quickly ate his food and finished his cup of coffee. The women quickly cleaned up the kitchen and then gathered their own coats.

"Now we can leave," Marie said.

Slade ushered everyone out and locked the door behind them. Rodriguez was standing on the sidewalk in front of the house.

"What do you want us to do with Staci's rental car? It's been processed, and I don't want to leave it in impound," Rodriguez asked Slade.

"Turn it in. She can drive my car until insurance sends her a check, which should be any day," Slade answered.

Rodriguez grinned. "Really? You're gonna let her drive your precious swagger wagon?"

Slade scowled at Rodriguez. "Shut up."

Rodriguez laughed boisterously as Slade climbed into his government SUV.

*****

As the group rounded the corner in the ICU hallway, Cassidy, who was in the front, suddenly pulled up and stopped, causing Slade to almost knock her down. Putting his hands up, he grabbed her shoulders to prevent disaster. He followed her gaze to where she was staring at Manny. He was sitting outside Staci's room, staring straight ahead, no expression on his face. When Slade saw him, he smiled and moved Cassidy out of his way, moving in Manny's direction.

"Yo, Manny. Thanks, man." Slade put out a hand, and Manny stood. They did a handshake that was more involved than the average shake, grasping each other's hand around the thumbs.

"No problem. Quiet night," Manny assured him. He was looking at Cassidy with some interest.

Slade recognized that look. "Nope, not gonna happen," Slade leaned in and told him softly.

Louder, he introduced Manny to the rest of the family. "This is a good friend of mine and also one of our best field agents, Manny Coronado. Manny, this is Ken and Marie Everly, Staci's parents." He pointed to Staci's sisters. "These are two of her sisters, Allison and Cassidy."

Manny nodded respectfully but gazed a little longer at Cassidy. Cassidy studied the man looking at her. He was only slightly taller than herself, wearing jeans and work boots and a leather vest over a long sleeved shirt. She could see tattoos on his hands and peeking out of his collar onto his neck. His dark hair was average length, and his brown eyes sparkled with intelligence.

"Nice to meet you, Manny." Cassidy stuck out her hand to shake his.

Manny took her hand and rather than shake it, brought it up to his lips and kissed the back of it, drawling, "*Enchanté.*"

Cassidy giggled, but Slade was not amused. He snatched Cassidy's hand away from Manny.

Manny smiled at Slade. "You gonna need me again tonight?"

Slade glanced at Ken before answering. "I'm not sure. Can I let you know?"

Manny stretched. "Sure. I'm going home to get a nap."

Turning to the family, he politely bid them good day and walked down the hallway to the elevators.

Cassidy turned and watched him leave, and Slade leaned into her ear and told her, "I wouldn't. He's a great friend, but I don't think he's your type."

Cassidy grinned at Slade. "He's upright and breathing. He's my type."

She turned to the family and asked, "Who's going in first?"

All eyes turned to Slade. He felt panic rising up. He couldn't see her, not right now. He wasn't prepared for seeing her so motionless, so helpless. He had no idea what he would say to her, even if she was still unconscious. He watched as first Ken and then Marie took charge and entered the room.

A doctor rounded the corner, and Slade approached him. "How's Staci Everly doing?"

The doctor glanced at the tablet he was carrying and flipped through it. He quickly read through it and brought his eyes back to Slade. "Still not awake or responding to anything. I'm sorry."

"Does she still have brain activity?" Slade could feel his adrenaline rising, and his hands start to shake.

"Oh yes, all of her vitals are actually great this morning. We can probably pull that chest tube out in a couple of days, and her EEGs are all normal. We just need her to wake up," the doctor assured him. Slade nodded.

When Ken and Marie exited, Slade let Allison then Cassidy go ahead of him. He was frantically trying to figure out what to say to the unconscious woman and coming up empty. Ken was dialing his phone and then walked out of earshot to carry on the conversation. Marie sat in the chair that Manny had occupied earlier.

Cassidy walked out of the room and told Slade, "Your turn."

TO DIE FOR HER

Swallowing hard, Slade nodded and walked to the doorway. Looking in, he looked long and hard at Staci. Laying in the bed, motionless, she was pale against the sheets. He could see the chest tube snaking out from beneath the sheet. He walked closer and then around the bed away from the machines that were beeping and clicking. Standing next to the bed, Slade noted her injuries. Her left eye was puffy and bruised red and purple and blue. There was a blue bruise in the middle of her forehead and just to the left of that bruise, a bandage covered the laceration on her head. Her face was swollen around her eye and her cheek where she had facial fractures. A slip of white bandage was across her nose. He saw the deep bruises around her throat. He could feel the fury rising up inside again.

Both of her hands had bandaging across the knuckles. Her forearms and biceps had random bruising as well. Sitting in a chair that was next to the bed, he scooted it close to the bedside. He gently lifted one of her hands into his.

"Staci, it's Mike," he softly told her. "I don't know if you can hear me, but I need you to know some things. Things I should have told you a long time ago. I need you to wake up and hear me. Staci, wake up, baby." No response.

Sighing, Slade pushed ahead. "I need you to know that I love you. Not like a friend. I am so deeply and uncontrollably in love with you, I am terrified. I never told you before now because I was so scared of what I was feeling, scared you didn't feel the same. But when I knew Carmichael had grabbed you, the fear I felt then completely erased any fear I had about loving you." Emboldened by the fact that Staci was unconscious, Slade continued, "When you wake up and get out of here, we're getting married. I'm not taking no for an answer. I don't care if we have a big wedding or we get married in some judge's office, but we *are* getting married."

Very slightly, very gently, Staci's hand squeezed Slade's hand. His eyes shot to her face, but the eye that wasn't swollen shut was still closed. Her squeeze spurred him on.

"None of this was your fault, you need to know this. I take full responsibility for not going with you to your appointment, not being by your side every minute until you were out of danger." No response. Slade continued, "Darlin', we lost our baby." Slade choked on a sob and laid his head on her hand. "Did you know?"

A squeeze. She was communicating with him! A squeeze meant yes; no response meant no or disagree. He gulped. He could do this.

"Were you going to tell me?"

A squeeze.

"I promise you, darlin', that once you're ready, I will fill our home with the most beautiful green-eyed babies. As many as we can handle. But only when you're ready. You can take as long as you need to grieve for the one we lost," he promised, his Texas drawl becoming pronounced.

Staci moved her hand to softly cup Slade's cheek. Slade covered the hand that cupped his face with his own and looked closely at her face. Small tears were coming out of the eye that wasn't injured.

"You won't have to do it alone, Staci. I will be there for you, to grieve with you, to help you through this."

Her hand fell back to the bed and squeezed Slade's hand again. Then a ragged sigh erupted from Staci's chest. Slade saw her slowly open her right eye. She took a minute to focus then looked at him. The white of her eye was mostly red, the petechia from the strangling filling it. Slade told her about her injuries, explaining why she couldn't talk, couldn't see out of her left eye, about her ribs, and her lung. She listened and very slightly nodded.

"Do you have any questions?" Slade asked.

Staci nodded her head, so Slade had to figure out a way for her to find a voice. "I'm going to list topics. When I say one you have a question about, squeeze my hand. Okay?"

A squeeze.

"Carmichael."

A squeeze.

So he told her everything Carmichael had bragged about, his role in everything. He left out the part about a second person being involved. Stacy formed her hand into a gun.

"He's dead. You didn't shoot him, but you did save my life. When you picked up my gun, you distracted him. Someone else shot him, not me, but only because I wasn't as fast as that other person."

212

TO DIE FOR HER

Staci tried to smile, but the broken jaw had been wired shut, so the smile didn't lift her lips on that side, making her face appear crooked. Slade grinned at her.

"You look like hell, you know that?" he teased her.

She squeezed his hand.

"Please tell me you're the one that messed up his face," Slade raised his eyebrow.

A squeeze.

"That's my girl."

Staci made a V with her forefinger and middle finger and showed Slade. He was puzzled. What was she trying to tell him?

"Peace?"

No response.

"Two?"

A squeeze.

"This is harder. Two times? Two guns?"

No response.

"Two people?"

A squeeze.

Slade stared at her, processing what she was telling him. "You know there's a second person?"

A squeeze.

"Do you know who?"

No response.

"How do you know?"

Slowly, Staci raised her hand to her ear and made a pretend phone out of her fingers.

Slade asked, "Did Carmichael call that second person when he had you?"

A nod of her head.

"You're safe. Please don't worry about that. I have someone who is keeping watch over you at night long enough for me to get some sleep."

A squeeze.

"Your family is here, well, most of them. They've all be in to see you. They're worried about you, baby," Slade told her.

A squeeze.

"Want me to send your mom in?" Slade didn't want to leave Staci's side, but he couldn't be selfish when her parents and sisters were just as worried about her as he was.

A squeeze. Nodding, Slade stood up and put her hand on the bed. "I'll send her in." He leaned over and put a soft kiss on one area of her forehead that wasn't cut or bruised. He lingered long enough to tell her "I love you." Then he left the room.

CHAPTER 17

When Slade exited Staci's hospital room and her mother took his place inside, Ken Everly motioned Slade to come closer to where he was standing several feet away. Slade sauntered over, feeling much more relieved now that Staci was awake and communicating.

"Yes, sir?" He ducked his head and glanced around. Nurses and orderlies were doing their jobs. No one was paying them any attention.

"We need to confirm that the person who answered that phone call last night was Carmichael's handler," Ken told him.

"Okay." Slade leaned against the wall next to Ken and crossed his arms. "I guess just asking him isn't going to be productive?"

Ken snorted. "No. He'll deny it then possibly come after anyone he thinks can identify him. It has to be done delicately. It has to be done so that he believes you have some sort of leverage."

"Don't you mean 'us'?" Slade looked straight ahead when he asked the question.

"There is no us as far as this guy is concerned. Understood?"

"Yeah, I got it." Slade switched the weight on his legs.

"We'll plan it, but you are the only one who can pull this off," Ken explained.

Slade nodded.

"Do you think you can do it?"

Slade nodded again.

"Do you think you can get him to meet you?"

Slade nodded a third time.

Ken left to speak with Marie briefly when she exited Staci's room. She nodded and patted his cheek. He walked back to where Slade was waiting.

"Let's go put this thing together," Ken said to Slade as he walked by without stopping.

Slade followed him to the elevators.

Cassidy watched Slade and her father get onto the elevators.

"Where are they going?" she asked her mother.

Marie turned to look in the direction that Cassidy was staring. She sighed and turned back to her daughter. "Oh, you know your father. Someone put his daughter in danger. He's just making sure she's safe," Marie answered.

Cassidy nodded and didn't ask any more questions.

*****

Approximately thirty miles north of St. Louis sits the small town of Alton, Illinois. A few community colleges and small businesses dot its landscape. There is nothing that makes it stand out. Ken Everly and Slade pulled into the parking lot of a nondescript bar at 7:00 p.m. They sat in Ken's car near the back of the parking lot.

"Just get him talking. Convince him the gig is up. We need to establish that he was Carmichael's handler and knew about the chaos Carmichael was involved in. That's all this meeting is about," Ken reiterated.

"Got it," Slade told him for the hundredth time.

"Once you know for sure, just signal me, and we'll leave."

Slade nodded. "Yep."

Slade exited Ken's car and sauntered to the door. He opened the door and walked in. He paused for a moment to let his eyes adjust to the darkened interior. There were a handful of people inside, including the waitstaff. He chose a table at the back of the bar. He sat with his back to the corner and signaled to a server.

When the server approached, Slade told her, "I'm still waiting on the other party. I'm going to need you to bring me your most expensive bottle of bourbon with two glasses with ice."

She nodded and left. He didn't have to wait long. The man Slade was waiting on walked through the door. Slade signaled him

TO DIE FOR HER

subtly. The man strolled over to the table where Slade was sitting and then stood next to the table.

"What's all this about?" he inquired impatiently.

Slade leaned back in his chair and gestured toward the chair that sat between the man and the table. "Sit. We need to talk," he answered.

The man sighed and rolled his eyes, but he pulled the chair out and sat. The server returned to the table with the items Slade had ordered. Slade leaned forward and opened the bottle of bourbon and poured a healthy amount of the amber liquid into the glasses over the ice. The man stared at Slade as Slade took a sip of his own drink.

"Staci Everly is laying in a hospital bed, beaten to a pulp," Slade told the man.

The man's eyes widened slightly. He reached for the bourbon. "What's the prognosis?" he asked.

"She is in ICU. Probably won't make it," Slade lied as he took another sip.

The man took a healthy sip and savored it as it slid down his throat. "That's too bad," he commented. "Do you know how it happened?"

"Yeah, remember Carmichael? On my team?" Slade raised one eyebrow at the man. The man nodded. "Yeah, he kidnapped her, beat her to a pulp, and he tried to kill me. He actually shot another one of my men twice."

"Oh my." The man took another drink. "Where's Carmichael?"

"Dead. Bullet to the brain does that," Slade told the man. Slade leaned over and poured more bourbon in the man's drink.

"Well, that's an interesting turn of events," the man remarked. He took another drink.

Slade nodded and took a sip. "Before he was killed, Carmichael told an interesting story." Slade kept his gaze on his glass of bourbon. "Claimed he was CIA. Went into graphic detail about the assignment he was on, working with Las Aranas in order to get money to fund some overseas projects. He bragged about taking a little of the money for himself. He also apparently skimmed some of the product, sold it, and made more money. Some for himself, some for the 'company.'" Slade used the common nickname of the CIA.

TARA BRITT

The man took another drink and leaned back. "Really? What does that have to do with our meeting now?"

Slade reached into his pocket and pulled out the cross he had yanked from around Carmichael's neck and Carmichael's cell phone. "I pulled these little trinkets off Carmichael after he was killed."

The man looked at the items as if they would bite him.

"Turns out these crosses have tiny little transmitters in them. They're GPS devices so somebody can track whoever wears one. We pulled crosses off every dead member of the cartel and off all three of the witnesses we are holding to testify."

The man took another drink of his bourbon and waited silently for Slade to continue.

"Turns out there is a jewelry shop in St. Louis where all of these passed through. Took some doing, but we managed to track who ordered them," Slade lied.

"Really," the man commented skeptically. He took another drink, and Slade refreshed his drink a third time.

"Yeah, really. And then, well, as you know, the federal government has an awesome cyber unit. They were able to trace where the coordinates from the transmitters were being sent and when they were being sent," Slade continued.

He picked up one of the crosses and twirled it slowly as if examining it. He glanced over at the man who was sipping the bourbon again. The man began to look uncomfortable.

"Guess where those coordinates came back to?" Slade challenged the man.

The man shook his head.

"To the same person who ordered these crosses," Slade told him. "Then we have Carmichael's cell phone." He picked up the phone and showed it to the man. "The last call on this phone was to the same person who ordered the crosses. Same person who was receiving coordinates from the crosses." Slade smiled sardonically at the man. He lifted up his drink and took another sip. "Wanna know who that person is?"

Slade paused. The man didn't respond. He just glared at Slade.

218

"You, Max. It all came back to you." Slade kept smiling. "You know why it came back to you?"

"I'm interested in your theory," Max responded.

"Really not a theory when it all gets monologued by a crazed rogue CIA agent. Every deep cover agent has what is known as a handler," Slade explained.

All this information came from Ken and not Carmichael, but Max needed to believe Carmichael snitched him out. "The handler is supposed to keep the agent on track, on point during the mission. The handler is directly responsible for that deep cover agent's actions or inactions." Slade stopped and took another sip of the bourbon and allowed for Max to do the same.

"You might recall how that went terribly off the rails with Kiki Camerena back in the '80s?" Slade mentally nudged Max.

Max nodded. Slade leaned over and poured another healthy dose of bourbon in both of their glasses.

"Yeah, so Carmichael a.k.a. Zorro went off the rails. His handler didn't pull him out of the mission, didn't put him back on track. In fact, his handler gave him vague orders in an effort to cover up what was going on. Vague enough that Carmichael had a lot of creative license, including killing a United States Marshal."

Max took another healthy gulp of the bourbon. "Well, that is certainly an interesting theory. Certainly, nothing that will stand up in court." He smirked at Slade.

"Don't forget, Staci managed to indict all others," Slade spoke slowly, "known and unknown. That would include you, Max."

"Well, if she's dead or at least out of commission, I don't see that indictment being tried," Max remarked with arrogance. He slugged back another gulp. His hand was slightly unsteady when he went to set the glass down.

Slade took notice of Max's speech; it was starting to slur ever so slightly.

"There're other assistants in your office, Max. Unless you kill it. That would look bad though, don't you agree?" Slade pushed Max verbally and refilled his glass again.

"You don't seriously think the government is going to allow any of that information to be public knowledge, do you?" Max rattled the ice around in his glass. "It's really beyond my control at this point anyway." He shrugged.

Slade smiled slowly. He looked up and glanced around the bar. He saw Ken sitting at the bar near the exit. Slade made eye contact with Ken and slightly nodded his head. Ken put money on the bar and left. Slade turned his attention back to Max.

"Well, you might be right about that, Max," Slade agreed. "I just wanted you to know that I know. I know everything. I also have genuine proof to back up this 'theory' as you call it."

"What do you plan to do about it?" Max took another sip.

"I have no idea. But I promise," Slade stood up, signaling the end of the conversation, "I will keep you posted when I decide."

Max finished the rest of the bourbon in one gulp and stood, swaying ever so slightly.

"You do that," he replied. "Thanks for the drinks. We'll have to do this again sometime soon." He walked to the exit and out of the establishment.

Slade sat back down and peeled back some cash to pay for the bottle. He waited another ten minutes, as the plan called for, and then left the bar as well. He walked to Ken's car. Ken was behind the wheel, waiting on him. Slade got into the car and asked, "Now what?"

Ken started the car. "Now we go home and get some sleep." With that, he pulled out of the parking lot.

*****

Slade woke up to loud off-key singing and the sun streaming into Staci's condo. Shaking off the fuzz in his head, Slade sat up and looked around. Allison and Cassidy were singing Christmas carols but off-key, off-pitch, off-everything.

"They sound like cats in heat, don't they?" Ken's voice came from behind Slade.

TO DIE FOR HER

Slade whirled around and Ken stood there, a coffee cup in one hand and a piece of toast in the other. "Uh, yeah," Slade cautiously agreed.

"You'll find that Staci doesn't sing any better," Ken warned him. "Get a shower so we can go see how Staci's doing."

Slade quickly obeyed, and when he descended the steps, his hair still damp, Ken was sitting on the sectional, clicking through the channels on the TV with the remote. He paused on a local news station. The picture on the screen was of a car that had plowed into a tree and had burned. The black pile of metal stayed on the screen while the reporter was discussing it.

"Hmm. What do you know about that?" Ken commented.

"What?" Slade advanced on the sectional to get a closer look at the television.

"You know someone named Maxwell Reilly? Isn't that Staci's boss, the US attorney here?" Ken asked, his face blank.

"Yeah, I do." Slade turned to stare at Ken.

Ken knew that. Ken knew that's who he met with and drank with the night before. Carmichael's handler.

"Apparently, he was killed in a car wreck last night. They are investigating it, but the responding officers smelled alcohol." Ken turned to look at him, his face devoid of emotion.

The difference between your woman and your child is that you would die for your woman. You will kill for your child. Ken's word echoed in Slade's mind. He looked at the television and back again to Ken.

"I'd say that's a hell of a coincidence, wouldn't you?" Ken asked him, staring pointedly at Slade.

"Yeah," Slade replied slowly, the situation dawning on him. "Crazy coincidence."

"Good thing he didn't show up to your meeting," Ken calmly told Slade.

"Yeah, it is," Slade agreed, staring back at Ken.

Ken stood up. "Well, we better get going so we can visit with Staci."

He took his cup to the kitchen and handed it to one of his daughters while Slade just watched, stunned at the turn of events.

221

EPILOGUE

Staci stood on the boat dock, one hand on her hip and one shielding her eyes from the warm June sun. She smiled as she watched the boat carrying her sister Meredith, Meredith's husband, Steve Vaughn, and her two nephews rock gently on the water. All of her sisters had gathered this last weekend in June at their parents' house on the Lake of the Ozarks before life once again separated them from each other. She breathed in deeply. The lake air was clean.

Two arms snaked around her waist. She smiled. She had sensed Slade before he had embraced her. His mouth came down to plant a gentle kiss on her shoulder, and she breathed in deeply, savoring his essence. His mouth moved to her ear and he whispered "Hey, darlin'" in that deep baritone voice.

"Michael," she replied in a tone she knew made his heart pound and his pulse race. She put her hands over his, which still held her around the waist. She felt his wide wedding band, and after three years, she was still amazed that this wonderfully masculine man had chosen her to be his wife.

"I think this is going to be the last time I squeeze into this bikini this season." She chuckled softly.

Slade leaned back a little to peruse the pink-and-white polka dot bikini that Staci still rocked like a teenager. Leaning forward again to speak softly into her ear, he told her, "That's okay. I like the emerald-green thong better anyway."

Staci snorted and replied, "That thong is what got us into this current predicament in the first place." She moved his hand over her just barely swollen belly. It was still a secret from the rest of the family, a secret they had kept for four months, but they planned to tell everyone this evening.

Slade threw back his head and guffawed loudly. "I do believe you are correct," he agreed when he had stopped laughing. "But it's not my fault we're both so fertile."

"I swear you just have to look at me and I get pregnant," Staci agreed with him.

His deep voice mellowed and dripped with sexuality. "If memory serves, it was a whole lot more fun than just looking at you."

A mere forty-eight hours after Ayala had taken a plea deal and the case that had brought them together came to a close, Slade and Staci found themselves at the county courthouse. Slade had put a wide gold band on her finger (wide enough there was no mistake that she was married, he had told her) and made her his wife. Due to work obligations and other circumstances, their honeymoon had been delayed until February of this year. Slade surprised her with a trip to Italy, Lake Como specifically, and they had spent a glorious week on the water, sightseeing, meeting up with friends who still lived there, and making love as often as they could. She had bought an emerald-green thong bikini for the trip, and it drove Slade wild.

Staci smiled when she remembered the look on his face the first time she had pulled her cover-up off on the boat they had rented. His eyes darkened as they always did when his libido was in control, and he couldn't take his hands off her. She had come back from Italy pregnant again.

Staci turned in his arms and put her own around his neck. She nestled into his broad, muscular chest and relished being held by him. Even after three years, it hadn't gotten old.

He leaned down to whisper in her ear, "Mmm. Maybe you shouldn't wiggle against me out here, or your family is going to find out what's in my swim trunks."

Staci giggled slightly and pulled back.

"Daddee!" a tiny voice squealed with delight, and Slade immediately let go of Staci and turned his attention to the shoreline where his father was walking toward them with a tiny little girl with dark curly hair and big green eyes in tow.

The child ran as fast as her chubby little legs could take her toward Slade. He grinned at her one-piece bathing suit covered in

TO DIE FOR HER

rainbows and unicorns. She was also wearing a cheap plastic tiara and pink sparkly sandals. It was a typical outfit for this child. He leaned down and scooped her up as she ran headfirst into his open arms.

"How's my best girl?" he asked her.

"Papa gots rocks!" She pointed at Slade's dad, who was approaching.

He held a couple of pebbles in his hand. Grinning, he held them out to show Slade.

"She insisted we had to bring them back to you," David Slade told his son.

Slade thought his dad looked younger these days. The more time he spent with his granddaughter, the happier his dad was. He remembered the first time his father had held her. He had come into the hospital room the day after she was born and taken a seat near the crib. Slade had picked her up and plopped her into his father's arms.

His father had teared up and said, "She looks so much like your mother. She would be on cloud nine if she was here."

Slade himself fought back a tear and told him, "Her name is Rubianna Marie." Rubianna after Slade's mother, Ruby, and Marie, after Staci's mother.

His father had smiled so brightly that Slade had to leave the room, choking up on the emotion on his father's face. Ever since that moment, for the last two years, David Slade had found reasons to visit them. At least one weekend a month, he was pulling up outside their home, ready to play with his granddaughter. Slade didn't blame him at all. Ruby was an amazing child.

He had been there for her birth, and the moment they placed her in his arms, all nine pounds and eight ounces of her, he finally understood what Staci's father had told him that night they left that first bar together, the night before Max had died in a fiery crash that had been ruled a drunk-driving event. "*The difference between your woman and your child is that you would die for your woman. You will kill for your child.*"

Slade had known the moment that Ruby had looked up at him for the first time that he would kill for her. It was a good thing Staci was such an earth mother, letting her get dirty, explore and some-

225

times get scrapes, and generally let her learn about life and her environment. Staci had already introduced a soccer ball to Ruby and was teaching her how to kick it. She had also started teaching Ruby how to swim and to row the kayak Staci had insisted they buy so they could go white river rafting. She was not only giving Ruby valuable skills but getting Slade out of his comfort zones. If it had been on him, Slade would have wrapped the child in bubble wrap and kept her close to him at all times, not letting her learn about cause and effect and consequences. She hugged his neck now and placed wet kisses on his cheeks, giggling when he tickled her.

Staci watched the exchange between father and daughter and smiled to herself. As soon as the doctor had given Staci a clean bill of health after she was discharged from the hospital, Staci had gone back to the US attorney's office to finish the case against Ayala, the only remaining defendant. In a surprise turn of events, he had chosen to plead guilty rather than go to trial. Two days later, she and Slade got married, and it wasn't long before he had gotten her pregnant again. Not sure how he would feel about it, she had made reservations at the steak house where they had first celebrated his birthday and told him over dessert. Instead of being disturbed by the news, he had grinned, his dimple prominent in his cheek, and had immediately jumped headfirst into planning for the baby's arrival.

Staci remembered he had been both annoying and charming about the entire pregnancy. He hovered over her until she had to tell him to back off. He worried about her continuing to run every day until the doctor told him it was fine as long as there was no spotting and Staci felt like doing it. He watched everything she ate, insisting on fresh produce and lean meats and whole grains. Staci found herself hiding to eat the foods she craved: ice cream, potato chips, fast food. She finally yelled at him about letting her indulge once in a while. She did make two concessions at his request. First, she stopped going to her kickboxing class, at least while pregnant, and took up yoga specifically designed for pregnant women. Second, she left the US attorney's office. She called up a couple of friends from law school, and they had formed a family-friendly family law firm

TO DIE FOR HER

that was finally starting to take off and make money. The best part was she could bring Ruby with her to work whenever she needed to.

On the day Ruby was born, Slade had been on assignment in another part of the state. A coworker had driven her to the hospital after her water broke. When Staci finally reached Slade to tell him of the impending birth, somehow he had made it to the hospital in record time and was able to be there for the last hour of labor before Ruby was born. He cut the umbilical cord, and tears rolled down his face when they placed her in his arms for the first time. Staci, exhausted physically and mentally, cried with him at the wonder of how their lives were evolving. He brought Ruby over to her, leaned down and kissed her heartily, then showed off their daughter to her.

"Look what we did," he whispered in awe.

Defying all DNA odds, Ruby's eyes had turned green within a month of her being born. When Staci had mentioned that the science dictated Ruby's eyes should have been brown, considering his DNA and her family DNA, he just grinned at her and said, "I promised you when you were in that hospital bed that I wanted to fill our home with green-eyed babies, not brown-eyed babies. I keep my promises."

Slade also made some concessions. He had cut back on his assignments, volunteering for less dangerous ones and being more cautious whenever an assignment placed him in danger. He and Vaughn and Rodriguez had gotten together and formed a security company, and as soon as it was showing signs of success, the three planned to leave the agency and devote their full attention to their company. Slade, never happy unless his hair was on fire, also decided to run for sheriff in the rural county where they now lived.

After Staci had become pregnant with Ruby, they sold her condo. They moved a little farther west, to the middle of the state, closer to her parents. They had bought property that had a few acres and an old farmhouse. On the weekends, they had spent their days renovating and upgrading the farmhouse, and now it was perfect for their family. Of course, Slade and Staci's father had outfitted both the land and the house with top-of-the-line security devices. There was also plenty of room to expand the family, Slade had teased Staci.

It was quiet and peaceful, with a large pond and plenty of space if they ever wanted to put in a garden or have livestock. Staci and Ruby loved to explore the wilderness, and they were constantly bringing home treasures to share with Slade when he got off work.

Slade had brought home a retired K-9 one evening, a Belgian Malinois named Brutus, who was anything but a brute. He loved the cuddles and the treats, and he adored Ruby. Whenever Ruby was playing outside while Staci was working in the yard, Brutus kept vigil. He would try to herd her if he thought she was too close to danger, and he would alert the adults if that didn't work. He would alert with loud barks if anyone or anything crossed the yard, day or night. Staci and Slade were currently looking for a puppy to grow up with Ruby and the new baby.

Staci's dad watched his family from the back porch of his lake house. Meredith was on the boat with her new husband, her belly stretched and swollen; her husband was smiling at her and kissing the belly that held his child. Her two children from her first marriage were being silly on the boat, pretending to gag and then laughing. He moved his gaze to Staci and Slade. The thought that he had almost lost her filled him with anxiety. She was always his scrapper, and she recovered from the physical trauma she had endured. Slade had proven himself as far as he was concerned, and their daughter, Ruby, was going to give her parents a run for their money. He knew Staci was pregnant again even though no announcement had been made as of yet. He could just tell. His eyes then sought and found Casey and her husband, Jeff. Casey was also pregnant, not quite as far along as Meredith, and she had her hands full with her two sons. Jeff was a big man, even bigger than Slade, but he was incredibly gentle with Casey and playful with his boys.

Allison and Isabella were walking together. Allison was carrying a bucket of something they had found. He hoped that they both would find love soon. They both deserved good men, men who would protect them and respect them. Men who would love them for their minds and their hearts. Finally, he watched Cassidy. She needed to figure out what she wanted before she could settle down. She would flit from man to man but never let one get too close. She

TO DIE FOR HER

was the biggest flirt of all his daughters. One day, she was going to fall and fall hard. He hoped he would be there to see it.

Marie sat next to him on the porch. "Penny for your thoughts, Pops," she teased.

"Just admiring the brood we have. You did an amazing job raising those girls."

"You did just as amazing a job. You just did a different job than me. It was just as important." Marie patted his hand. "Can you believe we managed to get everyone here under one roof for an entire weekend?"

Ken Everly just smiled.

ABOUT THE AUTHOR

Tara Britt is a native Oklahoman. After serving as a United States page, she received her Bachelor's Degree in Literature and her Master's Degree in Education from Northeastern State University. She taught English, creative writing, and drama to middle school children in Laredo, Texas, before attending law school at the University of Tulsa College of Law. She graduated with a Juris Doctorate in 1995 and has worked as a prosecutor in the Tulsa County District Attorney's Office for twenty-five years. She has served as director of the juvenile division, as a sex crimes prosecutor, and as the supervisor of the misdemeanor division of that office. She has taught cross-examination and trial practice on both the state and national levels. She is married to a man who was a police officer for thirty years before he retired. They have five children. She currently resides in a suburb of Tulsa, Oklahoma.

Printed in the USA
CPSIA information can be obtained
at www.ICGtesting.com
CBHW022328070924
13881CB00093B/478